BUSTING LOOSE

VANESSA M. KNIGHT

Busting Loose

Copyright © 2025 by Vanessa M Knight

Published by Inked Publishing

Cover Design by Najla Qamber Designs

Edited by Nancy Canu

Busting Loose is a work of fiction. All names, characters, places and events are the product of the author's imagination or are used fictitiously, and any resemblance to actual persons, living or dead, or to actual events or locales is entirely coincidental.

ISBN: 978-1-963575-01-9

*To Marcy, for being a great friend and sounding board.
Thank you for being you.*

CHAPTER ONE

"AND THAT'S when I knew I was going to be an insurance underwriter. I love assessing risk. It's an exciting field."

Leticia Ramirez ran a hand over the long sleeve of her dark blue cashmere mini dress. She'd actually dressed up for this—something she was slowly starting to regret with every word out of his mouth.

Phil rambled endlessly about his turtle, his new Prius and his "high-risk" job as an insurance underwriter. Apparently, the pun was intended. And he was not too happy when she didn't laugh out loud.

Since he was finally taking a breath, Leti decided to say a little something about herself. She hadn't had a chance to talk. Not once. It wasn't like she wanted to just talk about her life and her dreams, but maybe if he'd asked her one question, she wouldn't feel like she was a couture-wearing brick wall.

And then he smiled. It was a nice smile. Friendly. He grabbed his drink and kept talking—stuttering a little. It was almost sweet. He'd monopolized the conversation, but maybe the guy was just nervous. After all, it wasn't every day you got set up by someone's parent. Unless they were her parents. Her mother picked up a guy for her at the grocery store a few weeks ago and brought him home for a weekly dinner. Utter disaster.

This guy, her mamá met through the seamstress at her dry cleaners. She needed to stop agreeing to go on these "errand" dates.

He raised his drink to his mouth again, and Leti pounced on the short burst of silence. "I guess that's why I love being an accountant. I love numbers. And working for Busted Detective Agency, I get to explore all types of creative accounting practices." Numbers were stable. There was no ambiguity. They did what they were supposed to—unlike people.

Phil shook his head. "Does a small firm like that need an actual accountant?"

"Yes and no. I also have experience that helps when analyzing data."

"So, you're not doing *real* accounting." His chin tipped back in arrogance, or maybe he was trying to get to the fresh air of a higher altitude. Jerk. "Some people just don't get it. Playing with numbers doesn't make a person an accountant any more than guessing at probability makes someone an underwriter. No offense. I'm sure what you do is delightful."

Delightful? Offense taken. That was one step away from cute. What she did wasn't cute or delightful. She brought down thieves and embezzlers.

Although, she was actually studying to get her CPA. Soon. Well, soon was relative in this case. Once she got the certification, there'd be no reason for her to stay at Busted. Her parents would expect her to get a "real" job. They even had one lined up for her with one of their neighbors. A stable job. Something they could be proud of. And since she was currently living with them until she could get back on her feet, she needed to keep them happy. It was probably time to become an adult anyway.

Leti tried to smile and hoped it didn't look as awful as it felt. "I am a real accountant. The analysis I perform gives a complete picture of company or personal financial health. It's irrefutable proof of sales and expenditures. Not relying on assumptions based on historical data." *Like underwriters do.*

The guy grimaced. "We'll just have to agree to disagree."

Yes, let's do that. Leti took a sip of her wine. These were the times she wished she was more of a drinker. If she was, this night might not be the equivalent of a root canal. Unfortunately, alcohol just made her tired. This date didn't need any help on that front.

Phil smiled and took a drink of his wine.

Leti tipped her glass and matched him gulp for gulp. She might not be a drinker, but she needed something for her hands to do instead of checking the time on her phone. If she had to guess, she'd been on this date for three hours, at least. But since they hadn't received their food yet, it was probably more like forty-five minutes.

"I should run to the bathroom." Phil pushed back from the table and walked off.

Taking the opportunity, she grabbed her phone. Twenty minutes. She'd been sitting here for twenty minutes. Her finger hovered over the chat app. All she had to do was ask her business partner and high school friend Maggie Lane to call and fake an emergency.

Her friend would do it. She owed her. The only snag might be if Maggie was with her boyfriend. But honestly, they were always together. They could use a little time apart to let their libidos miss each other.

"How's your date?"

She knew that voice and it wasn't coming from her phone. She'd grown to hate that voice. Kevin Lane. Maggie's annoying older brother. He'd just come back from the military two months ago, and he hadn't wasted time settling in at the agency— and with the many women of Chicago. He was incapable of keeping his love-muscle to himself. Which sucked because he was pretty darn cute. And ALWAYS around.

"Have you resorted to stalking me now?" She might give him a bit of that attitude back. But he'd started it. Yes, *she'd* resorted to thinking like a five-year-old...

"You're like Starbucks, everywhere I look, there you are. Why would I need to stalk you?"

...but really, could anyone blame her?

"Why does anyone need to stalk anyone?" She'd found out he hated when people answered a question with a question. So, naturally, she did it as often as possible.

He moved closer to the table and therefore closer to

her. She could smell the sandalwood soap he used. Or maybe that was just how he smelled—musky and spicy. Each whiff made her want to jump up and down on him like a pogo stick. Every inhale dropped her IQ a few points. She didn't want to join the harem of women notching his bedpost.

"Hot date?" He nodded toward the bathrooms as his tongue slid along his bottom lip. It was almost hot. Almost made her want to slide her own tongue along that plump, pink lip. Except for the smirk. He knew what he was doing to her. How could he not tell? Her breath came in slow stutters. Her mind blanked. If it wasn't for that look on his face, she'd be a panting pile of goo.

Instead she wanted to smack the smirk right off of his face. "Yes."

"Really?"

"Yes. He's nice and he's very interesting. I could talk to him all night." She was so lucky to be indoors. God generally didn't send lightning strikes into buildings. But with this whopper, she might have to watch herself in the rain for a while. "In fact, we might just talk all night. Or maybe we'll find other things to do beside talk."

Her cheeks burned. What had she just said? The implication of not talking with this guy, that they'd somehow do something else, was not something she would ever say.

To. Anyone. And she could barely converse with the guy. There was no way any "other things" were going to happen tonight or any night.

"Really? Is that why you looked bored?"

"I don't know what you're talking about. It's not boredom. This is just how I look."

He smiled, and his face practically lit up. Good granola, the man was nice to look at. Dark blond hair that had grown longer since he left the military, but still didn't quite hit his collar. According to his sister that was the goal, and Leti hated that the thought got her excited. That blond hair swishing along his collar would look good. Like Thor. Nummy.

Not that Kevin was anywhere near as swoon-worthy as the Norse god.

But he so was.

"Just hush."

Kevin's forehead pinched in confusion. "Hush? I didn't say anything."

He hadn't. Fantastic. She was arguing with herself out loud now. "I could tell that you wanted to say something rude." *Nice save.*

"Have fun on your interesting date. See you around." He smiled and walked to a table across the room. He sat across from a woman. Not a woman. A goddess with long red hair and a size zero waist. She was probably a model or a weather girl.

And Leti was here with Phil. Who wasn't bad to look at, if you got past the sweater vest and the baggie corduroy pants. And if you ignored the fact that he hadn't asked her one question at all. And after twenty minutes they'd already had to agree to disagree.

Wasn't promising.

She watched Phil walk out from the bathroom with

a scowl on his face. He turned and faked a smile before sitting at a table. Not her table. But one in the next row. A woman with long dark hair, obviously also Latina, stared at Phil like he was crazy.

And he might be, if he set up another date in the middle of this one. He leaned in and grabbed the glass of wine on the table. He whispered something to the woman in front of him. She looked frightened and overall confused. Holy moly.

He. Did. Not.

"What are you doing?" The woman asked in a low voice that barely reached Leti.

"Aren't you my date, Leslie?" He put the wineglass down and looked around when she shook her head.

He. Did.

Phil didn't even know her name. Or what she looked like. She was just an interchangeable Latina woman. Leti raised her pointer finger to get his attention. Although, having him come back to the table now was just ridiculous. She didn't want him here and he didn't want to be here. But she was not about to get stuck with the bill.

Once her date saw her finger waving, he nodded. She could think of another finger she'd like to wave right about now. Which would be bad. What she did was even worse. She turned to the man sitting across from the fashion model on the other side of the room. The man whose attention was laser-focused on Leti.

Her face flamed. Since her date was a monumental failure, naturally Kevin should be there to witness it.

She couldn't just live this mortification in private. Nope.

"Your twin was sitting over there," Phil said, tipping his head toward the other table. The woman rolled her eyes and gave Leti a head shake that clearly told her she could do better. That might be Leti's own assumption, though.

With the exception of their hair and skin color, they were nothing alike. Leti was curvy, with high cheekbones and full lips. Her neighbor was rail thin with a narrow face. Most normal people could probably pick them out of a lineup. Then again, most normal people could remember the name of the person they were on a date with.

The server came up to the table and placed their food in front of them. Leti could barely look at her plate. She wasn't hungry. She wanted to get out of here and watch Hallmark movies.

Phil's phone rang just as he poked at his plate of food. "I should take this." He pulled his cell phone out and held it to his ear with a dramatic flair. "What?... No, the hospital... I'm very busy, but family comes first." He nodded and mouthed *I'm sorry* as he put on a Razzie-worthy performance. He stole her move. It was her idea to get pulled away by a fake emergency—and for the record, had she done it, the acting would have been much better. "I'll be there in fifteen minutes."

Fifteen minutes? There weren't any hospitals within fifteen minutes of the restaurant. Not with Chicago traffic. Made her wonder what the play was going to be.

"I'm sorry, but my mother fell down the stairs and I have to meet her at the hospital."

"Which hospital? I can go with." She was never ever going with, but messing with him could be fun.

"Oh, no. I wouldn't want to put you out." He lifted his hand and snapped his fingers. "Waiter! Waiter!"

The server came by without glaring at the crazy snapping man. The guy deserved an award—or at least a huge tip.

"Can you wrap this up? I need to leave."

The server took Phil's plate and looked over at her. She could stay here and finish alone. Which didn't sound bad, but then she'd have to watch Kevin and his hot new trophy canoodle—which did sound bad.

Oh, and she had a new Hallmark movie just begging to be watched at home. She had options.

Leti nodded and pushed her plate toward him. "Please wrap mine as well."

The server took both plates and scurried away. Leti and her date sat in silence as they both stared at the door to the kitchen. She was praying for the server to come back so she could leave. She could only assume he felt the same way.

"Well, it was nice to meet you, Leslie." He started to rise as the server dropped the leftovers on their table and placed the bill on top of his bag.

Phil pushed the bill to the side and opened the plastic bag to check the contents. He was going to leave without paying. For real? Where did her mother find these guys?

Dry cleaner. That's right. Her mamá needed to

start being more selective or Leti needed to buy her a gift card for laundry delivery. Maybe if she didn't leave the house, she'd never meet these "great" guys.

He picked up the bag. Oh. Heck. No.

She just needed to hold him up for a second and then run. She made an awkward grab for her bag of leftovers, swung the bag and tapped his wine glass. Wine everywhere. "Oops. I'm sorry." She got her purse while Phil was spluttering. "This was great." She turned and walked toward the front door.

"Leslie?" He called after her, but she didn't answer. It wasn't her *frogging* name. He must have gotten the hint because he stopped talking. She turned briefly, saw him sit down and open his wallet. He hemmed and hawed as he pulled out one bill after another.

She was pretty sure the guy was too cheap to leave a decent tip. She detoured to the host stand and pulled out two twenties, handing them to her server as he walked past. "Thank you. Sorry about all that."

He smiled, all white teeth. He was nice looking. He had a good job. "You had to sit with him. I think you ended up with the short end of the stick on that one."

She couldn't help the smile that spread across her face. Now that she was about to be free from the prattling-nightmare-date, she was feeling better. And this guy was kind and cute. She glanced down at his finger. And married.

"Have a great evening." She turned away as the server headed back to the tables.

Being a single woman was never easy. The men were either married or gay or narcissistic man-children.

She might have a bit of bias. Her sister and mother had found good ones. She just needed to find her own. It just wouldn't be tonight.

THE NEXT MORNING, Kevin Lane needed coffee. Not just any coffee, Cuban coffee. He'd missed the good stuff. The coffee shop he'd found in Kabul was amazing, but since he was nowhere near Kabul, he had to take what he could get. In the States, there was a chain on every corner. But the chain crap wasn't going to cut it.

Café Colao was his favorite when he was in town. And it was convenient. He needed convenient this morning after staring at the ceiling most of night. The scene at the restaurant last night with Leti kept replaying in his mind. At first, he'd thought it was funny, until that dumbass went to the wrong table.

What a jackass.

Then the jerk had barely had enough money to cover the bill. He haggled over ten bucks, making a scene until the server told him to just leave. The cap on the whole thing was when he mentioned no pussy being worth it.

Holy hell. Kevin was ticked. If he hadn't been with Robyn, he would've followed that guy out and kicked his ass. But he couldn't take that chance. She'd been through so much already. She didn't need to see him lose his shit on some asshole.

He threw the door open of the café, and it snapped

shut behind him. The place smelled like coffee beans and sugar. He could live here forever, but they probably wouldn't let him sleep on the floor—among other logistical problems, like running out of cash.

"Welcome to Café Colao." The woman was cute. Young. Maybe in college. And she popped her gum as her fingers hovered over the iPad sales terminal.

"Coffee black, please."

"Sure, sweetie." She clicked some buttons. "Eight sixteen."

He handed over the money and stood back against the counter. There was not a chair to be had in the packed café—unless he wanted to share a table. Which he didn't. He needed time. Five minutes of solitude to get his head on straight before he faced his sister and her cronies.

Not that he hated working for Maggie at her detective agency. It wasn't a bad place, but it wasn't what he wanted to do with his life. Watching cheaters and dealing with distraught wives was a service, but it wasn't the service he wanted to perform. He wanted to get into law enforcement. So he was just biding his time until he got the results from his written test with the Chicago Police Department. Which wouldn't be a big deal, but two of the guys he'd tested with had already gotten callbacks to start recruit processing. They were scheduled to take the power test next week.

He hadn't heard a damn thing, and it wasn't like he could follow this path forever. He was thirty-five years old. Most agencies stopped taking recruits after they turned thirty-six. He was at the cutoff. Had he known he wouldn't make the military his lifetime career, he would've left a long time ago and tested for law enforcement when he was younger, and his legs were fresher.

Instead he was on his own, trying to piece together his life in a place where he didn't feel like himself. He was used to bullets flying and decisions being life or death. His adrenaline was flatlined and it made him jumpy.

He smiled at the cute barista as she handed over his coffee. Her number was written along the side in looping letters and a heart over "I" in Tina. He didn't bother saying anything further. He wouldn't call. He wasn't good for anyone right now. He needed his life back on track before he could even think about sharing space with anyone else.

He took a gulp of his coffee, burning his mouth, but couldn't seem to care. He just wanted to sit down and caffeinate his head on straight before he headed to work. He looked around the room for a chair. A laugh tickled over the low murmur of the patrons. A laugh he recognized. He'd never heard it aimed his way, but he knew Leti could laugh. She'd laughed enough at Busted —with her partners, with the clients.

No matter what he did, though, he couldn't get her to laugh. Although he was a master at getting her to glare. If that was a skill that paid, he'd be up to his eyeballs in gold coins. Instead he was here watching Leti laugh at some guy in a suit sitting across from her.

She rested her hand on his arm. A breakfast date?

First thing in the morning. Or was it the topper to a late night? Crap.

The guy in the suit stood up at the same time as Leti. She managed to embody all of Kevin's hot-teacher fantasies. Narrow black skirt that hit right above the knee and clung to hips that curved in all the right places. Just a glimpse of the long legs that hid underneath. Tight satin shirt buttoned just low enough to show taupe skin that looked fucking edible. Long hair pinned into a bun and glasses on the bridge of her nose.

She looked better than the coffee in his hands.

Then the guy looked into her eyes. There was no more laughing. Somewhere along the way, the conversation had gotten serious. And then this guy stared at her until he wrapped his arms around her waist and kissed her cheek. It was smarmy.

And Kevin didn't like it. Not that it mattered what he liked. She wasn't his. And from what he could see, he never would be.

She liked smarmy suit guys and sweater-vest assholes. Kevin didn't own a suit and wouldn't be caught dead in a sweater vest, even if he did own one. He wasn't a lawyer or dentist or whatever the tool who was walking away was. He was just him, and she'd never be into him because...

Oh yeah—she hated him.

That fact almost made him turn around and leave. Almost.

CHAPTER TWO

LETI STOOD in the coffee shop with Enzo leaning into her. Somehow, the smell of coffee and carbs was overpowered by his clean scent. He smelled better than her mother's pozole on a cold winter's night.

"I just need you to sift through the financials. But keep it between us." He was a good-looking man, and from what she just learned he smelled good too. And he was nice. Too bad he seemed to already be taken.

Him and Jessi Xu, the woman who worked the front desk at Busted, had some love/ hate thing going that bordered on adorable. He'd come to her rescue, and Jessi pretended he hadn't. They seemed to hover around each other, waiting for something to happen.

"This could be dangerous. You have to be discreet." His eyes crinkled with concern. "Are you sure you're okay with this?"

She smiled. "I can handle it."

He stepped back. "I'll send you the numbers from

his different companies. Anything you find, bring directly to me."

"I will."

He smiled and grabbed his briefcase. "Thank you."

She slid the USB and paperwork he'd given her into her bag and sat back down. She wasn't about to start looking at classified information out here in the open, but she couldn't head back to the office just yet. She wanted to finish her coffee in relative silence.

There were murmurs from patrons and the hum of the cappuccino machines, but it wasn't a noise she had to respond to. She could block it out. Not like at Busted. She loved her friends, but they could be a bit much when she needed to concentrate. And she worked with numbers; she generally needed to concentrate. No distractions.

As soon as she walked into that office, they'd want to talk. And she didn't want to talk about her date last night. It was going to end up being a thing. All gossip was a thing.

"Good morning." The voice that had been grating on her nerves for the past couple months interrupted her mellow. His was the picture next to distraction in the dictionary—as well as some other words she didn't like to think out loud.

"Good morning."

Kevin sat on the bench Enzo just vacated. Without invitation.

"Yes, please sit down. I wasn't enjoying some alone time."

His face fell. That gorgeous smile gone, leaving a

hole in Leti's chest. "I'll leave then. I'm sorry to interrupt." He went to stand up.

Okay, fine. It was sad. She was evil. He hadn't done anything but sit down and be friendly. "No, please stay." Alone time was overrated.

"Okay." He sat down and leaned back, and a smile spread over his lips. "Why do you need alone time? Don't you live alone?"

It wasn't that he asked if she lived alone, it was how he asked it. It was the arrogant turn of his lips. Like she couldn't find someone to live with. "I don't live alone."

"Who do you live with?"

My parents hung on her tongue, but she could only imagine the smirk getting larger. It's not like she had to live at home, it just made more sense to save some money after the divorce. Granted, the divorce had been finalized two years ago, but her bank account was so happy with her living sitch that she ate her pride like ice cream in July.

Her sanity wasn't as excited. "I'm at my parents' house."

He didn't say anything, just kept looking at her. The staring was disconcerting, but the confusion was annoying. She leaned to the side to pull her half-eaten breakfast close—she tore an end off the tornillo and popped it in her mouth. His eyes stayed on her. She came back to center and leaned the other way.

She felt like she was looking at the Mona Lisa. His eyes just kept following her. "What?"

His eyes cleared as he played with the coffee in front of him. "So, dating again, huh?"

"Why wouldn't I be?"

"I'm just surprised you tried dating so soon after the disaster last night."

"Last night wasn't that big of a disaster." It was. It was like the Deepwater Horizon explosion, complete with blowhards. Not that she'd tell him what a complete cluster it had become. He'd already seen too much.

"Is that why you tried again this morning?" The right side of his mouth tipped up in that smirk.

"Tried?"

"Another date." Kevin nodded to the door. "Although that date appeared to go better. At least that guy got a little hug action."

Hug action? She huffed. "There was no action. What about you and gorgeous redhead from last night?"

"We're not talking about me. Does that guy know there's no action? He looked pretty excited to have his hands all over you."

Leti didn't know what to say. She wasn't supposed to tell her partners about the work she was doing for him, but she also couldn't let them hear she was after the man. Jessi would kill her. Enzo would kill her if he thought Jessi was upset. "If I didn't know you better, I'd think you were jealous."

"Good thing you know better." He brought his coffee to his lips so she couldn't read if he actually meant that. He probably didn't do jealousy. And he wouldn't get jealous over her. "So, who was the suit?"

"Who was the redhead?" She wasn't going to answer without him answering first.

"Fine. Robyn. She's the wife of an old Army buddy of mine. He passed away in Afghanistan and I like to check in on her every now and then. She had a rough time of it at first since they have three kids."

"That's nice." And it was.

"Her new husband thinks so, too."

Even nicer. Leti nodded.

"Your turn," Kevin practically sang as he leaned back.

"Not that it's any of your business" —she'd better tell him who he was before rumors of some dating thing swirled around the office— "but the suit, who seems to be gaga for Jessi, needed some advice."

"What kind of advice?"

"I wouldn't be a good friend if I gave away everyone else's secrets." She'd stand up and walk away, but she wasn't ready to go into the office. She had a tornillo. A flaky, pudding-filled tornado-looking thing. She pulled off another piece and slid it in her mouth. It was delicious.

"Do you give everyone advice?"

"Just those who ask." She slid another bite into her mouth. It really did make unpleasant interrogations tolerable.

"What if I wanted advice?"

She almost laughed. Like he would want advice from her and like she'd be willing to give it to him. "What kind of advice?"

"Let me see." He took a long pull from the coffee in his hands.

She could almost see the wheels creaking in his head. "Don't hurt yourself. If you don't need advice right now, you can always ask later."

"I might take you up on that." He laughed. "When I can come up with something I want your opinion on."

"Well, I might offer you one if you can come up with something I want to give you an opinion on." *Jerk.* She finished her coffee and popped the last piece of the tornillo in her mouth. "This has been as delightful as a migraine, but I should get to work."

"Come on now, talking to me isn't that painful."

"I should go." She stood up and grabbed her bag. His comment didn't deserve a response. "Goodbye, Kevin."

"See you around, Ramirez." He pulled out that smile. Not *that* smile—the annoying smirk one. No. She could handle the annoying smirk. He broke out the honest smile. The one that looked sincere and made his eyes sparkle. The man looked sweet and innocent when he smiled like that. Dangerous.

Which meant he looked hot. Not that she saw him as hot, but if a woman was into that type of thing— dark blond stubble lining a strong chin, green sparkling eyes—he could be. His face relaxed when he laughed.

And dad-gum it, she was totally into that type of thing. She was into him. And she was thinking words like dad-gum.

She was so dad-gummed.

TWO WEEKS LATER, Kevin sat at his sister's desk at Busted. He'd tried to talk to Leti about the date he'd witnessed with that jerk, but she refused to talk. She hadn't even told his sister yet. Either she was feeling a certain way about it, or she wanted to pretend it never happened. He couldn't blame her either way.

He was uploading pictures of some cheating jerk with his tongue stuck down the throat of a more-than-willing woman—who wasn't his wife.

The guy's ring finger was lighter and indented where his ring should be, but the woman didn't seem to care or maybe she didn't notice.

Either way, Kevin had a meeting tomorrow with this guy's wife. He got the joy of telling her that her husband was a slimeball. He hated this job sometimes. But it was probably a good idea to practice. When he made it onto the police force he'd have to deliver messages that weren't always pleasant. Chalk it up to experience.

He clicked at the mouse as he printed the best shots onto eight by ten sheets. He poked at the keys trying to write a report that would probably take Maggie five minutes to complete. Instead he was hunting and pecking at the letters.

"A gorilla could type faster." Maggie sat in the chair next to him and rammed the arm of her chair into his. "Move back." She pointed at the center drawer.

"Can't it wait?" Where the hell was the P? There were twenty-six letters and he was positive one of them was a P. What kind of keyboard didn't have a P? Screw it. They didn't eat at a pizza place, it was a restaurant now.

Really, when a woman found out that her husband was cheating, did she care what they had for dinner? All she cared about were the pictures and finding a good divorce lawyer.

"I've been waiting. For. Hours. You are taking forever to write one report." She stretched her long neck like a giraffe and stared at the screen. Then she moved her long tentacles and grabbed the mouse. "You have one paragraph done."

"Maybe if the keys on this keyboard had the letters on them."

"The letters are on most of the keys." She minimized his document and opened folders and files.

"Most. Have you thought about buying a new one?"

"Have you thought about buying your own, so you can leave my shit alone?" Maggie clicked print on a document as she elbowed him.

A bony-elbow-shaped pain burst through his chest. "Ouch. You're getting cranky in your old age." Another elbow hit him in the same spot.

Maggie added a slap to his shoulder. At least that one didn't hurt. "Why are you such a jerk?"

A loud snort came from across the room. Leti stood at the printer sifting through the paperwork.

"What's so funny?" Kevin knew what she was laughing at, but he wanted to hear her admit it.

"This paperwork." She waved her pages at him as she handed Maggie the papers she'd printed.

"Accounting joke? Is that even a thing?"

"Yes. Accountants can be quite funny." Leti raised her chin, and she looked so damn hot when she set her jaw. It was defiant and strong.

"When are accountants ever funny?" Maggie howled.

Leti giggled. "Your retirement planning is pretty funny."

"See. Not funny." Maggie shook her head.

"I find it hilarious." Leti laughed, deep and sexy.

Kevin felt a laugh bubble in his chest. Maggie's retirement plan was probably kind of funny. He wanted to show Leti his retirement account and see if he could get her to laugh like that again. He'd been paying into it since he was eighteen, so it had to be better than his sister's. "Ouch." Another elbow hit his chest. "Stop doing that." He was tempted to bodycheck his sister, but he hadn't done anything to her since he was ten and his dad whipped his ass for shoving her.

Never did that again. Didn't mean he didn't want to on occasion.

Maggie stood up as she sifted through the paperwork. Her phone beeped at her hip, and she pulled it out. Smiled at the screen. "Well, guys and gals, my work here is done. I'm heading out to dinner with Chase."

Apparently, his sister met the Chicago detective several months ago while working a case. So far, he seemed to be a good guy. And his sister was completely loopy over him. She slipped out the back door and the room went quiet.

Leti went to her desk, put on her reading glasses and started typing, then printed out a stack of pages. Kevin watched as she wrote, stapled, and sorted. She was all single-minded focus, like a teen texting her boyfriend.

He looked at his own screen, but the step-by-step description of a cheating husband wasn't exactly holding his interest. He was almost jealous of her determination and interest in her work. He wanted to feel that. But given she worked with numbers, he couldn't imagine what she had was any more exciting than his philanderer's handbook. So why he asked, "What are you working on?" he had no idea.

"Nothing important." She sat over the pages, her highlighter poised for action. For something that was "nothing", she was awfully focused. The highlighter slid across the page. Line. Line. Line. She grabbed a pen and wrote along the edge of the paper.

"What's nothing important?"

"Uh-huh."

"Is it the answer to the universe?" He stuck out his neck, trying to see what was so damn interesting that she obviously wasn't listening to a word he said.

She pulled out a red pen and underlined. "Uh-huh." Breaking out the red pen was apparently much more exciting than talking with him. He wanted a little excitement.

Walking over to her desk, he couldn't help himself. He leaned over her back. Her hair smelled amazing.

Not that he was smelling her hair. That would be weird. But she did smell good. Like sugar cookies.

If she smelled this good, he could only imagine how she tasted. And he'd have to imagine. She'd rip off his tongue and slap him with it if he even thought about giving her a lick.

Her red pen slid under a grouping of numbers. Not that there was any difference between those numbers and the thousands of others that covered the page. Lines and lines of numbers with small breaks between. Highlights covered some and lines were under others. How she knew what the hell she was looking at was rather impressive. She underlined another grouping. She didn't turn to him or tell him to go away. Either she didn't notice, or she was starting to like him.

"What ya doin'?"

Her body flew up, temporarily airborne. He pulled back to avoid a head-butt to the nose. "What the... good gravy. Have you lost your mind, sneaking up on me?"

Verdict in—didn't notice. Not that he thought she all of the sudden grew to like him. That would require some sort of divine intervention or a miracle.

"I was talking to you. It's not my fault you weren't paying attention." He leaned in closer. "What are you working on?"

"I believe we had this conversation already." She held her hands over the pages as red crept up her face. "Nothing."

"Is it secret?" He looked past her fingers to the page beneath. "What does the Wacker Children's Association have to do with it?"

"Nothing. Don't you have work to do?" She piled all the pages in the center of her desk.

He inched forward—his breath blowing a piece of her hair—for no other reason than he wanted to. The glare she was giving him said she wasn't liking it. He wasn't liking being lied to. Like his father always said, lies of omission were still lies, and don't let anyone tell you different.

"My dad did some work for that organization a few years ago," he admitted. "The precinct ran a fundraiser to get the kids off the street. Are you looking into them?" He was prying, but he had to get her to talk somehow—especially since she obviously didn't want to. Which was what made it so fun.

She huffed. "Why do you care?"

"Why won't you answer me?"

"Look, Enzo asked me to keep this quiet."

"So, this has to do with hug action. Why does he want you to look into Wacker Children's?"

She stared at the desk, almost like she was hoping for it to swallow her whole. "Are you seriously not going to drop this?"

"Nope." He knew her stuff would be more interesting. Her reaction solidified that assumption.

"I don't think he'd mind me sharing it with anyone here at Busted, but you need to keep it quiet outside of the office. He didn't ask me to look into Wacker Children's Association. He asked me to look into his boss, Stanley Welford. It looks like he might be infusing the charity with personal funds."

"So, he's donating money to his own organization. That's not weird."

"No, but he's moving that money to an offshore company. It's not staying within the organization. It looks like it if you go by the profit and loss statements, but Danni found some account information offshore that shows money being funneled out, not being spent as it should."

Danni Stein was another partner at Busted. She was the brains behind the computer and tended to operate on both sides of the law. She'd almost lost it all last month when her now-boyfriend had some run-ins with Chicago's finest. At least that was the gossip around the office. But Danni's gossip wasn't nearly as interesting as the jerk funneling money.

"So, he's stealing from kids." It was bad enough when people stole, but stealing from homeless kids was a new kind of low.

Leti shrugged one shoulder. "Not...exactly. I don't think so. I think he's funneling his own money through the organization."

"But doesn't it look like more money is going to the children than there is? 'Cause he's reporting that the money is going to the kids, but it's not."

She sighed. "Yeah, you're right. He is."

"So, we have to stop him."

"Stopping him might be harder than it sounds. He's a partner in one of the biggest law firms in the city. He has more friends in high places than I have books."

Kevin felt the smile inch along his lips. "So, you like

books." He could picture her with her hair up, wearing pink pajamas, curled up on a big fluffy chair.

"What?"

"I'm just picturing you reading in front of the fire with your glasses on and hot chocolate."

She shook her head. "I don't drink hot chocolate."

"Why do you want to ruin my nerd-girl fantasies?" He was pouting, but it worked.

Leti laughed as she pushed her hair behind her ear. The sound was amazing. "So you finally admit I'm in your fantasies."

He wanted to say no, but despite his best efforts he could admit she'd been part of one or two fantasies. But he had a feeling she'd run screaming from the room if he actually admitted to it.

"What do you fantasize about?" He sat on the edge of the desk and leaned toward her.

A glint passed through her eyes as she smiled. "What or whom?"

Whom? Her lips curved around the word like they would a popsicle on a hot day.

Every instinct told him to lean down and bridge the distance between them. Every nerve in his body wanted to touch his lips to hers. If he wasn't so afraid she'd punch him in the balls, he would.

Her smile disappeared. Her tongue slid along between her lips, leaving a shiny trail. Heat scorched the air.

He could practically taste her as he leaned in. The smell of vanilla circled and dragged him in. Inches. His lips hovered over hers. Her breath gasped from between her lips but she didn't pull away.

Closer. Her eyes drilled into his as she leaned in. Slow puffs of thick air stuttered in his chest.

There was a reason this was a bad idea, but he couldn't remember why. And he couldn't think of one reason why he cared.

Ring.

Bells were ringing, and his lips had barely touched hers.

Leti's eyebrows arched in confusion as she pulled back. Not exactly the reaction a guy wanted when he was leaning in for a kiss. She turned to the side and stared at the phone on her desk like it was speaking Russian.

She moved back, away from him. Toward the damn ringing. She picked up the phone and the air cooled. The moment was over. If the fact that Leti wouldn't look at him told him anything, it was that the moment had been torpedoed and blazed.

And maybe that was for the best. If only his body had received the memo.

CHAPTER THREE

TWENTY MINUTES LATER, Leti dragged her purse out of the bottom drawer of her desk. She sifted through the insides, moving aside her wallet and a half-eaten bag of peanuts. Buying time. Hoping Kevin would get bored and go home.

No such luck.

Kevin stood over her desk. Waiting. "Are you ready to go yet?"

She didn't want to leave with Kevin. He'd been inches from her less than a half hour ago. She'd been millimeters from sticking her tongue down his throat. If he had moved in for the kiss, that most definitely would have happened.

So putting herself into that situation again was not at the top of her list—or maybe it was—which was why she could not be alone with him. She pulled out a pen and double-clicked it before sliding it back in her desk. "I'm just getting my stuff together."

"You've said that for the past ten minutes." She

could feel him breathing down her neck like a dog waiting for dinner time. And it was probably his dinner time. They'd missed dinner while they were working. "How much stuff do you have?"

"I have normal amounts of stuff, but I didn't realize we were in a hurry." She pulled out her phone and stared at the screen. No alerts. Nothing. "Why don't you go, and I'll follow behind?"

"Really?" Kevin's eyebrows launched up to his hairline. Thank goodness for his hair or they might have left his darn face. "It's eight o'clock at night in the city of Chicago."

She'd admit Chicago at night wasn't a ride over a rainbow by unicorn, but if you practiced situational awareness, Chicago wasn't as dangerous as some media outlets liked to paint it.

"You shouldn't be allowed to leave alone at night."

"Shouldn't be allowed?" Was she a toddler? He'd implied this before, the night they'd met. Like she was incapable of handling the streets of Chicago. "I grew up here."

"So did I."

"In Beverly." The laugh bubbled in her chest and burst out her lips. "That part of the city is practically the suburbs. You might have grown up on the South Side, but I grew up west of Pulaski. You have no idea what the city really is."

"No you didn't. You grew up in Lincoln Park."

"I know where I grew up."

"Do you?" Kevin frowned.

He knew what she'd told everyone, but very few

people knew the truth about where she'd grown up. She wasn't embarrassed, it just didn't come up very often. And her parents pretended like their time next to the stockyards never existed. "We moved to Lincoln Park when I was sixteen. Before then I was in the Back of the Yards." Why did she tell him that?

"Back of the Yards, huh."

"Huh, what?" Back of the Yards had a bad reputation, but it was full of good, hard-working people. When her parents came to this country, they had nothing. They'd worked hard and built a life for themselves and their three children.

His eyes traveled up her body—not in a sexy, *I want to have your babies*, kind of way. It was more assessing.

This was why she didn't tell anyone where she was really from. There was pity or judgment or recrimination. He was so hard to read. She couldn't tell which one was swimming in that one look. And that look was unnerving. She wanted to cross her arms to cover herself, but she refused to give him the satisfaction of seeing her squirm. "What?"

"I'm just surprised. I can't picture you growing up without a Neiman Marcus nearby."

"I don't always wear designer stuff." Only when her mother bought it for her. Otherwise, she was just as happy with cute little dresses from Target. "But thank you for appreciating my style."

He hadn't really said that, but she wasn't above taking liberties.

"So are you ready?" He hadn't moved. He was still

hovering, taking all the air from the room. Still annoying all the sanity from her body.

"Fine." She stood and hung her purse on her shoulder, whipping it just a bit too hard so it aimed right for his... body.

He twisted to the side, avoiding the collision. He smiled as his hand waved her forward.

"You know I leave here alone all the time," she pointed out.

His brows pinched together, but he didn't say anything. Something told her he didn't like that. Which was sweet. Except when it interfered with her plans.

He moved to the back door and held it open. His cologne or the smell of his body circled her head and made her lean toward him. Spicy and musky. Delicious. Not that she was obvious-like as she smelled him in. That would be weird. Just a little lean and a subtle inhale.

"Get any closer and I'll have to carry you."

Arrogant ass...tronaut.

She stopped and spun to face him, intending to give him a piece of her mind. And froze. There were no more mind pieces to give. His body was hard against her chest. His green eyes darkened. No humor. No smirk. She swore he was looking at her like he wanted her. Like she wasn't the only one feeling this pull. This need. Everything went blank. His lips were inches from hers. His eyes stared deep into hers and she hated to admit it, but she liked it.

She watched his eyes darken further as her tongue slid along her bottom lip—an open invitation for him to take over. Her lips tingled. Her breath spindled from her body in reedy strings. Heat from his body circled hers and pulsed at her core. Too much.

This was too much. Her vision darkened at the edges as need throbbed in her veins. She needed him to touch her. To want her. She needed him to wrap his arms around her and relieve the ache. She stood there. So close to him. To what she wanted.

A door slammed outside. The neighbor's voices carried across the lot, pulling his eyes from hers. She stepped back.

"We should go." His words held an edge of regret.

She'd like to think there was a bit of regret. That regret was weighing on her hyper-aware body about now. She hated leaving like that—all horned up and no one to blow...

Where in tarnation did that come from? This is what he did—made her all foul-minded and desperate. Blow? She'd need to do at least ten Hail Mary's to wipe that from her memory.

The back lot was close to empty. Kevin's truck sat in a diagonal spot along the building. Her little green Honda Accord hybrid was wedged between a fence and a garage across the alley. The soft glow of overhead lamps gave some light, but there were still too many shadows and too much darkness.

Not that she'd ever admit it to Kevin, but he was right. She hated leaving the building at night. The night was lonely and creepy. It was nice to have a body-guard. Her shoes crunched on the gravel as she angled past the sidewalk and walked the length of the diagonal parking spaces.

"Good night," Mr. Bodyguard called from behind his truck, arms crossed over his chest. He looked good. Almost good enough for her to walk the two steps she needed to get to him, and then... Well, that was where the problem lay. In the "and then." She wasn't exactly the love 'em and leave 'em type. And he wasn't the sticking-around type.

She smiled his way. The "and then" didn't stop the grateful swirling through her chest. And he wouldn't move. He just kept waiting, watching her walk to her car.

"Good night." She turned and stepped into the alley.

Squealing tires.

Lights flooded the gravel lining the road.

Leti turned, deer-in-the-headlights style. All she saw was light coming closer. No sounds but the deep rumble of an engine. She needed to move. She'd never make it. The car was too close.

A body slammed into her. She flew. She crashed. Her chest scraped against the gravel. Her head jerked, making contact with the concrete.

She couldn't move, her body flattened beneath a large weight. A large weight that was hard and breathing heavy.

"Stay down." Kevin's voice tickled her ear, and Leti turned her head to see what the blazes was going on.

Kevin angled above her, one arm propping him over her body. The other arm held a gun.

The lights disappeared. The sounds faded. They stayed down for what felt like an eternity, until Kevin holstered the gun she hadn't known he carried.

"Are you okay?" He lifted off her completely, and reached down to help her stand. "Anything broken?"

"I'm okay." She thought she was okay, anyway. She looked down as she shook her arms and legs, brushed bits of gravel and leaves off her clothes. She lifted her hand to her throbbing temple, and the sting yanked a hiss from her mouth.

"Hold on." He pulled her to his Silverado and opened the passenger side. "Sit."

She would argue but she was staring at her hand. Her bloody fingertips. Kevin disappeared around the back of the truck and returned holding a first aid kit.

"This might hurt a bit." He pulled a wipe from the bag and ran it along the sting at her forehead. "Does that happen a lot?"

"What?" Pain needled at her, making it hard to think.

"A car trying to run you down?"

"No." Leti's eyes watered as the evil wipe cleaned the scrape. She couldn't stop staring down the blurry alley looking for headlights.

Kevin stared at her forehead like he was performing surgery. "You should call the cops."

"Why?"

He went into his bag of tricks, pulled out a cotton swab and a tube of gel. He gently spread the cool ointment along the wound with the swab, his tongue peeking out the side of his lips as he concentrated on the task. "Someone tried to run you over."

"It was probably just a distracted driver. They whip around here all the time trying to avoid the traffic on Kedzie Avenue." She hoped it was, anyway.

She shivered as his hand disappeared and he went back to his bag. The evening was a bit chilly, but at least when he was standing between her legs, she was warm—not that she was thinking about him between her legs or anything. Her head was throbbing too much for that. And a car just tried to run her over—or did it?

"Why would anyone want to run me over?"

"That was going to be my question for you." His touch was so soft as he taped a piece of gauze to her forehead. So patient as he guided her hair away from the tape. So intent as he avoided her eyebrows.

"They wouldn't. No one would want to run me over." She was pretty darn boring.

"What about that Welford guy?"

"What about him? He doesn't even know I'm looking into him." No one knew—except for Kevin, Danni, and Enzo.

"Are you sure?" Kevin pulled out a packet and ripped it open.

"How would he know?"

"I'm not sure, but that didn't look like a distracted driver. They generally don't speed up when they get closer to a person." He sighed as he handed her two pills. "This is Tylenol. It'll help with the pain." He pushed everything back into his first aid kit and tossed it on the backseat.

"Maybe it was the Testy Tenant." Leti took the pills and jiggled them in her hand.

"Who's that?" He reached across her for a water bottle from the center console and twisted it open.

"Sal, from Sal's Delivery Service." She pointed at the trucks lined up along the building. Sal rented the other half of the Busted building from Maggie. He liked to call her a slumlord, a cold-hearted bit... yeah Leti couldn't even think the words. "But he hasn't whined in months. Ever since Chase had a little talk with him. We don't think the guy likes cops."

Kevin held out the open water bottle. "Would he have a reason to run you down?"

"I parked in front of his garage a few weeks ago, but he didn't say anything, just glared." Leti took the water bottle from him. "I only parked for five minutes, so I don't think he would resort to murder for that."

Kevin nodded. "We should get you home. Grab what you need from your car and I'll drive."

"What?" Leti swallowed the pills with some water. "Why can't I drive?"

"Because you were nearly run down. Because you hit your head. Because it would make me and the city of Chicago feel better if you weren't behind the wheel until we know if you have a concussion."

"I don't have a concussion."

Kevin turned on his cellphone flashlight and pointed it at her eyes. She blinked as he moved the light from one eye to the next. "Does this hurt?"

"No, but I will hurt you if you don't stop."

"Fine." He chuckled. "I don't think you have a concussion, but we'll want to keep an eye on it."

"Okay." Her eyes weren't blurry or crossed as she stood up. The pain in her head was tolerable, but very much there. She walked toward the driver's side of her Honda. If she stayed off major roadways, she could probably make it home without incident.

"What are you doing?"

"I'm heading home." She opened the door and tossed her purse across to the passenger seat.

Kevin stormed over. "If Maggie hit her head like that would you let her drive home?"

"No." She hated when he made sense.

"Grab what you need and I'll take you home."

"How will I get to work tomorrow?"

"I can pick you up." He opened the passenger door and stole the purse before heading toward his truck.

She closed her eyes. The pain in her head wasn't ebbing. The smart thing to do would be to not drive after a head injury. But getting into a car with Kevin didn't exactly feel like the smart thing to do either.

Her eyes flew open when a hand touched her back.

"Are you okay?" Somehow he was at her side, all concern and furrowed brows.

"I'm fine."

"Maybe we should head to the emergency room."

"I'm really okay." She wasn't going to be driving herself tonight. And if she didn't let him drive her home, she'd have to spend the next five hours at the hospital for them to tell her she was fine.

She closed the car door and clicked the locks. "Let's go."

Kevin led her across the alley to the passenger side of his truck. He opened the door and waited as she slid inside. He pressed the door closed and jogged around to his side of the cab.

He started the engine and pulled into the alley and onto Kedzie. They didn't say a word as he maneuvered through traffic. The lights bouncing and pinging in front of her eyes made her head swim a bit. There was no way she could have driven home.

"Thank you." Warmth spread through her chest.

His shoulders sagged as if they were weighed down by guilt. "For knocking your face into the cement?"

"For making sure I wasn't embedded in the hood of that car." She smiled. "For making sure I didn't wrap my car around a tree."

"You're welcome." He laid his head against the headrest. "It scared the hell out of me."

"What did?"

"Seeing the car coming for you." He tapped his hand against the steering wheel. "I didn't know what to do. I just knew I had to get you out of the way."

Leti reached across the cab and rested a hand on his knee. "And you did get me out of the way. I'm still here."

"I don't know what I would have done if it would have hit you." He shook his head, lost in some thought that was bringing the corners of his mouth down to his shoulders.

He turned to her and the hand that was resting on

his knee. The hand that somehow started to rub back and forth trying to soothe whatever thought was in his mind away. It felt so natural. "You don't have to find out."

He removed one of his hands from the steering wheel and wrapped his fingers around hers. "Thank you."

"For what?"

"I needed to hear that." He smiled.

Leti leaned her head against the headrest and closed her eyes. Tonight had been rough, but feeling Kevin's hand stroking hers was somehow making all the hurt go away.

LIGHTS FLASHED and disappeared as Kevin drove the nearly empty streets of Chicago. Well, not empty, but empty by Chicago standards. This would be a regular rush-hour in any other city. Cars weren't bumper to bumper, but there was barely room to switch lanes.

Leti sat in the seat next to him. Quiet. She had been right. People flew down those alleys like they were qualifying for the Daytona 500. But what happened in that alley wasn't normal.

The headlights had turned on and then he'd heard the engine rev as the car had barreled toward Leti. It hadn't been a texting driver or some other normal distraction. They'd been sitting in wait.

He needed to know who was after Leti and why.

He didn't think she'd let him drive her around the city of Chicago for the foreseeable future, even if it was his attempt at keeping her safe.

She'd barely admitted something had happened tonight. She wouldn't exactly jump at having him hanging around. Which meant he was going to have to leave her alone tonight—and every other night. Alone with someone after her. The thought made his stomach knot and his head ache.

Who would be willing to run her down? He needed to know before they tried again. This was when he missed being in the military. In Fallujah, when he needed intel, he had contacts. He'd work the streets. He'd call on one of his friends in intelligence. Now he had no one.

He drove past the condominiums in Lincoln Park that cost more than a mansion in the suburbs. Old buildings with grand columns and ornate gargoyle statues set against freshly manicured lawns. In the daylight they looked monumental and stately. At night they were downright ominous. Or maybe it was just tonight. Because everywhere he looked, he saw potential danger.

Those damn gargoyles could fall from the roof and do some serious damage. She could walk into one of those grand looking columns.

He just had to get her a few more blocks to her quiet neighborhood, surrounded by her parents. Although that didn't really solve the problem of keeping her safe past tonight.

Red light washed over the front of the truck as they sat at a stop light. He needed more information, and he knew only one name.

Kevin turned down the side street to her parents' home. The lights were out. The houses blazed but the lamp posts were dark. Only on her street. Something was wrong. "Is this normal?"

"No." Leti looked around the area like her head was on a swivel.

He watched all the cars parked along the street as he passed. No movement. But that didn't mean someone wasn't hiding.

The smart thing to do would be to get her far away from the mundane. Switch up her routine so whoever was after her couldn't find her.

"Do you want to stay at my place tonight?" It was technically Maggie's, but he didn't think his sister would mind.

"I think I'll be okay?" She said it more as a question. "I'm taking Krav Maga at the YMCA. It's great cardio."

He smiled. "I appreciate your martial art prowess, but it's best for you to not be where the danger is. Is there somewhere else you can stay?"

"My parents would worry." Leti attempted a smile —a very poor attempt as the corners of her eyes pinched in concern. She picked up her purse. "Do you mind walking me to the door?"

Like he would have left her alone in the darkness. "Not at all."

She didn't get out immediately, which gave Kevin a chance to parallel-park into a spot. He slid the Beretta from the side holster as he jumped out of the truck and walked to the passenger side.

She slid out and closed the passenger door as he checked from right to left. No movement on the street. Although it was hard to spot anything with all the darkness surrounding them.

Her heels clicked along the sidewalk as they walked toward a two-story tan brick house. Lights from inside washed over the front yard. A black iron fence surrounded the property. It was elegant. And although the gate didn't appear to have a lock, the security company sign in the window made Kevin feel a bit better about leaving Leti here alone.

Not that an alarm meant he wasn't going to keep working on figuring this whole situation out. But at least he might be able to sleep tonight.

She walked up to the gate, pausing at the mailbox. She tipped the lid and pulled out a handful of letters before opening the gate.

"Are your parents home?" he asked at the same time she turned to him and said, "I just wanted to say thank you." She smiled.

"You're welcome." His body hummed from that look on her face. It was aimed at him, and didn't that just turn him on. It made his night—hell, his year.

"I'm pretty sure my parents are here. The lights are on." She started toward the stairs. "Let me check."

He followed her up the narrow steps to a brown

door. Leti turned the handle and the door popped open. She stuck her head inside and smiled. "They're here."

"Good." He nodded. Part of him wished they'd been out so he could stick around a little bit.

Leti stepped closer. "I really can't thank you enough."

He could think of a lot of ways for her to thank him. And although some of those ways included them both being naked, a lot of them just included that smile —maybe one of those laughs she threw out earlier.

"Just keep yourself safe until we figure this thing out. And make sure you set that alarm." He nodded to the sign in the window.

"If it will make you feel better." She smiled.

He couldn't help the smile that spread across his lips. "It will."

She leaned in and rested her lips on his cheek.

His eyes slid shut. Her lips were soft on his skin. She slipped away quickly, but his body hadn't quite figured that out. He was in need of one hell of a cold shower.

"Thank you for getting me home."

"No problem." He stepped down the stairs and headed for the street. He couldn't stop himself. He needed one more look—just to see if she was still there —he turned around.

She smiled. "Bye, Kevin."

"See you around." He couldn't believe she'd caught him.

He closed the gate and walked to his car. Once there, he watched the house until he was certain no one was going to follow her in.

Or maybe to make sure she wasn't going to come back out.

CHAPTER FOUR

LETI WATCHED KEVIN WALK AWAY, and she technically kept watching long after it was needed. But who could blame her. He had a great behind. He was easy to watch.

And the whole driving her home and saving her from moving vehicles had her all hot and bothered. Which was why she'd kissed him. On the cheek. If she was like Maggie or Danni, she would have fused her mouth with his. But she wasn't that bold.

So she'd leaned in and kissed his cheek, hoping he'd realize how thankful she really had been. It didn't matter why that car flew through that alley, all that mattered is he'd pulled her from the danger.

Inside her parents' house, laughter came from the formal living room. It sounded like more than just her parents.

And it was more. The sideboard was covered with a stack of small plates, coffee cups and typical coffee paraphernalia. It was like her parents decided to throw a Humpday Get-together. Which was weird, they rarely had guests over in the middle of the week. Too much work to do.

"Leti." Her mother got up from the table and walked to the doorway. Her movements choppy and her face pinched. It was her disappointment face. The one saved for Leti, since she seemed to get it aimed at her the most these days. "You're late."

"I was working." Leti leaned down as Pork Chop came running. Her adorably sweet white ball of fluff toy poodle made her smile. Her mother, not so much.

Her mother leaned in to whisper, "How did you get dirty at work? And that bandage—"

"I dropped my keys and they rolled under the car. I bumped my head trying to get them." There was no way Leti was telling her mamá about the almost car accident.

Her mamá would start to pace or scrub the floor—a legacy from generations of stress-cleaners. "You should be more careful." She fluffed Leti's hair and slapped at the dirt on Leti's arms.

Stress cleaning.

"Yes, Mamá."

"Do you remember Lilah and Steve?" Her mamá turned to wave at her bosses, the doctors at her office. Even though her mother had run their practice for years, they hadn't been over for dinner in months. Which was okay. Why bring work home with you?

"And this is the new doctor, Doctor Giovanni Ricci." A guy approached Leti and smiled. She shifted her purse and the mail to one hand and reached out to shake his hand.

"Nice to meet you." He took Leti's hand and kissed the back. He was nice looking, early thirties like her, with an unbelievable Italian accent. And smoldering eyes that never left hers.

"Nice to meet you, too, Doctor Ricci."

"Please, call me Giovanni."

"He's single," her mother whispered. That's why she'd brought work home with her—to introduce their new acquisition and present Leti with the latest prospect in her arranged marriage fiasco.

Although, this one actually had potential. A doctor. Gorgeous. Swoony. But he wasn't a muscled guy with blond hair and a cruddy attitude. Somehow, someway, that had become her type.

Or maybe just Kevin was her type. Either way, she wasn't in the mood to entertain her mother's new coworker. "I should go upstairs and get some work done."

"You just got here." Her mother's disappointment was masked by the edge of annoyance in her tone. It was a common occurrence. Her mother was often disappointed and therefore angry.

"I just want to grab something to eat and head to bed."

"Fine. Why don't you take Giovanni into the kitchen with you? You can serve the rice pudding."

"Sure." She tried to smile. But the thought of serving the dessert before getting the chance to eat was making her stomach grumble.

They walked into the kitchen, and Leti could practically feel her mother's eyes boring into the back of her head as she dropped her bag and mail onto a side counter right inside the doorway.

She pulled the little glass dishes of rice pudding from the refrigerator and set them on the counter before reaching for a serving platter in the cabinet.

"Can I help?" Giovanni stood off to the side.

"Sure." She pushed the platter toward him. "Put the glass dishes on the platter."

She pulled out the cinnamon sticks and the honey as he lined them up. "Nice plating job." The six bowls were arranged in a heart-like shape. Although it might just be a V. She was feeling a bit romantic after her near-pancake experience.

He laughed. "My momma taught me well. Presentation is important."

"Does she live in Chicago?" Her hand swung to her stomach as it growled. Hopefully he had shoddy hearing.

"No, Italy. I just came back to the states to live with my Zia until I can find my own place." His dark brown hair hung over his light chocolate eyes. The man was put together well, that was for sure.

She drizzled the rice pudding with honey and added a cinnamon stick to each bowl. "Well, these are ready to go." She capped the honey and put it back in the pantry.

"I'll take them out to the party, and let you make yourself some dinner. It was lovely meeting you." He lifted the platter. "Maybe we'll see each other again."

"Maybe." She smiled because that didn't seem like such a hardship. She'd like to see him again. He seemed pleasant enough. At a minimum, he'd helped. Her ex had only come into the kitchen to nag her that she didn't cook as well as his mother.

Probably why he'd left her for her best friend, who had been a pastry chef before she'd died. That story was something she didn't like to think about. Ever.

A yawn ripped from her chest. Maybe dinner was overrated. Tonight had been terrifying and exciting, and it seemed it might need to be over. Sleep was sounding better and better. She grabbed a bag of treats for Pork Chop, a bottle of water for her bedside, and moved the mail from on top of her bag.

A letter fell from the stack. Her name written on the envelope. No return address. No stamp. She opened the letter. A single sheet of paper, folded into a square.

Leti spread the edges until the page was open. Four words. That was all.

STOP OR YOU DIE.

FOUR WORDS that made her wonder what she'd gotten involved in. Maybe the car earlier wasn't an accident. Maybe Kevin had been right.

Fear wrapped around her chest, pushing any thoughts of sleep away. She didn't want to die, but she had no idea what she needed to stop. She was working a few cases right now: a couple cheating spouses and researching a corporate takeover. Nothing out of the ordinary.

Enzo's case. He'd said it would be dangerous, but she never pictured this. It was time to talk to him and get some answers.

KEVIN SAT in the coffee shop the next day. He'd texted Leti to see when she wanted him to pick her up for work, but she'd said she had a ride. So he'd hoped to run into her here at the coffee shop —get a chance to talk about what happened last night. He hadn't been able to sleep. The more he'd thought about it, the more he was sure it was intentional. She needed protection—at least until whatever was going on blew over.

He took another drink of the second iced mocha of his day. He was one gulp away from jittering off the chair, but that could have been nervousness. He didn't look forward to the conversation with Leti, but that didn't stop him from wanting to see her.

He liked the fire in her eyes—the way she didn't take any shit. And she was smart. He couldn't get over the brains on her.

He waited until the last drop was gone before he left the coffee shop and headed into the office.

When he walked in the back door of Busted, there was laughing. Lots of it. It looked like an office sleep-over. Leti leaned back in her chair, her stockinged feet propped on her desk. Maggie sat on her own desk, legs crossed, and Jessi lay on the leather mini-couch they'd recently put against the wall for walk-ins. Danni sat on the floor, her back against the couch, her left Tardis boot-slipper twirling as she laughed.

It was going to be one of those type of days.

"...and then he looked around the room and saw me sitting a few tables over," Leti said.

"He. Did. Not." Maggie hung on every word. "No."

Leti pointed at Maggie. "Exactly! Then he stood up and walked over to my table."

Jessi ran a hand through her short black hair and rolled her eyes. Danni angled forward. "He didn't apologize to her?"

"No." Leti shook her head.

Not that Kevin needed to hear any of this. He'd watched it, but he didn't want to interrupt, and they hadn't seemed to notice he was standing there. And honestly he was glad she was finally talking to someone about it.

"He called me Leslie and sat down. Then he got a fake call and tried to leave, sticking me with the bill."

Maggie slapped her desk. "You did not pay for his dinner."

"No, I spilled his wine on his leftovers to distract him, gave the waiter a big tip for having to deal with him, and ran out the door."

Jessi laughed. "Did he try to stop you?"

"I'm not sure. He was too busy yelling for Leslie."

"Leslie! Leslie!" Danni screamed, doing an excellent Rocky Balboa imitation, and kicked at Leti's desk with her cartoon slippers. They all fell over in giggles.

"Where did you find this guy?" Maggie rolled on her desk like a buoy. It was a miracle she hadn't fallen off.

"My mamá found him through the seamstress at her dry cleaner."

"Never find a guy through the dry cleaner." Jessi pretended to write on an invisible piece of paper. "Check."

"You could always just say yes to your lawyer. Enzo's a good guy." Maggie pinned Jessi with a stare. Enzo, aka Hug Action. Kevin wasn't all that thrilled with him right about now and it had little to do with the hug, and more to do with the car that about ran Leti down.

"Enzo and I are not a good match," Jessi snarled. "You could always stick your tongue down Chase's throat and mind your business."

Maggie laughed. "I could. But Chase isn't here and it's more fun to guide your love life."

"I don't need a guide."

"Yeah, it's going so well." Danni rested her British phonebooth-covered feet on the desk as she clasped her hands behind her head and leaned against the couch. "When was the last time you had a date?"

"Not everyone can find a rich computer nerd." Jessi huffed. Apparently, over a month ago, Danni and an old friend, Marek, had found each other—it wasn't without drama though. "And anyway, I had a baby."

"Ten months ago." Maggie's huff matched Jessi's.

Leti shook her head. "If you don't watch out, you'll

be a middle-aged woman with a son in college, talking about how you can't date because you had a baby."

"What?" Jessi popped up to a sitting position. "Is that supposed to be bad, *Leslie*?"

"Ahem." Kevin drew the attention to him before a brawl broke out. "Working hard?"

"We're discussing a psychological study of human behavior." Jessi flopped back down on the couch, closing her eyes.

"Yep." Danni pulled out her phone. "Important stuff."

Maggie grabbed the keyboard for her computer and placed it in her lap. The keys clacked as she hit the buttons.

"Do you have a minute?" Kevin leaned into Leti.

"Right now?" Leti looked around at the women in the office, but if she thought anyone cared that he needed to talk to her? They didn't.

"Yeah, I need to talk to you about that infidelity case." Hopefully, she wouldn't ask which one. He had so many cases and too many other things on his mind.

"Sure." She stood up and walked out the back door.

The crisp air slapped him in the face as he followed. "I just wanted to see how you're doing."

She paused. Almost looked at him like she didn't know what he was talking about. "Fine."

"You sure? You don't seem convinced of that."

"It's just... Nothing."

"I think we should talk about what happened. Revisit having someone watch over you for a few days."

"Thank you for worrying about me. But this is my problem. I'll deal with it."

"Your problem is my problem." He thought that was a valid argument.

"I can't talk about this now." She turned and walked back inside.

Kevin didn't know what to even say. She wouldn't listen. Maybe he needed to adjust what he'd said. Make her see that what happened last night wasn't normal. Or maybe it was. He'd feel better if she had someone watching her back, just so they could validate someone wasn't out to get her.

He walked back in the office. He'd ask her to talk again. This time he'd make her see. He opened the back door and walked inside. The women hadn't moved since he'd been in before. All except Leti. Leti had her head down as she stared at the computer screen.

A click came from the front door of the office before a man came around the wall. Dark suit. Dark hair. Speak of the devil.

"Am I interrupting?" Enzo paused at the front of the room. His eyes started at Maggie but ended with Jessi. The look he gave her made Kevin regret any not-jealousy he might have felt. This guy was not after Leti. He only had eyes for Jessi. And those eyes were sappy as hell. He had it bad. Poor guy.

Jessi looked up and then turned away. There had to be a story there, not that he had any plan of finding out.

"Not at all." Maggie stood up. "What can we do for you?"

"I actually need to see Leti."

"Well isn't she the popular one." Maggie smiled.

"What?" Enzo looked confused.

Kevin could understand. He found himself confused a lot around these women.

"Nothing." Maggie pushed some papers together.

"I have work to do." Jessi disappeared from the room faster than a puff of smoke.

"Yeah, I've got code to write." Danni shuffled her slippers across the room and up the stairs to her lair-slash-office.

Maggie leaned over and snagged her purse. "I have a house that won't watch itself." She smiled at Kevin. "Hey, brother, want to drink a large coffee and watch a house collect dust all day? I'd bet money this chick went out of town, but her husband swears she's in town."

"Sounds intriguing." Read: torture. Six-plus hours in a car with his sister. No thanks. He loved his sister... and he'd like to keep it that way.

"Really?"

"Nope. I have my own house to watch."

"Have fun, then." Maggie opened her purse and stuffed the papers inside. She carried her large cup of coffee out the back door—leaving the three of them alone.

Kevin knew he should have followed the women out the door—any of them—but he didn't want to leave Leti alone. Not with this guy. Enzo already managed to put a target on her back. Kevin didn't want Enzo to get her involved any further.

Leti smiled at Enzo. And that smile was gorgeous. It killed him it wasn't for him.

Damn. Kevin was starting to sound like an ass. He really wasn't controlling. He just seemed to be playing it on TV. He didn't want her to get involved with Enzo, because he was dangerous. It had nothing to do with the fact that he was a good-looking man.

He most certainly was not jealous. That was his story...

Kevin felt Leti's eyes follow him as he walked over to Maggie's desk. He needed some information on the stakeout he had tonight.

What? He did. He wanted to make sure he had the right address.

Even he didn't buy his own BS.

Leti watched Kevin as Enzo sat down in front of her desk. "Don't you have work to do?" she asked.

"I'm working." Kevin sat in Maggie's chair and clicked the computer to life.

"Working?"

"I have to look up an address." That wasn't exactly a lie.

"We need privacy." Leti's words clipped at the end —like she was annoyed. Join the club.

This Enzo guy was dangerous—at least whatever he was getting Leti involved in was dangerous. She had to see that. Yet she was going to sit here alone with him.

Not on his watch.

Kevin didn't say a word as he located the folder with the open cases. He found the Williams' case and located the address.

Yep. The address matched what was on the printout from yesterday. So what if he'd printed out the screen this morning. Maybe they'd called and asked Maggie to change the address in the last hour. He was being proactive.

Leti cleared her throat. "Are you done looking up that address?"

Kevin didn't say anything as he clicked the file closed and locked Maggie's computer. He was done. And he couldn't think of another thing to keep him in the room.

"If you need more time, you could use that handy-dandy cell phone in your pocket." She picked up her cell phone, pressing at the screen before turning it to Kevin. "This app right here gets you to the internet."

And yes, she was pointing at the app icon with a forced smile on her face.

He almost called her out on it. But Enzo just sat there picking lint off his suit like she wasn't talking down to him. And there was no way Kevin was going to let her win.

"Thank you." Kevin picked up his phone and sparked it to life. "I always forget that app is there."

Leti's smile faltered.

Kevin shook his head. He'd perfected the confused-soldier-in-distress overseas. It was easy to disarm a person with a little assumed vulnerability. "Do you think you could show me how to use it?"

Leti glared. Definitely not disarmed. Maybe a little funny.

Her lips pursed as she dropped her hand to the side

of her desk. She waved at him discreetly and pointed at the door—her hand a frantic pendulum. Her upper body still as she tried to hide her frenzy from the suit.

Okay, it was a lot funny. But Kevin kept his laughter to himself. She'd either kill him or never speak to him again. Neither sounded like fun.

"I think I'll figure it out on my own." Kevin picked up his phone and poked at it. "The Army taught me how to be shrewd. I can figure out a little phone."

"Then go." Leti's hands were resting on the desk. At least she wasn't swinging her arm any longer.

Kevin walked toward the back door and turned around. "I'll be a phone call away if you need me."

"Thank you." Leti nodded and looked back at Enzo.

Kevin was being dismissed. And that just sucked.

CHAPTER FIVE

"SO THAT WAS INTERESTING." Enzo looked over at Leti with a grin on his face as he leaned back in the chair across from Leti's desk.

"Not at all."

"He seemed to be sticking around for some reason. You don't find that interesting?"

Leti had no desire to talk about Kevin or how interesting that interaction may or may not have been. And she knew how to end the discussion. "How's Jessi?"

"Touché." The smile on his face dried up. "You wanted to talk. But obviously not about that guy."

"I found something. But I'm not sure if you want me to tell you about it."

"Why wouldn't I?"

Leti slid her hand into the briefcase under her desk and pulled out the slip of paper she'd stared at for most of the morning—heck—for most of the night. It was bad enough she was getting threats, no one else needed to be under the gun. "Someone sent me this."

"'Stop or you die.'" Enzo's eyebrows furrowed and lips pursed. "Where did you get this?"

"It was sent to my home."

Enzo stared at the paper. Leti knew that look. She'd perfected it over the past twelve hours. "There's more."

"More?"

"Someone tried to run me down last night." Thinking about that car and how the lights just appeared and the way the engine gunned, Kevin was right. The car sat in wait and aimed for her. "A car was waiting for me outside the building after work."

"Are you alright?"

"Yes. I got out of the way before it hit me." He didn't need to know how she got out of the way. He'd just give her another look and talk about how interesting it was.

"Good. I'm glad you're okay. I understand if you don't want to look into this anymore."

"It's not that." She took her reading glasses from the corner of the desk and tapped the edge of the frames on a file.

"What is it?"

"I found something." She turned her glasses over in her hands. She wasn't sure if she should share any of this. She didn't want anyone getting hurt, especially her friends.

"Great. And?"

"Are you sure you want to know? Someone is trying really hard to make sure that I stop looking. I don't want you to get involved if you don't have to."

Enzo seemed to think about that for a minute as

he stared at the paper in his hand before setting it on the corner of her desk. "I understand your concern, but I'm already involved. This is something I have to do."

"Okay then." She pulled out the spreadsheets she'd been working on for the past few days. Highlights and red marks colored the documents. She nodded and put on her readers. "You were right to think that there's something fishy going on. If you look at the deposits in yellow and the transactions in red, it looks like he's depositing money and then withdrawing ninety percent of it for this miscellaneous security expenditure."

"What do you mean?"

"I wouldn't have even noticed it, because security is at the heart of all companies these days, however, look at the amount of money going out. It's exactly ninety percent of the third deposit every month." She pointed to a three-million-dollar deposit and then to a two-point-seven-million-dollar withdrawal. "It's like this every month."

"The charity had a security breach a year ago. They lost all donor information and had to revamp the firewall and all the security around the servers. They even hired an Information Security team. Could that be what this is?"

"Secure-shot?"

"Yeah. I think that's it."

"They fall into a different bucket." She turned to the page she needed. "They're considered a vendor expense. And the server upgrade and purchase would have been on last year's balance sheets. This year, the expenses for upkeep would be in operating expenses."

"Then what is security?" Enzo turned page after page, all of them showing the same anomaly that Leti had found. A deposit, followed by ninety percent of said deposit used to cover miscellaneous security expenses.

"I don't know. But would anybody question miscellaneous security expenses?"

"Probably not. I wouldn't have questioned it, if you didn't say anything. That breach was all over the news. A lot of work and money went into making sure something like that wouldn't happen again."

"I'm sure a lot of money went into it, but not three million a month."

"Thanks for this." Enzo gathered the paperwork and rolled it into a tube. "I'll keep looking."

"Are you sure you want to go down this road?" Leti could admit the whole night of danger made her question her own involvement.

Enzo stared at his hands as they twisted the pages tighter and tighter. He was thinking about something, or just lost in thought. Leti wasn't sure which, and she didn't want to interrupt. "Can I ask you a question?"

"Sure." Leti wasn't sure at all. No question was good when someone had to ask if they could ask it.

"How do you know that someone tried to run you over? Maybe it was a drunk or someone on their phone."

"That's what I thought at first, but the lights didn't turn into the alley. The lights just popped on as the tires screeched to life. The car didn't slow down when the driver saw me. The closer it got, the faster it went." She nodded to the letter he had placed on the corner of her desk.

"How would they know you were working on this?" His knuckles whitened as he spun the pages around and around.

"I was thinking about last night. I had to make some calls to get the records. A friend of mine works for Chicago Charity Watchdog. They monitor charities in the Chicagoland area."

"Would she have said something?"

"I don't think so, but it can't be a coincidence all this happening."

Enzo's face turned an interesting shade of ash—which was especially impressive with his Mediterranean complexion. "We should stop."

"I know." Another thing Leti had been thinking all last night. "We really need to stop."

Enzo stopped his paper assault and stared at her. "There sounds like a but is in there."

"We can't stop." Leti also knew this to be true.

"This sounds personal."

"It is. I had a friend who was adopted when she was a child, and her adoptive parents were abusive. The adoption agency did nothing when they found out."

"That wasn't your fault."

"No. I was her family, for a long time." Until they weren't. She didn't want to let Erica down, despite how things ended between them. She'd never had the chance to say goodbye, but at least she'd get a chance to help others like her.

"This isn't the first time they've threatened some-one." Enzo shook his head. "It won't be the last."

"What happened?" Leti's heart rate sped up. Maybe she was in over her head. This was way over her skills unless she could spreadsheet her way out of it.

Enzo stood up. "I was on a date with... a woman and they took us to a cemetery and left us there."

"They took you to a cemetery?" Leti wasn't sure how that equaled *threatened*.

"It was at gunpoint," Enzo added as if reading her mind.

"That..." *must have been terrifying* "...sucks."

"It wasn't my best night." Enzo sighed. "I don't want anything to happen to you or anyone here." His attention moved to the wall separating the back room from the front. His eyes glazed over as he just stared. No words were needed.

Leti knew that this was none of her business, yet the words kept coming out of her mouth. "Have you told her how you feel yet?"

He shook his head, his eyes clearing. He crossed his arms on the desk before his head dropped to his fore-arms. When it came to Jessi, he seemed defeated. "I just can't put any of you in danger."

"I get it." Leti reached across the desk and laid her hand on his forearm. Her desk phone buzzed at her side, but she didn't bother answering it. She needed to deal with this first. "But we can't let them get away with this, especially if that money isn't going to the children."

"Leti..."

"Enzo, we can do this." She was pretty sure her voice sounded more confident that she was feeling, but she was a terrible actress when her life was on the line. "I can do this."

She must have been a better actress than she thought. His head still down, he nodded. "Okay." He raised his head to stare directly into her eyes. "But you have to tell me if things go sideways or if you feel threatened in any way."

They were in trouble if feeling threatened was the bar. She already felt threatened. She just hoped it didn't get worse. "I will tell you if it gets to be too much."

"Okay." Enzo rested his hand on hers. "We got this."

Ahem. Jessi stood in the doorway. Her eyes laser-focused on Enzo's hand on Leti's.

Leti pulled her hand away—but not as fast as Enzo leaned back. The fear on his face would have been adorable if Jessi didn't look like she was ready to kill someone.

Hopefully not Leti.

"Leti, there's a call for you on line one."

"I should probably go." Enzo raised the paperwork and nodded at Leti.

"I'll keep digging and see what I find."

Enzo walked up to Jessi and smiled. "It's good to see you."

"You too." Jessi waited in the doorway, staring at Leti, as Enzo left the room. Not that she seemed angry.

"Everything okay? There wasn't anything going on between us." Leti had no designs on Jessi's man.

"Everything is fine." The front door dinged as someone, probably Enzo, walked out. Jessi turned toward the front. "And it wouldn't matter if there was something. He's not mine."

"I don't think he's gotten the memo," Leti mumbled as she grabbed the phone from the cradle.

"What?" Jessi's head popped from around the corner.

"Nothing. Just thank you for transferring the call."

Jessi's eyes narrowed as she slipped back around the wall and into her office space.

Leti hit the button the phone and her mother's voice chirped across the line. "I don't know where she is."

"Mamá?"

"Oh, there you are."

"Yes, I'm working."

"You would think they'd let you take five minutes to speak to your mother." Because the world stopped for mothers.

"What can I help you with, Mamá?"

"I met someone."

"Won't you miss Dad?" Leti almost started laughing.

"Don't be obtuse. He's a lawyer."

Leti actually felt her mamá's eyes roll—if that was

even possible through the phone. "Mamá, I don't want any more set-ups."

"Why not?"

"Phil, Mamá." Leti hadn't had the heart to tell her mamá about the entire nightmare of a date that was Phil, just the highlights.

"One bad apple doesn't mean you throw out the whole lot."

"I'm not giving up on all men, just the ones you find at the dry cleaner."

"I didn't meet this one at the dry cleaner. I met him at the salon."

"The hair salon?" Leti wasn't sure that was much better.

"Yes, he was taking his mother to get her hair done. He knows the value of family and how to take care of his mother."

"That is a good trait, Mamá."

"So, you'll meet him for dinner?"

"I can't. I'm too busy with work right now." Leti shook some of the papers in her hand near the phone. It made her sound busy, at least.

"You don't have to work late every night."

Which was true, but she'd gladly work every night to avoid going on another date with her mother's strays. And anyway, this case with Enzo was turning into something a bit more urgent than she thought. "It's a big case, Mamá. I just don't have time right now. Maybe in a few weeks when we have all the research done and the numbers reported."

"I don't know why you can't get a nice nine-to-five job. Then you'd have time for a husband and children."

Leti didn't want to tell her mamá that she did have time for those things, she just hadn't found the right guy. Not that she'd spent a lot of time looking. She had a job she loved. She wanted to make more money, and when she got her CPA, she would. She'd miss her friends, but it was a small price to pay for success. "Mamá, I have to get back to work."

"Fine." Her mamá sighed over the line. "But you'll have to tell him yourself. I already gave him your phone number."

Of course she did. "Fine."

"He has a very nice voice. Very manly."

"What does that mean?"

"I don't know. He had a manly voice. I thought you'd like that."

"Sure, Mamá. I like manly voices." Leti tried to hide the sarcasm, but she had a feeling it was dripping from every word.

"You mock now, but try marrying a man with a girly voice. You'd hate it. My friend Griselda..."

"I should get back to work."

"Wait. Did you text Doctor Ricci?"

Giovanni? "No. Was I supposed to?"

"How are you going to get to know each other if you don't text?"

"How am I supposed to text him if I don't have his phone number."

"Why didn't you ask him for his number?"

"Mamá, we were serving dessert last night, not exchanging personal information."

"That's all part of communication." Her mother sighed and whispered, "No wonder you're not married, you don't even know how to ask for a phone number."

"I heard that."

"You were meant to hear."

"I have to get back to work."

"We're having chiles en nogada. So don't be late."

"Am I ever?"

"I won't answer that." Her mother clucked her tongue before hanging up the phone.

Leti closed her eyes and held back the sigh that wanted to escape her lips. She loved her mamá a lot. She was a strong woman, smart and reliable. Leti could always count on her. But sometimes talking with her was the equivalent of a brain-freeze. Painful and unpleasant and you just had to close your eyes and wait till the discomfort was over.

"Mother problems." Jessi peeked around the wall and smiled.

"You could say that."

"I have one of those. I get it." Jessi leaned against the wall. "I was thinking of grabbing a slice over at Giordano's. You want?"

"Yes." A slice of pizza sounded great about now. Anything to stop her from questioning why she even got up today.

CHAPTER SIX

A FEW HOURS and a slice of Chicago deep dish later, and Leti was working. At least she was trying to work. Her eyes were fighting the carbs to stay open.

She leaned back in her chair and closed her eyes. Unfortunately, the carbs were winning. She just needed to keep her eyes open. The further she dug, the more she hated this guy and his whole "charity".

The numbers usually didn't lie. And they didn't lie here either, but so far they didn't make sense. She could see most of the money going to the offshore accounts. A small amount actually went to the children's homes. She was still tracking those offshore accounts, but it wasn't looking good.

She needed more help.

"I need a drink." Danni's slippered feet shuffled down the stairs and across the office to Leti's desk.

"You were just the person I was thinking of." Leti lifted her head, but it felt like a chore.

Danni's hand flew to her lips and started to tap. "Good thoughts or bad thoughts?"

"Depends what type of drink were you thinking, and are you going to get me one?"

"Coffee." Danni tsked as if it was obvious and waved her wrist. "And hell yeah."

"Then they were good thoughts."

Danni moved the chair in front of Leti's desk to the far edge. She dropped down to the seat and plopped her Ren and Stimpy slippers on Maggie's desk. The only reason Leti didn't complain was because Danni knew not to put her feet, slippered or not, on Leti's desk. Ever. "If I said I wasn't going to get you a drink?"

"Definitely bad thoughts."

"That's impressive how you knew what to think before I told you my intentions."

"I'm honing my ESP." Leti tapped her head. Wouldn't that be wonderful? She wouldn't need to do hours of research, and she'd take down so many more bad guys.

"That could be useful in this business."

"Yeah." Just what Leti was thinking. "I could actually use a bit of the ESP right now. But since I don't have it, I could use some of your high-tech research abilities."

"I do have a few of those." Danni smiled. "What kind of debauchery am I looking for?"

"It's not pretty."

"I have a feeling my not pretty and your not pretty are not the same." Danni had shared some of the cases she'd dealt with over the years. Anything having to do with children and pornography could not be easy. Hopefully, this case wasn't going in that direction at all.

"It's not pretty in the sense that these people are laundering and bilking money out of children's charities. I'm trying to find where the money goes, but I keep hitting brick walls. Can you look into it for me?"

"Sure. Marek has some interesting programs that should help."

Leti didn't want to see anyone get hurt over this. "Just be careful."

"Why?"

How much to share? "I might have almost been run over." Yeah, she was downplaying it a bit. But maybe it had been a figment of her imagination.

"What do you mean? Like a car swerved and tried to move you off the road?"

"No, like a car tried to hit me while I was walking across the alley the other night."

"Shit." Danni shook her head. "Are you sure this is worth it?"

"I don't know. But if you can find anything without anyone noticing, then I want to see if it's something that we should pursue. Something tells me there's more to this."

"This is my jam. Looking in corners and not getting caught is what we do. It's our Saturday night." Danni smiled. "Marek and I got this."

"How are things going with Marek?"

Danni and Marek were old flames who had found their way back to each other despite being shot at and wanted by the law. Luckily, they hadn't been hurt and the law stopped looking their way when they found the real bad guys. But it was still a high stress meet cute. Well, re-meet cute, since they already knew each other.

"Things are good." Danni's cheeks tinged an adorable shade of pink.

"What's with the look?"

"We spend a lot of time at his place."

"I'm sure playing video games and eating Cheetos." Leti had no desire to think about what other wild things the two of them did at his place.

"Yep. It's all about the video games and eating Cheetos." Danni smiled and leaned in. "So which one is the euphemism for sex? Video games or Cheetos?"

"Neither. I thought you both would be abstaining since, well, you know, you're not married and you've only been dating for a few weeks." Leti couldn't help the laughter that bubbled up out of her chest and within a second Danni joined in.

"I thought you were serious." Danni shook her head. "How many times have we heard about Maggie and her sexcapades. How did you hide you were such a prude?"

"Well, I wouldn't say I'm a prude, but no one needs to share their sexcapades as much as Maggie does."

"Amen."

"Ahem." The sound of a man clearing his throat made both Danni and Leti's heads snap around to look at the back door.

Kevin didn't exactly look happy. To be fair, they had just been talking about his sister's sex life.

Danni waved. "Hey, Kevin. How long have you been standing there?"

"Long enough."

"You might want to announce your presence? Get a bell?" Danni tapped her fist against the desk. "Knock?"

"You want me to knock at my own job?" Kevin walked over to Maggie's desk and pushed Danni's slippered feet off the edge.

How many times did Leti want to do that?

He walked around the desk and sat in Maggie's chair. Leaning back, he stared at Leti like she ate his canary. She hadn't even told him she wasn't giving up on the case yet. This was going to go over really well.

Danni glanced between Kevin and Leti. "Well, I should grab our coffee so I can get back to work or head home or go anywhere but here."

Not that Leti was doing anything. She wasn't glaring or staring or any other *aring* words. "You don't have to leave."

"Oh, but I do." Danni grimaced. "I need caffeine and you have..." She made a vague gesture with one hand as she walked to the back door. Paused. Waggled her fingers in Kevin's direction and whispered, "That to deal with." Like Kevin was some secret. There was no secret.

Danni's slippers scuffed up the stairs and silence took its place. Kevin continued to stare.

"What?" Leti had no idea what he was waiting for. But she had a feeling she was about to find out.

KEVIN DIDN'T HEAR Danni leave. He didn't care if she was still there. He remembered the conversation last night clear as a bell. Leti had said she'd stop working this case. It was too dangerous. Funny, but he could've sworn that wasn't the message she was chirping today.

He needed to hear her say it. "Do you want to tell me something?"

"I don't think so." She actually looked confused.

Fire burned in his veins. He'd heard the conversation with Danni. The part where they'd talked about his sister's love life didn't bother him. He'd learned to block out that part of his sister's existence in high school when she'd posted half naked posters of Hansen on her bedroom wall. It was the other part, the one where she was bringing more people into this hell-case. After she'd said she'd stop. "I thought you were dropping the Enzo case."

"Oh that." She actually looked contrite. That was good. "I can't." Those words, not so much.

"Why can't you?"

"I wish I could." She took a deep breath, which was distracting. "The money he's stealing is from kids. I think there's more to it."

"But you're not sure." Why would she put herself in danger if she wasn't sure?

Leti flipped both hands up, palms out. "If Stanley Welford is behind all of this, would he risk coming after me" —she touched her upper chest— "for money laundering? I don't think so. He's powerful enough to hide that. There's got to be something I'm missing."

The logic wasn't helping. Logic was not helping when he wanted to argue. Logic was not helping his blood pressure. "You're not going to stop even after what happened."

"Especially after what happened. Someone is hiding something." She leaned forward. "I can feel it in my bones. Something is wrong. And I need to figure out what it is."

He wanted to argue. He wanted to grab her and wrap her in bubble wrap or Kevlar. He wanted to shield her from whatever was out there.

Except how many times had he trusted his gut? How many times had he acted on his hunches? How many times had they saved his life? And if she was right, if there was more to the story and they just walked away, horrible people would get away with terrible things. That wasn't who he was. And he'd like to think he knew Leti pretty well, and that wasn't who she was.

It was one of the reasons he liked her so much. "Fine."

"Fine?" Her eyes narrowed.

"Fine." He ran a hand down the back of his neck. He might be fine with all of this but the stress in his body hadn't quite gotten the memo. "I get kids are involved, but it's your life on the line and we don't know what we're even dealing with. Are you sure it's worth it?"

Leti stared at her desk and didn't say anything for a bit. Kevin could almost see the wheels turning in her head. Her fingers flicked the papers and envelopes in front of her, not really moving them. "Did Maggie ever tell you about my husband?"

"No." He knew Leti had been married, but not the details.

"This isn't easy for me to talk about." Leti peeled an address label off an envelope, staring at it intently. "I had a best friend in college, Erica, who was adopted. Her stories were...awful. Her adoptive parents were abusive, and they stole the money she'd borrowed for tuition and books and everything. She almost had to drop out of school. The financial aid office was able to help, but it was close. She was packed and ready to leave." Leti took a breath. Let it out. "Move forward ten years. My husband left me for another woman."

"That sucks." So did his response. He wanted to tell her that had to have been hard and that it wasn't fair. But he had no idea how to say it, so instead he said, "I'm sorry."

"It was for the best." She shook her head, lost in a memory. "He and I weren't getting along, and he wasn't all that nice to me. I wasn't all that upset he left. I *was* upset he left me for Erica."

Kevin had no idea what to say to that, so he didn't say anything and let her continue.

"She knew that he and I were having problems. She kept trying to talk me into leaving him. I thought she cared about me. But she just wanted him for herself." Leti swiped at her eyes. "I refused to talk to her after that. She tried. She apologized over and over again, but I couldn't get past the betrayal."

"That's… It makes sense. How do you trust someone who hurt you like that?"

"Yeah. Last year, she was diagnosed with stage four breast cancer. She died a few months later. I never had a chance to say goodbye. I was never able to tell her that I forgave her." Leti shuddered and shook her head, rolling her shoulders. "She went through so much at the hands of the adoption agency and her adoptive parents. That's why I can't let them destroy these children's lives. If she had seen a healthy, loving family, maybe she wouldn't have made the choices she did. Maybe I would've helped her through her last months. Like in *Beaches*, just without the singing."

"Beaches?"

Leti smiled and finally looked up from the envelope in her hand. "Old reference."

Kevin got it. "So you need to keep going on this."

"I do." Her eyebrows arched as she stared at him. "Why do you care if I stay on this case?"

He'd say the stress, but it wasn't about him. It was true he didn't want to lose her. But he didn't want her parents to lose her. He didn't want her siblings or her friends to lose her. She was well loved—in a friendship, family kind of way. Not that he was in love with her or anything. As he said before, this wasn't about him. "I don't want to see you hurt. Or worse. Is that so unbelievable?"

"No." Leti sighed. "I just can't let this go. I can feel something isn't right in my gut. All I know is that these kids deserve better. I want to follow it through."

"Okay." Kevin ran a hand down the back of his

neck again, still trying to get the knot there to release. That thing wasn't going to dissipate without a good masseuse or without this case disappearing. "But if you're going to stay on the case, so am I."

"You don't have to…"

"I don't have to do anything. But I'd feel better knowing someone is watching your back."

"Someone, or you?"

He knew the answer. He knew what he wanted to say. But he was afraid she'd run away and tell him to pound sand. But she kept staring at him with those eyes. And he couldn't keep the words inside him any longer. "Me."

She didn't say a word. She didn't flinch or cringe or scream. She was like a statue. And that made him feel just as bad as if she'd run away screaming.

He shrugged. "If that's okay."

"That's okay." She smiled and wiped what was left of her tears from her face.

"Good." He smiled. He wanted to remove that pain from her eyes—the pinch in her forehead and the frown on her lips. He motioned to the space in front of the other side of her desk. "If you're going to stick with the case, I want to show you some moves." Come here real quick

Leti stood up. "I got moves. Barry thinks I'm a natural."

"Barry?"

"My Krav Maga instructor."

Kevin had plenty of self-defense training in his time—in the military, not at the YMCA, so he was pretty sure they sugar-coated everything. She needed to be able to do some real damage if the time came. "Well, I'm sure Barry is great, but I need you to be prepared if one of these guys comes after you again."

"I don't have a way to stop a car." Her hands were on her hips. And what lovely hips they were.

That train of thought was not helping.

"Well, if it's you and a car, first of all, look both ways." He stood in front of her. A foot in front of her to be exact. He wanted to be closer, but his mind was already having a hard time concentrating with her this close. "Next, jump out of the way."

Leti's face was blank, no anger, no humor. She looked like she wanted to haul off and hit him, but at least he knew she was listening and not stuck in her memories.

"When you've got someone who wants to hurt you, the amount of force needed is equal to the adversary's actions and intentions."

She blinked. "Huh?"

"What's the saying, don't bring a knife to a gun fight? So if someone just wants to annoy you, maybe they're jawing at you—"

"Jawing?"

"Talking crap. They're not looking to hurt you, just get under your skin. You don't need force at all. But somebody comes at you with a knife or a gun, you have to assume they want to kill you. You need to be prepared to use enough force to extricate yourself from the situation. Make it out alive. That's your goal."

"Okay." She nodded.

"Now come at me."

She raised her hands. Reached for his arms. He grabbed one of her hands and twisted the wrist. She bent over. "Ow."

Kevin snorted. "I didn't even twist as hard as I could. We're just playing around. If I wanted to, I could twist that wrist till it breaks."

"Could I do that?"

He smiled. "Of course you can."

"Will you show me?"

He showed her where to put her hand on his wrist. "Now twist away from the body. Trust me, it will bring them to their knees."

She tightened her grip and twisted. Kevin leaned to the side and dropped to his knees.

"Like that?" Leti's smile lit up the room.

"Just like that." He stood up, right next to her. His face inches from hers. His breath stopped. He wanted to lean over and kiss her. He wanted to take her in his arms. He wanted so many things.

She smiled and stepped back. "I should get back to work."

He nodded. "Get me before you leave tonight." He didn't wait for an answer. If Leti wanted to follow this path, he wouldn't stop her. She was a grown woman. But he didn't have to stand by and wait for someone to take her out, either. He could make sure she had the support she needed. Starting with finding out all he could about Stanley Welford and Wacker Children's Association.

CHAPTER SEVEN

THE SUN WAS SETTING as Kevin waited for Leti to finish crunching her numbers. She'd spent a little time on the Welford case, but then Maggie had brought in a high-profile divorce and needed all hands on deck.

Normally they would have given the client a jump drive of incriminating information, but the wife—the client—was old school. She didn't have a computer—or she didn't know how to use it. Either way, Kevin helped print out bank account records and credit card statements so Leti could do her magic. She was currently creating a lying, cheating paper trail that led to half the working girls on Cicero Avenue.

Now he was just in the way, so he came outside to get some air. Or maybe he just wanted some quiet to make a call. Maybe both.

He pulled out his cell phone and dialed an old army buddy who'd managed to land a job at the FBI.

Grayson Porter had been in same unit with Kevin. They'd had each other's backs and fronts. They were brothers in every sense of the word but blood. Kevin knew Grayson would take a bullet for him. Not just would, had.

"Gray."

"Lane. How the fuck are ya, brother?" Gray tended to be the life of the party, even in the middle of the desert with semi-automatic assault rifles aimed at his head.

"Hanging in there, man."

"That's good. You working?"

"With my sister." Kevin hated that he was still working with Maggie, but he'd known getting into the Chicago Police Department was long and drawn-out process. He had just hoped it wouldn't take the better part of a year. Between the background checks, the psychological testing, medical testing and power test, he could've gone out and started his own police department faster.

"Working with the hot PI, huh? That's got to be interesting."

Kevin was choosing to ignore the hot comment. Every guy on the team had taken a turn drooling over his sister, not that they'd normally say anything to his face. He'd given up defending her honor. She had her cop boyfriend now and if she didn't kick a guy's ass for gawking, the cop would.

The job thing, he should address though. Interesting was a stretch. "It has its moments."

"Does she have any hot PI friends?"

If he only knew, not that Kevin was about to tell him. "They're my sister's friends."

"Yeah, don't want to dip your nib in the family circle."

There was so much wrong with that sentiment. "They're not my family."

"Ah, so you got your eye on one of her friends?"

"No." He didn't have his eye on anyone. He might like looking at Leti, but that was something different. "No one's dipping anything in anyone."

"Eh, worth a shot." Grayson laughed. "You're a funny guy, Lane. So how is the whole cop thing going?"

"I applied. I'm waiting." The waiting was killing him, but he wasn't giving up hope. Not yet.

"Where? I can see if I can help..."

And he would, but Kevin wanted to do this on his own. He'd even asked his father, the Chief of Police at CPD, to step back and let things play out. "No thanks, man. I've got this."

"I'm sure you do. They'd be stupid not to take you, brother. If they knew half the shit you've accomplished, they'd be throwing money at you."

Wasn't quite how it worked, but wouldn't that be nice. "So far, I'm just going through the process."

"Yeah. They do like their processes. So if you don't want my help with the job, what can I do for you? You want me to set you up with a woman from my book club?"

"You're in a book club?"

Grayson wasn't exactly the book club type. He was the type books were written about.

"How do you think I met that girl Sheila?"

"The one you took to Miller's funeral?" Who

brought a date to a funeral? Then again, Grayson showing up with a busty blond was right on brand.

"Yeah with the big—"

"I get it." Kevin could just imagine what Grayson's hands were doing—cupping air in front of his chest. Grayson was a sexist pig, but he was loyal to his friends and he was a great friend—as long as he wasn't trying to sleep with you. "I actually was hoping you could look into someone for me. Stanley Welford. Some hotshot lawyer here in the city."

"What's his deal?"

"He's stealing from kids and I'm pretty sure he tried to run over one of my sister's friends." He wanted to find the creep and beat the shit out of him just for the possibility of him hurting Leti. But he needed to find out what Welford was up to before he showed his hand.

"Is this the friend into which you don't want to dip your nib and isn't family?"

Why did Grayson have to be such a dick? "Yeah."

Grayson didn't laugh. He didn't say anything that would make Kevin want to punch him. Surprisingly. "I got you, brother. I'll get right on it. Tell your lady we'll take care of it."

"She's not my lady."

"Sure. I could feel the anger all the way through the phone, brother." This time Grayson did laugh. "But you keep telling yourself that."

Grayson hung up before Kevin could get another word in. Which was probably good. Grayson and the men from his platoon knew Kevin better then he knew himself most days. So if Grayson heard anger, there was anger.

Kevin was angry with Welford or anyone else who threatened Leti. She was his sister's friend. That's all.

And maybe if he kept telling himself that, one day he'd actually believe it.

BY TEN O'CLOCK THAT NIGHT, Leti could see the lines of a spreadsheet everywhere she turned. It was like the grids were following her—the lines in her desk, the lines in the air conditioning registers on the wall, and the lines from exhaustion etched on her face.

Well, she couldn't see those lines, but given the yawn that just broke loose a minute ago, she was pretty sure they were there.

"Great job, Leti." Maggie slid pictures into a binder as her own yawn stretched her mouth. "Go home. I'll hand this over to the client tomorrow morning."

"Do you want some help with the scrapbook?" When a client asked for a hard copy of the file, there were three major sections. One, the album, usually surveillance photographs. Two, communications, which was information gleaned from social media or phone records. Three, the financials. They called it the scrapbook. It sounded more fun than dossier or something more clinical.

"You did your part," Maggie slid another picture into the plastic holder in the album section. Leti had finished writing up the financial section a half hour ago. "I'm going to finish with the pics and then head home."

Leti leaned sideways in her chair grabbed the pair of heels under the desk and slid them back on. She'd lost those about five hours before and didn't care. Between running from the printer to the desk and then upstairs to get more data from Danni, her feet had been about ready to secede from her body.

"There aren't any more shots we can use." Kevin walked into the office, clicking through the pictures on the camera in his hand.

"None?" Maggie stood up and held out her hand for the camera.

Kevin handed it over. "Unless you have super-sonic-special vision that can see through darkness, we got nothing."

"Shit."

"Yeah, shit."

Maggie stared at the tiny screen as her finger poked at buttons. "Well, we have these here. You can tell it's him."

"But you can't see her in that shot."

"There's her ear." Maggie sighed as she pointed at the screen. "You can see her in this one."

Kevin sighed. "You can see something. I guess."

"It's what we have. Between that and the hotel rooms, fancy dinners, trips, and the car Leti found in the numbers, the wife should be able to make a pretty good case."

"Isn't Illinois a no-fault divorce state?" Kevin asked.

"It is, but she's filing where they own their winter

home." Maggie leaned back and smiled. "She's going to nail him to the wall in Florida. It's illegal there."

"Hell hath no fury like a woman scorned." Leti felt this to her bones, and if they played this right so would their client's husband.

Kevin crossed the room and dropped onto the couch, resting his forearms on his thighs.

"Tired?" Maggie set the camera on her desk and went back to the scrapbook.

"It's been a day." Kevin might have said those words. It was hard to understand him with his head down between his knees.

"You should go home. I got this covered."

"I'm not leaving you here alone." It was good to know Kevin treated his sister the same way he treated Leti.

"Chase is on his way. He doesn't want me here alone at night."

"I'll wait till he gets here."

"For goodness' sake, I'm a grown-ass woman." Maggie stepped around the desk and stomped over in front of Kevin.

"I'm not arguing that—"

Maggie's fist hit his shoulder before both hands landed on her hips. "I was a Chicago police officer. I carried a gun and protected and served."

"I know." He leaned back, his arms up probably to defend himself from another attack.

"I have gotten myself home, on my own, a hundred times."

"I'm not arguing that either."

"Don't you have that hot date tonight with the busty blond? So, head home and I'll see you tomorrow." Maggie crossed her arms. Her chin was raised in defiance, just daring him to contradict her.

"See you tomorrow." He nodded at his sister before looking at Leti. "Ready?"

"I can get home alone." Leti picked up her bag. She had no desire to be escorted by a man who had a date with a busty blond. Not that she could say anything about it. They weren't together.

Kevin curled his lip. "Nice try."

Leti looked at Maggie for an assist.

"Don't look at me." Maggie sat back down at her desk. "If you want to lose Mr. Chivalry, lose him on your own."

"Fine." Leti hiked the bag higher on her shoulder. "I'm going home. Alone." She practically ran out the door. "See you later, Maggie."

"Bye, Leti." At least that's what it sounded like Maggie said. It was a blur of sound as Leti streaked through the office and whipped open the door.

She was halfway to her car when the back door creaked open again. Leti could tell it was Kevin without looking back. "You don't have to follow me."

"Are you going to keep looking into this case?" Kevin's voice came from behind her.

"Yes." She looked both ways—twice—before crossing the alley—making sure to check for parked cars lying in wait to jump up and run her down.

"Then I'm following you. If you want to lose me, drop the case."

Leti opened her car door and slid inside. Part of her wanted to start it up and drive away. If she accidentally ran over Kevin, that would be tragic, but he shouldn't be standing in front of her car.

The police wouldn't believe that excuse. Not that she'd actually run him over. That was just crazy.

"Are you trying to run away?"

Exasperation left Leti's lungs in a long sigh. She wasn't going to get rid of her shadow and she wasn't going to let him know she was bothered. "Not at all. I just want to go home, and you shouldn't have to follow me around. Isn't there a busty blond waiting for you?"

"I'll cancel."

"Don't bother on my account." Leti turned the ignition and wanted to close the door, but there was a man in the way.

"It's not a bother." Kevin leaned down into the car. He was pretty close. All she had to do was lean forward and her mouth would be on his.

Not that she was going to do that.

"I want to make sure your safe."

"You do?" Warmth spread through her chest. He wanted her to be safe. That was the sweetest thing she'd ever heard. If she hadn't thought about leaning in and kissing him before, she was thinking about it now.

"Yeah." Kevin leaned against the car door, keeping it open. "We don't know what we're up against. I don't want anything to happen to you. Your family would miss you. My sister would miss you."

Right. Because he was being chivalrous and protecting her for his sister. Not because he cared about her or anything. Not that she cared. "Well, it's late. We should head home."

"Yeah." He stepped back, but kept his hands on the door. "Are you going to give me a minute to get to my truck or do I need to get someone to stand in front of your car?"

"What about your date?"

"I'll have her meet me later. Just...don't drive off."

"I'll wait." Not that she wanted to, but she wasn't going to be a pain. Not now. She wanted to go home sooner as opposed to later.

"Are you in?" He still had both hands on the door.

"Yep."

He shut the door and walked to his truck. Leti started her car, watching as Kevin backed out of his spot. He angled his truck so it was facing the same direction as Leti's car. With a tap of the horn, she pulled up to the end of the alley.

She headed north, Kevin's lights following behind. The streets were filled with cars. People heading to food or heading home from work. Leti wasn't a fan of Chicago traffic, but she loved the drive home. It was quiet time. Time to unwind. When a girl spent all day looking at spreadsheets, she needed time to look at anything but numbers.

Her cell phone rang through the car speakers. Unknown flashed on the car screen.

It was probably Kevin. She clicked the phone button on the steering wheel. "Bad enough you're behind me. We have to talk the whole way, too?"

"I'm sorry?" The Italian accent told her it wasn't Kevin.

"I'm sorry, I thought this was a friend of mine." They *were* just friends. She wasn't a busty blond.

"Well, I'd like to be a friend." The accent was drool-worthy and almost made her forget it wasn't Kevin. "This is Giovanni, we met at your parents the other night."

"I remember you." Tall. Dark. Handsome. How could she forget? "I'm Leti."

"I know." He laughed, a low, deep laugh that shook her insides. "I called you."

He did. That laugh made her insides feel all warm and mushy. It almost made her not care how he'd gotten her phone number. Almost. "How did you get my number?"

"I hope it's okay, I asked your mother if I could call you?" His voice held an edge that was hesitant, almost nervous.

"Sure." Part of her thought that was so incredibly sweet. Part of her wondered if asking her mother was going to be a habit that would continue throughout their relationship. Not that this was a relationship.

Ugh. She was overthinking.

And she was pretty sure he asked a question, but she hadn't heard a word because her brain was too busy rambling for her to pay attention to the hot guy on the phone. "I'm sorry, did you say something? I missed it."

"I really should get a new phone. It cuts in and out sometimes." He cleared his throat. "I uh, I asked if you'd like to go out to dinner sometime this week?"

"With you?"

He laughed again and her insides warmed. "Yes."

Leti stopped her car at a light and watched the truck lights pull up behind her. Part of her wanted to say no, that she wasn't interested in dinner, but she couldn't figure out why. Why wouldn't she be interested? It's not like she was dating anyone else. She didn't even have any other prospects. It's not like she wasn't interested in Giovanni.

He was good-looking. He was nice. He was successful. He came highly recommended by her mother.

Well, everyone had a flaw.

There was not one good reason for her to say no. She could go to dinner and get to know him. It couldn't hurt. "I would like that."

"Great." His tone actually changed. Leti could almost hear the smile in his voice. "How is Thursday at eight?"

"Perfect."

"Great. I'll see you then."

"See you then." Leti couldn't help but smile as she clicked off the call. She had a date. Today had been a nightmare of stress, but tonight ended with the prospect of a date. She'd take it.

CHAPTER EIGHT

A FEW DAYS LATER, Leti sat at her desk questioning her life choices. She was being babysat like a toddler and they hadn't found a thing. Either her gut was lying to her or this guy was really good at hiding his indiscretions.

She'd found the financial anomalies, but a good accountant could come up with valid reasons for every one of those inconsistencies. She needed more, which was leaving her cranky. Or maybe she was cranky because she was freaking out a bit.

"So tonight's the night." Danni smiled as she sat in the chair across from Leti's desk.

Tonight was indeed the night. Hence the reason she was freaking out.

"Ooooh, that's right." Maggie looked up from her computer. "You're going out with smoking hot guy tonight."

"He has a name."

Maggie and Danni looked at each other and smiled. "Gio...vanni," they sang together.

Why Leti had told them anything, she had no idea.

Jessi's head poked around the front corner. "Giovanni is tonight? Oh, I know!" Jessi disappeared in the direction of her desk, and less than a minute later she appeared around the front corner, running toward the back office. She stopped in front of Leti's desk and dropped a row of condoms on the desk. "Don't use them all in one place."

Maggie laughed and high-fived Jessi. Danni clapped, then started making kissy faces. Maggie wrapped her arms around herself and rubbed up and down. She cooed and oohed. They were like horny teenagers. No, more like clueless middle-schoolers. Ugh.

"Why do I tell you anything?" Leti picked up the condoms and threw them at Maggie. Jessi might have been the messenger, but she was not the brains behind the prophylactic. Jessi was too nice to do something like this. Maggie had been harassing Leti for years.

"Why'd you throw that at me?" Maggie picked them up and tossed them back.

Leti batted them away. "Because I'm sure you talked her into giving them to me."

Maggie's mouth dropped open. "I did no such thing. I'll admit I like watching you turn red, but that was all her."

Leti looked over at Jessi, who just smiled. "With a name like Giovanni, you're going to need those."

Maggie went back to making out with herself.

Danni made more kissy faces. Leti picked up the strip of condoms, trying to figure out who to throw them at first.

"Everything okay in here?" Kevin stood at the door.

A fierce blush clawed Leti's skin. Her face was practically pulsing. She dropped her hands to her lap, hoping that he didn't see the rubbers. But the crinkle of the packaging and the size of his eyes told her he saw. It also told her she was never going to be able to face him again.

"Leti is getting ready for her date tonight." Danni waggled her eyebrows.

"I am not." Leti wanted to rip those eyebrows out and beat her with them. She opened her drawer and tossed in the crinkly evidence. "I am trying to get some work done, and my coworkers are acting like children."

"We're not the ones throwing rubbers around like it's a gym class." Jessi looked so innocent. Such a lie.

Maggie nodded with a straight face. So serious. "Really Leti, that's not how you play dodge ball."

"Yeah," Danni said. "You wait till Giovanni puts one of those on and then you duck and weave. Dodge his balls. Dodge them balls." All three of them began cackling.

Kevin didn't laugh. He looked ready to run. "I don't know what's going on here, and I don't think I want to know." He turned around and walked back out the door he'd come through barely a minute before.

Leti looked at each of the women in the room. She didn't know what to say or do. So she laughed. And they all joined in.

"If I knew that's all it took to get rid of my brother, I would have done it years ago." Maggie wiped at tears in her eyes.

"I think we might be onto something." Danni laughed. "A way to scare men away."

"We'll be rich." Jessi giggled.

The phone up front began to ring. "Darn it. Work beckons." Jessi ran for her desk.

"Yeah, we should probably get back to work." Maggie pulled her bag from the bottom drawer of her desk. "I'm going to sit on the Merrill house for a bit.

"Merrill?" Leti asked.

"New case." Maggie slid her camera into the bag hanging off her shoulder. "Call me if you need anything."

If there wasn't a financial component to a case, Leti wasn't always brought in. Merrill must not be hiding money, only hiding the salami.

Danni still sat in the chair in front of Leti's desk. She hadn't made a move.

"Everything okay?" Leti sat back. It wasn't like Danni to linger, not without cause.

"I think I found something, but I'm not sure." Danni chewed on her lower lip.

Leti had never seen her like that, and the woman had been chased by the cops a few months ago and hadn't flinched. Now she was flinchy. "What is it?"

"It started about ten years ago." Danni poked at her cell phone.

Leti's email dinged. She opened the app and entered her password to get the documents.

"The first article is from a shelter over on the South Side. There was talk that a child died in their custody. They claim it was an accident. The shelter closed right after that."

"Could it have been an accident?"

"Maybe." Danni didn't look convinced. "The next article's from a children's shelter a few miles away on the south-west side."

"Another death?" Leti would read them both, but she wanted to get Danni's take on them first.

"Another accident."

"What kind of accident?"

"It's not the accidents that stand out." Danni shook her head. "The first one, the little girl fell and hit her head. That happens. The second one, the little boy had an allergic reaction to a bee sting."

Leti frowned. "That could happen to anyone."

"Like I said, it's not the accidents. The children were living in filth. There was barely any food. Per one report, the little girl wasn't taking her prescribed medication. But another report didn't even list that she had medication to take. It doesn't add up. So I looked deeper. They lost files. Children's files were just gone. Years of files, missing."

"Missing, or are they hiding them?"

Danni made a face. "I don't know. That's what we need to find out."

"Why would they hide them?" Leti knew there was always a reason for hiding things, but why this? She had no idea. All she knew was that it couldn't be good that they were tampering with children's files. In fact, it had to be pretty darn bad.

"I don't know."

"Well, whatever they're covering up, they've managed to do it for years. How are we going to find anything?"

"They didn't actually hide everything. People just didn't connect the dots." Danni waggled her eyebrows. "We're smarter. We know what to look for."

And if that was true, then she couldn't stop looking even if she wanted to—not that she wanted to at this point. "So what are we looking for?"

"The missing documentation." Danni leaned back and closed her eyes. It was like she had something to say but she just didn't want to say it.

"What?"

"I don't know how to say this."

"Just say it."

"I don't know what we're going to find, but I think they might have done it to cover up something."

"Like?"

"Uncared for children? Missing children?"

Leti didn't know what to say to that. "Is that just a theory or you do you have proof?"

"Nothing yet. It's a feeling."

"Where do you think the missing docs are?" Leti had no idea where to even start.

Danni shrugged. "If I was hiding paperwork, I'd burn it."

"Well, then we're in trouble." This was looking worse and worse.

"I don't think they're that smart." Danni shook her head. "I think they might have held onto it."

"Why do you say that?"

"The second article said that the boy who was stung by the bee wasn't on record as living there. That's when the documentation disappeared. But then his file was found, supposedly a glitch. When the reporters asked about the other documentation, the shelter said it was lost in a fire."

"You think they lied."

"I think if they were talking, they were lying." Danni leaned forward in her seat and pointed at Leti's computer screen. "I think we should check out these shelters."

"The two where the children died?" That felt obvious even for arrogant politicians trying to get away with...well... murder.

"The one on the south-west side is now an admin office. The South Side location is still a functioning children's home." Danni leaned back again. "If you can check out the locations and see if you can find anything, I'm going to focus on trying to get into their files."

"You mean...hacking?" Leti knew Danni did some questionable things to get information, but this was highly illegal.

"I mean poking around. It's not my fault if their firewalls aren't configured correctly."

"Can you do that?"

"I can. It's more should I do that?'"

"Should you?"

"It's only illegal if I get caught." Danni winked. "But I don't get caught."

"I don't think that's how legality works." Leti was glad Danni worked for the good guys or she'd be a menace to society. Leti wanted to share Danni's confidence, but she was a numbers girl. "How do I get inside the shelter?"

"I have no idea. That's not my realm." Danni stood up. "You're smart. You'll figure it out."

Leti didn't believe that at all, not that she had to believe it. She just had to do it. She had to get in and find any information she could. This was going to be a cluster...thing, but she didn't have time to worry about that now. She had a date.

———

LETI SAT at a small table in a small Italian bistro. Photos of Italian vistas in black frames lined the off-white walls above a dark blue chair rail. Dark oak beams stood in the corners of the room and ran across the ceiling.

Giovanni sat across from her on a light-green fabric chair. A small basket with garlic knots sat in the center of the two-person table. It was like all her other dates. But not.

He smiled, gorgeous lips and sparkling brown eyes. She could get lost in those eyes if given the chance. And don't even get her started on those lips. "I would love to work with my friends every day, but we'd never get anything done. Your job is fascinating, but it sounds dangerous."

"I don't know about dangerous." She didn't want to think about the car that pulled a Christine on her the other night. "Maggie and Danni have had a few run-ins with some bad guys, but I work behind a desk."

Which was mostly true. If anyone would have asked her a week ago, that would have been absolutely true. She wanted to say the car was a fluke. She was in the wrong place at the wrong time. Delusional? Maybe. But it was her delusion. Let her have it.

"It still sounds exciting finding anomalies." Giovanni took a drink from his glass. "Numbers never lie."

It was like he read her mind.

The waiter came up to the table, carrying two plates. He slid her chicken pesto in front of her and Giovanni's surf and turf in front of him. Then the waiter produced a cheese grater from his apron. "Parmesan, signora?"

"Yes, please." Leti leaned back and let him coat her dish with cheese. There could never be too much cheese.

The waiter tapped the grater. "Enough?"

She wanted to tell him to keep it coming, but she didn't want to look like a crazy cheese person. Not on the first date. That was more third date territory. Although, Maggie once gave a waiter twenty bucks to keep the grater on the table during the whole meal. Leti and Maggie had eaten the entire block of cheese.

Kevin would get a kick out of that story. She

wanted to tell him, but he wasn't here. She looked at the waiter as he stood over her, an expectant look on his face. "I'm sorry?"

"Is there anything else I can get for you?" The waiter smiled when she said no, and turned to Giovanni. "Parmesan, signore?"

"No, thank you."

The waiter nodded and walked away.

"That's why I love my job. I'm a big fan of numbers. They're impartial." Leti brought the conversation back to the last thing Giovanni had said. "How about you? Why did you become a doctor?"

"I didn't have much choice. My mother is a doctor. My father is a doctor. It was expected that I go to medical school."

"Do you like it?"

"I've learned to love it. I made it my own." He smiled and took a bite of food. He didn't seem to be done with the thought, so Leti took a bite of her own and waited for him to continue. "My parents are both surgeons. I went into private practice. My version of lashing out."

"You rebel." Leti giggled.

"I hear you're a bit of a rebel yourself."

"My mother told you that?" That was surprising. Usually her mamá was so busy telling men how perfect she was. Her mamá didn't have time to tell them the truth—what a disappointment she was.

"No, I heard it from your father."

"That makes more sense."

Giovanni laughed. "Your dad seemed proud that

you aren't a CPA, and your mother is very disappointed."

"I'm not sure how that came up, but I'm glad he's proud." She wasn't sure how to even take that.

"Your mother kept mentioning you were working on getting another job."

Or as her mamá would say, a "real" job.

He continued. "She mentioned you were getting your CPA. I think your dad wanted to make sure I didn't want you for your credentials."

Leti felt the laugh bubble in her chest and pressed her linen napkin to her mouth. After she finished her bite of food, she draped the napkin back over her lap and picked up her fork again. Her other hand stroked the base of her water glass. "Are you sure you're not after my CPA?"

"Once you get your CPA, I'm going to be all over it." He smiled and slid his hand over hers. "For now, I think I'll just be after you for you."

His hand was warm and strong. She wanted to kiss those fingers up and down. She wanted to feel those hands on her body. All over. She pressed her legs together to keep the excitement at bay.

He laced his fingers through hers and rubbed his thumb along the back of her hand. The nerve endings fired all along her arm, landing straight in her belly. After a moment he let go of her hand and reached for his fork. Her hand was cold, but it made eating a heck of a lot easier.

· · ·

LATER ON, the waiter brought the check and set it down in front of Giovanni. Sexist? Yes, but that didn't stop her from reaching across the table. Her hand was on the folder when Giovanni grabbed the other side.

"Can I get tonight's dinner?" He didn't pull. He just kept his hand on his side of the folder. "How about you get next time?"

"That sounds like a deal." She couldn't help the smile on her face.

Giovanni stuck his credit card in the folder and handed it to the waiter.

"Thank you for dinner." Leti took the napkin off her lap and folded it on the table.

"You are very welcome." Giovanni smiled. "Anytime you want to grab dinner, I'd be happy to do this again."

"So would I." And she meant it. He was nice guy and dinner had been effortless. The conversation fun. She hadn't been on a date that didn't end in disaster in so long, she forgot how fun they could be.

"Maybe next time you can take me to your favorite restaurant."

"Deal."

"Deal." Giovanni smiled as the waiter slid the folder back on the table. He signed the bottom and put his card back in his wallet.

She stood and picked up her purse. Once they were outside the restaurant, she led him over to her car.

"So, is this you?" Giovanni rested a hand on her green hybrid.

"This is me." She opened the driver's door and tossed her purse onto the passenger side.

He ran a hand along the roof. "Nice car."

"Thanks. I like it." She turned so her back was against the door opening.

One of his hands rested on the door and the other on the roof. She was boxed in, and she could admit she liked it.

"I had a really great time tonight." He leaned in, really close. He smelled so good.

She wanted him to close the distance. She wanted to feel those lips on hers. She wanted to feel him on her. "So did I."

"I want to kiss you. Is that okay?" His eyes grew heavy as he looked at her like she was ice cream on a ninety-degree day.

"Yes." She would've said more but she didn't have to. His lips were on hers and they did not disappoint. Soft. Firm. Warm. All the feels.

CHAPTER NINE

LAST NIGHT HAD BEEN amazing and Leti was still floating. Well, she was standing behind a dumpster looking at an empty building, so maybe floating was a bit of an exaggeration.

The morning sun sliced through the broken glass of the windows. She double checked the address. Avalon Ave. Yes. This was the address. She was back at exaggeration. The building wasn't just run-down, it was uninhabitable. And obviously hadn't been inhabited for a long time.

Her cellphone rang. She checked the screen. Kevin. She'd sent him a text earlier that she was running late. He didn't need to know why. She was just driving around the city. Nothing exciting. And maybe stopping here and there.

It had been over a week since the car incident. Maybe time was giving her a different perspective. It could have been an accident. Maybe the person sped up when they got into the alley. She'd done that before.

Turned from a cramped road into the alley and sped up. She was sure that was it.

That didn't matter right now. Right now she needed to know why a building that had a sign on it that said it was condemned was on the charity's list of active locations on their website. She walked around the dumpster, avoiding the crevices and stones of the parking lot. With the crack pipes and used needles everywhere, all she needed was to fall and get some sort of bloodborne disease.

She inched her way over the hypodermic obstacle course, stepping over a curb and avoiding a used diaper with something crawling out of it. Literally. She jumped back. There was something moving.

Gross. She headed toward her car.

This wasn't her scene. Maggie did disgusting stuff like this. Jessi, as a PI in training, did stuff like this. Leti sat at a desk and looked at numbers. She was anchored to her desk. She didn't sneak around, tracking down information. At least she didn't before.

She thought of Erica, and all the kids who could be in danger.

Her body stopped its trek toward cleanliness and hand sanitizer. Although it might take more than sanitizer to clean this place off her. She stopped before she opened the car door. She should take a look inside the building. See if it was in use. Because there was no way she was coming back here.

She could do this. It was a building. She just had to avoid anything that moved. Which meant avoiding the diaper. Easy-peasy.

Heading toward the right side of the building, she saw an archway. The outer door hung from a single hinge on one side, but she managed to sneak past. A blanket was shoved in the corner of the space, covering a pile of clothes and probably hiding a person's entire livelihood. Whoever was squatting there must have gone out to find food.

She avoided the pile of stuff and peeked in through a filthy window next to a plywood-covered door. Inside, the building was empty. No furniture. A beam hung down in the center of the room. The condemned sign wasn't lying.

"Hey!" a woman screeched.

Leti dipped underneath the sagging door and stepped away from the building.

A woman stumbled toward her, through the drug paraphernalia wasteland. A tattered coat hung from her body. Fists covered by fingerless gloves waved in the air. "Get away from my house!" The woman staggered closer.

Leti ran straight for the car. She would not fall. Not in this lot with the glass and needles. She made it past the rattling diaper. Rattling. Oh no, Leti was so out of here.

The woman yelled and kept coming.

Leti was faster but somehow the woman was gaining on her. It was like being stalked by Pepe Le Pew with all the smell and without the love. She was either going to have to get away or she was going to have to use Krav Maga on a homeless woman. That felt wrong.

She threw open the car door and slid inside. She slammed the door, and the locks closed with a click. High-pitched mumbling wafted into the car through the closed windows. Her heart hammered in her chest.

The woman slapped at the glass. "Get out!"

There was no way she was leaving this car. Leti fumbled the key into the ignition and started the engine. Shoved the car into reverse. She backed up, barely avoiding running the woman over. Slammed the car into drive and hit the gas.

Given the woman was still running after the car and waving her fist, she didn't seem injured. Thank goodness. The woman disappeared into a dot as Leti drove away.

As her heartbeat slowed to a normal rate, Leti's mind cleared. She'd only been at the paraphernalia building a few minutes. She had time to check out another location.

Her phone rang. She ignored it. She had one more errand to run and then she'd head to the office.

A HALF HOUR LATER, Leti pulled into a parking spot at the second building on her list. The good news was this one wasn't condemned. It was inhabited. Cars were in the parking lot.

She sat in her car and watched as a man walked in the front door. Inside, people lined up along the front window. A sign that said "Administration" poked out of the ground to the right of the door. This place was hopping. She needed a plan.

Looking in the windows wasn't going to cut it this time around. She needed to get inside. And with all the people milling about, stealth wasn't going to work. She'd have to do obvious and head-on.

Which wasn't exactly her strong suit. She did under the radar, behind the scenes, not front-and-center pretending to be someone she wasn't. She hadn't acted since second grade, and even then she was a tree. She was a great tree, but she was always scenery for a reason.

Another person entered the building, followed by a woman in a tracksuit with a toddler in tow. These were normal people, doing normal things.

She could do this. Ask a few questions. Blend. She'd be a tree—with talking. An Ent, or whatever those talking trees were.

Leti left the car and went inside. The first building was dirt and destruction, this one was the opposite. It was immaculate. She walked up to the front desk, where a woman sat behind the counter. Her employee badge said her name was Mildred.

"Hi, honey. Can I help you?" The woman smiled. Her curly gray hair was pulled back with a metal headband. Her yellow collared shirt was covered with ice cream cones.

"Hi, Mildred." Leti smiled back. "I was hoping you could help me."

"Well, that's what I do." Mildred smiled.

"I was writing an article about the shelter over on Avalon Avenue. When did it close?"

"It's not closed, honey. They're remodeling it."

Really? "But the building is empty."

"Well, yeah honey, they can't remodel with people inside." The pout on Mildred's lips said the words that she didn't say. Basically, bless Leti's heart.

Blessing people in lieu of out-and-out mockery—not just for the south anymore.

Leti didn't need sympathy or blessing. She really needed to look up the definition of remodel versus condemned and show it to Mildred, but now wasn't the time.

"I hadn't heard that. Thank you." Leti smiled and tried to think of another question. She should have had them all lined up.

"Did you need anything else?"

"According to your website, this is an active shelter as well."

"They changed this building to administration last year. It was a godsend. Now all the business offices are in one place instead of dispersed all over the city."

"That does sound more convenient." Although Leti appreciated the information, this wasn't exactly helping. She needed to look around. Maybe if Mildred stepped away... "Do you have a list of shelters that are active?"

"We have the list online."

"But it doesn't seem to be up to date."

Mildred's smile slipped. "What did you say you needed this for?"

Leti was losing her. "I'm writing an article about all the good the shelters have done for the city over the years."

Mildred smiled again. She was back on board. "I'm sure I have an active list somewhere." More smiling. "Let me check in the file room. I'll be right back."

The file room. That's what Leti needed.

Mildred slowly angled up from her chair and ambled to the back of the room. She walked down a side hall, and Leti watched her go. No one was left in the front, so she followed. Leti walked behind the desk and down the hallway, but Mildred was faster than she looked and nowhere to be found. A door stood open on the left. She tilted her head around the jamb, looking for Mildred or a set of file cabinets. The room was empty.

She continued down the hall and found another door. She opened it, bumping right into Mildred. "I'm so sorry."

"Why are you back here?"

Leti couldn't just say she was looking to go through file cabinets. "I must have misunderstood. I thought you told me to follow you."

"I couldn't find what I needed in there, but I have one more place to look." Mildred pointed back toward her desk. "Please go back to the front office and I'll get you that list."

"Of course." Leti nodded and took a few steps. Once Mildred disappeared at the end of the hall through another door, Leti turned and slipped into the file room.

Ugh.

File room? There was one double-sized file cabinet. One. She opened the top drawer, but the thing contained nothing but takeout menus and old empty forms. The second drawer wasn't much better—office supplies. It was overflowing with pens, notepads, and binder clips.

She leaned down and opened the third drawer. Bingo. Actual files. What a concept. She thumbed through the tabs. Electric company. Gas company. She pulled paperwork out of each folder. It looked like bills, although what did she expect in the administration building? They probably paid the utilities for all the locations.

Leti slid the drawer shut and turned around in a circle. There had to be another cabinet, but no—there wasn't another anything.

"Excuse me." Mildred lurked in the doorway with a scowl. Since Leti wasn't back at the front where she had been told to go, she wasn't surprised by the anger on the woman's face. "You shouldn't be back here."

"I'm sorry. I wanted to tell you I was in a hurry."

Mildred didn't smile as lifted her arm to indicate that Leti should leave the room. Leti led the way and stopped at the front of Mildred's desk.

"So, I was able to find a list." Mildred hugged the paper close to her chest.

Leti held out her hand. "Thank you so much." Her hand stayed empty.

"You're welcome." Mildred handed over the paper like she was handing over state secrets—which, if she knew half of what was going on within the organization, might actually be the truth.

Once Leti had the list, she folded the page and slid

it into her pocket. She had what she needed. So she could push the boundaries now. "Is there a basement?"

"Not that I know of." Mildred ambled back down the hall. "Why do you care? This building has nothing to do with the shelter."

"Oh, this has nothing to do with the article. I'm interested in old buildings. Is this a Frank Lloyd Wright?" He was the only architect she could think of.

"I don't think so." Mildred's smile was starting creep Leti out. "He makes such lovely buildings."

"He really does." Now what?

"Have a nice day." Mildred sat down at her desk and focused on the screen in front of her. And with that, Leti felt as if she'd been dismissed. Because let's face it, she had.

Her phone rang again. Kevin.

She better get back to the office before he sent out a search party. She sent him a text. *On my way.*

That should at least buy her some time to figure out how she'd tell him where she'd been.

ON MY WAY.

Kevin stared at his phone. He was tempted to throw it, but it hadn't done anything to him. He'd tried calling Leti. He'd tried texting. He was on the verge of sending smoke signals when she'd finally texted.

She was supposed to wait for him this morning. He went to her house, and she'd already left. He'd tried Café Calao and she wasn't there. Add all of that to the fact that she wasn't answering her phone, and he was worried. That last text made him feel a bit better, but he wouldn't feel okay until he could hear her voice and know she was safe.

He stared at the screen in front of him and tried to concentrate on the Facebook stalking he was trying to do. He was looking into a cheating wife, and he was looking for clues on social media before he staked out her house and office. No need to waste all that time watching her house if she posted pictures with some re-occurring guy in the background at the gym or at work.

He poked at the keyboard. It looked like he might have hit the jackpot. There were a few photos with her girlfriends, and the same guy seemed to be lurking in the background of a few pictures taken at the gym. One big coincidence, or she was using her friends as an excuse to see her sidepiece.

He should be happy. He'd found the smoking gun. It looked like she was spending her afternoon with her friends and her boyfriend. This afternoon he'd post himself outside of Flextime Gym. Instead of feeling that happiness, he was restless. He wanted to pace. Or call. Or run.

"If you hit that keyboard any harder, we're going to have to report you for aggravated assault." Maggie sat in the chair at Leti's desk.

He hadn't heard her come in over the sound of his thoughts and the clicking of the keyboard. "When did you get here?" He drew his hand back. If he kept his hands near those keys, he'd keep beating them.

"I just got here—stopped to see how things are before I meet with a client."

"Things here are fine." He attempted a smile, but it must have fallen flat because his sister didn't get up and walk away.

She frowned. "Are you okay?"

"I'm fine."

"Do you want to talk about it?"

Part of him wanted to unload, but he knew it wouldn't do any good. It would just lead to questions that he wasn't able to answer—or maybe he didn't want to answer. "There's nothing to talk about."

"Okay." Maggie stood. "If you need to talk. I'm here."

"I know." He truly smiled this time because he knew she meant it. She would listen to him anywhere, anytime. "Thank you."

Maggie slipped her sunglasses on as she walked to the back door. She stopped and turned. "Oh, we're cooking out tonight. You're coming to Dad's, right?"

"What if I'm too upset?" He could use his mood to get out family obligation. Not that it had ever worked in the past.

"Too late. You said you're fine." She slid her sunglasses down her nose and looked at him over them. "Unless you need to talk about something?"

"That sounds like coercion."

She smiled. She knew she'd won. "So, I'll see you at Dad's at six tonight."

"Yeah."

Maggie disappeared out the back door with a "Hey,

I'm heading to see a client." The door opened again and in walked Leti.

Kevin kept himself glued to the chair. He wanted to jump up and give her the third degree. "Where were you?"

"I had an errand," she snarled.

His hackles went up. "I thought you were going to wait for me this morning?"

"It wasn't anything I needed help with." The snark in her voice said she was angry.

"Did it have to do with the case?" To be fair, he was angry too.

She didn't answer as she put her bag in the bottom drawer of her desk and turned on her computer. "I went to check on two of the shelters."

"And?"

"One is abandoned. The other is now the administrative offices." She sat at her desk.

"Okay. Do we need to check it out? We can go there tonight."

"I already did." She didn't look at him.

"You snuck in on your own?"

"I didn't sneak. I walked in and asked for information."

"Why would you do that? The last time you asked around, they came after you."

"We don't know that's what happened. And I need to find these old files."

"Old files?"

"Danni found an article online where they mentioned that a couple children died, but the weird part is that the shelter couldn't find any of their files. Then all of a sudden they found the ones they needed. So we think they're hiding them."

"You think they have hidden files." He leaned back. Hidden files was not a good thing.

"Yes."

"Did you think they'd hand over these hidden files if you walked in and asked?"

"No, I poked around while the receptionist looked for a list of active sites. I mentioned the location on Avalon Avenue was uninhabited, and she said being renovated, but it's condemned and the dust bunnies collecting on the 80's style furniture says there hasn't been anyone there for years."

"So you drew attention to the fact that you're looking into the site and that it's empty?"

"I just asked for a list."

"Did you get one?"

"I did." She pulled out the list from her pocket. She unfolded the page and stared at the information.

He stood over her shoulder and looked at the benign piece of paper. Addresses lined the sheet. "Couldn't you see that online?"

"They weren't correct. This list is supposed to be updated."

"So, you put yourself in danger because they didn't update their website?"

"I didn't put myself in danger. I asked a woman some questions and got a piece of paper. That's it."

"I don't like it."

"Well, it's done." She turned to the computer and

began tapping at the keyboard. She seemed to be done with him. Well, he was done too.

"Fine."

"Fine."

Kevin stormed out the back door. It was bad enough she didn't wait for him. Then she put herself in danger again. And she didn't even seem to care. Well, then he didn't care.

He had a job to do. Flextime Gym wasn't going to stake itself out. If he was lucky, Cheating Christy would be at her two o'clock Pilates class and hook up with background guy afterward.

Either way, he'd be doing something useful. Sitting here wanting to protect a woman who didn't want his protection was not useful at all. And he was done.

CHAPTER TEN

LETI STOOD at the small counter, aiming her dart at the board. With a flick of her wrist the dart sailed into the red double-ring on the twenty slice of the target. The screen above the board dinged and sparkled as forty points were added to her total.

"Nice shot." Giovanni held up a hand for a high-five.

Leti slapped his hand. "Thanks."

"How do I follow a beauty like that?"

"The shot was pretty awesome."

Giovanni pulled three darts from board. "I wasn't talking about the shot."

She could feel the heat crawling up her cheeks. Leti grabbed her beer and took a slow pull to cool down. This date was turning out to be better than the first. She didn't think that was possible.

Turns out eating food and playing a couple games of darts at the Bullseye Club was not only fun, it was somehow romantic. Or maybe it was just romantic because of who she was with.

The last dart hit the board and Giovanni smiled. "So close." Twenty points flashed on the screen, but he only needed ten, so the twenty dropped, leaving the ten points still listed under his name.

"I only need twenty points." Leti pulled out the darts and moved back to stand behind the counter.

Giovanni leaned in. His breath heated her cheek. "You got this." He rested his lips on hers. Soft, warm kiss.

Her brain scrambled.

Her body melted.

Her guilt flared.

He wasn't Kevin. Why was she thinking about him at a time like this? He wasn't thinking about her. He was probably out with some gorgeous woman. She hadn't had the heart to ask how his date went with the busty blond, she didn't really want to know. Well, she did, but if he said good, she'd die a little inside.

So she ignored it. Just like she had to ignore any other feelings when it came to him. Giovanni was here and he was nice. He deserved her full attention. And so did she.

Operation Just-Giovanni was underway. No more thoughts of He Who Must Not Be Named.

"Ready?" He pulled away.

She smiled. She was here with Giovanni. Kevin was not.

"Your turn."

She stared at the mini-daggers in her hand. "You're cheating. You kissed me so I'd forget how to throw."

"I doubt just a kiss would make you forget how to throw a dart." He leaned in. "Unless that kiss was extra special."

"Maybe we should do it again to see if it was extra-special." She needed a do-over. One where she wasn't thinking about another man.

"I would." He inched closer. His mouth hovering over hers. "But I don't want to be accused of cheating."

And then he was gone. He stepped back and took a drink of his beer.

Leti wanted to scream that he could cheat all he wanted. She wanted another shot at a kiss. Although, if she won this game they could finish the kissing back at her place.

She set the darts on the counter and selected one. She twisted it between her fingers as she looked at the board. She needed one twenty, two tens, or three of anything that equaled twenty.

The sooner she finished this thing, the better.

She angled her arm back, flicked her wrist and let fly. The dart landed in the black space under the twenty. The television lit up like a Christmas tree as bells rang and choirs sang. Well, there might not have been a choir coming from the television, but Leti could hear angels.

"Nice job." Giovanni smiled and slid his hand along her arm. "Did you want to play again?"

"I had other plans."

"What kind of plans?"

"I thought we could watch a movie at my place. My parents are out tonight. Canasta."

"I never thought canasta was a beautiful word till now." He slid his fingers through hers. "Let's go."

"Let's go." She grabbed her purse and followed him out of the bar. He flagged down a taxi and they headed to her parents' house.

THE RIDE WAS LONG. Giovanni's thumb stroked along her knuckles. It was nice. Her head rested on his shoulder, but she wanted to turn her head toward him and kiss him. She wanted to put her hands all over his body and forget all the things she needed to forget.

The taxi pulled down the street of her parents' home. "Thank you," she said as Giovanni slid a credit card through the reader on the back of the seat and followed her out of the cab.

Hand-in-hand, they walked up the steps. She used the key for the front door and walked in. Her mother always left the light on so she could see once she came into the house, which meant the hall light was on, but nothing else.

"I'll grab us some drinks." Leti leaned into Giovanni and kissed his lips. Slowly. Ever so slowly. A soft groan came from his throat. And she could admit it was a great kiss.

He pulled away. "Skip the drinks."

"Sounds good." She grabbed his hand and pulled him toward the couch. Her lips were totally on board with Operation Just-Giovanni. She wanted to kiss him and then she realized she could. As she pulled him forward a man came into view.

A heavy-set man all dressed in black stood in the living room. A ski mask covered his face, and he held a giant serrated knife.

Leti screamed, and Giovanni turned to look.

"Please don't hurt us." Leti raised her hands to show she meant no harm. At least she meant no harm now, just until she could figure out how to get them out of this.

She was a master at Krav Maga. Okay, not a master, but she'd kicked Sheldon's butt in her last class. Despite his name, he was pretty agile. But maybe between that and Giovanni's muscles, they could knock this guy on his backside.

"How many times did we tell you to mind your business, sugar?" The bad guy stalked closer to Leti and turned the knife on Giovanni. "Maybe you need to be punished for not keeping her in line."

Giovanni threw up his hands. "I just met her. I don't know what you're talking about." He inched closer to the front door. "I'm going to go. This is too much for me."

"You're not going anywhere." Bad guy waved the knife.

Leti was between Giovanni and the bad guy. She was basically a human shield, and the look in Giovanni's eyes said he was going to use her and make a run for it.

Giovanni looked over at Leti as he said, "I'm sorry." He shoved her toward the bad guy and ran for the door.

Shoved her.

She tripped, and righted herself before she fell on the guy's knife. Giovanni threw open the door and shot outside, leaving her there alone with the bad guy. Who had a knife.

Bad guy didn't follow him. He didn't run at all. He just trained the knife back on her. "Where did you find that guy?"

"My mother set us up." She winced. Not the time for sharing.

"Phew. Honey, I thought my mom had bad taste." He shook his head. "Stop looking into things that don't concern you. Next time I won't just come after the dog, it'll be someone you care about." He drove the knife into the couch cushions and sliced down the center. Her mamá was going to have a conniption.

"Where's Pork Chop?" She wanted to tell him to stop, but maybe if he sliced up the couch, he wouldn't slice up her or her dog. Where *was* Pork Chop?

A skinny guy came in the back door. He also wore a mask, but had a gun in his hand.

Things just went from bad to worse.

"Let's go," skinny guy said.

The bad guy and partner disappeared out the open front door. She waited a beat to make sure they didn't come back shooting, then ran to the door and slammed it shut. Locked it. Slid to the floor.

Her heart hammered in her chest.

Air chopped in and out of her lungs.

Pork Chop.

No jingling. No nuzzling. Oh no. No, no, no.

She scrambled to her feet and tripped across the living room. "Pork Chop!"

Nothing.

She ran into the kitchen. "Pork Chop!"

Nothing.

She flung the back door open. Gasping little barks filled the air in between the jingle of a collar.

Pork Chop's leash was wrapped around his neck and nailed to the deck. Leti dove for her dog. Yanking the leash free, she picked him up and ran with him back into the house. "Are you okay, honey?"

She unwound the leash ran a hand along his body, making sure they didn't do anything else to him. He didn't appear to have any injuries aside from a little matted hair on his neck.

"I'm so sorry, honey." Leti flipped the lock on the back door and held back the tears she knew she wanted to cry. She was alone and they might come back. She needed help. Since Giovanni the runner had left, she needed someone else. And she knew who that someone else was going to be.

KEVIN COULDN'T WAIT to get out of his father's house, but given they hadn't even eaten yet, he didn't think he was going to be sprung anytime soon.

"Uncle Kevin, play ball with me." Michaela ran into the living room carrying a big yellow rubber ball. Her black curls bounced as she ran.

"Don't run in the house!" her father yelled, and Michaela skidded to a stop.

Kevin's niece was the cutest five-year-old on the planet. He might be biased, but with the attitude and the brains, she was the full package. And she absolutely drove her father—his older brother, Kyle— crazy. Bonus.

Not that Kevin didn't love Kyle. He did. It's just that his brother was a dick growing up, and watching Michaela drive him up a wall was satisfying in so many ways.

"Here." Michaela handed Kevin the ball and then crossed the room. Her arms were open wide. "I'm ready."

Kevin bounced the ball toward his niece. Her arms flailed as it passed her by, and she scooped it up off the floor. "Got it."

"You did."

She threw the ball to Kevin. Sort of. Throw was being generous. The ball left her little hands but headed straight for the retro glass lamp that used to be his mother's favorite. Kevin jumped at the ball and caught it one handed.

His dad would have a coronary if that lamp broke. Not that it was the first time it had been broken. Kevin broke the darn thing when he was eleven. He and Kyle had gotten into a fistfight over a girl.

His mom had glued the thing back together and made them both swear that they'd never fight over a woman again. And they hadn't. They'd found other things to fight about over the years, but never a woman.

With all of his mother's breakables lining the shelves in the living room, throwing a ball probably wasn't the best idea. Nobody said there was a problem with rolling a ball, though.

"Maybe we should sit on the floor and play there." Kevin moved to the floor and waited for Michaela to sit. He rolled the ball to her.

She grabbed the ball and smiled. "I got it."

"Great catch."

Michaela attempted to roll the ball back to him. It bounced off his foot and took a new trajectory right back to her.

She held the ball up and wiggled. "I got it."

"You got it." He wiggled back and forth, mimicking her move, and she giggled.

"You're silly."

"Silly?" Kevin rolled his eyes to the left. He smacked the side of his head and immediately rolled his eyes to the right. It was something he used to do to impress girls. They had been impressed. Given the laugh and way Michaela kicked out her legs, he still had it.

"Mommy! Mommy!" Michaela jumped to her feet and ran into the kitchen. "You should see what Uncle Kevin can do."

She came back a minute later, pulling Tatiana behind her into the living room. Tatiana was an amazing woman. She was smart, driven and sweet as could be. And Kevin had no idea what she was doing with his brother. She had dark brown skin, beautiful brown eyes, and curly black hair pulled away from her face in a ponytail.

Tatiana sat in the Queen Anne chair next to the lamp. The furniture was older than the house, but it was what his mother had loved. And his father refused to change anything. "So, I hear you have hidden talents."

"I don't know about that." Kevin got to his feet. He rolled his eyes and hit the side of his head, repeating the trick.

Michaela jumped up and down and Tatiana laughed. "You should take that show on the road."

"I would be the new hit for all the kids under six."

"I bet even six-year-olds would jump at that." Tatiana stood up. "I'm going to go finish making the salad."

"Can I help?" Michaela followed her mom out of the room.

"Of course, sweetheart."

Kevin stood in the living room. Alone. He dribbled the big yellow ball—thump, thump, thump. It gave him something to do.

Thump.

Thump. The sound was soothing. The alone was soothing.

His brother was manning the grill out back, with Maggie's boyfriend Chase. He could go help, but that might give his brother the idea that he wanted to talk. Kevin had no desire to talk. His life wasn't exactly going in a direction that led to happy discussions.

"Don't play ball in the house." His father stood in the doorway.

Kevin grabbed the ball and the thumping stopped. He should have found somewhere to hide while he had the chance. He couldn't leave now—not without being rude.

"You're good with her." His dad leaned against the chair Tatiana just vacated.

"Thank you." Kevin didn't really know what to say to that.

"Once you get your career on track, you should find a woman and create a few of them. Not now obviously, you have bigger priorities."

Kevin pressed the ball between his hands as he tried not to get mad. He didn't need any added pressure, and his dad was the master of pressure.

"There isn't any one woman in your life, right?"

This wasn't a discussion he wanted to have with his dad. Of course he wanted a family, and had every intention of settling down some day. He just wasn't sure it would be anytime soon. The whole job thing was part of the problem. The lack of potential bride was also an issue. "Of course not."

"Good. Smart." His dad nodded. "So, where are you in the process?"

Kevin knew exactly what process he meant. What he didn't know was why he was asking when he could find out himself. "Can't you just ask your staff?"

"I could." His father sighed. "But my son has tied my hands and asked that I not step in. I figured if I asked about the status of your CPD application, they might take it as an indication that they should show you favoritism."

"Thank you." And he meant it. He really wanted to do this on his own. His dad could snap his fingers and get him a job on the force. The fact that he was taking a back seat had to be tough for the man. He was controlling. Which made him a great Chief. Didn't always make him a great father. But he seemed to be trying.

"I passed the background check and the psych eval," Kevin said. "My medical evaluation is next week."

That's why this was taking forever. Every step seemed to take weeks or even months. And when one step was complete, another waited around the corner.

His father shook his head. "That's ridiculous. I could see what I can do. Get you in sooner."

"Dad, I want to do this on my own."

"Fine, but police work is in your blood. You've only got a few more years left before you age out of the system and you can't join the force."

"I know, Dad." The fact that Kevin was getting older and not a cop was weighing on him every day.

"You'll have to work twice as hard to get ahead. Most guys your age have made detective by now. You'll need to be laser-focused if you want to succeed. You don't have time for distractions."

"I get it, Dad." Kevin couldn't handle distractions. Leti was one of the biggest distractions right now.

"I know you're frustrated, son, but you should be out doing police work on the streets."

"I am working on the streets. I'm working as PI."

"That's not police work."

"Are we doing this again?" Maggie walked in the living room, glaring at her father.

"What you do serves a purpose, but it's not police work." Her father sighed. "You want to take this route—I don't get it—but I let you do it. Your brother wants to be a cop. He should be."

"I don't disagree, Dad." She seemed to think for a few seconds, like she wanted to say something else, but instead she shook her head. "Dinner is ready."

"Great. I can't wait to have one of Montgomery's famous burgers. I'm famished." Kevins' father clapped his hands together as he walked toward the kitchen.

Kevin watched his sister, who was watching his father walk away. "You okay?"

"Why do I let him get to me?"

"He's been practicing our whole life. He's really good at it."

"At what?"

"Getting to us."

Maggie nodded as she stared through the doorway where her father had disappeared. "Sometimes I think he's more proud that I'm dating a cop than that I have a successful business. It's like my only accomplishment is landing a detective that can make a good burger."

"I think he's proud of both, it's just that only one of those things can operate a grill."

She smiled.

Kevin sighed. "I think he's fine with you owning your own business and being a PI. It's me he has a problem with. I'm working for my sister. I think that's the issue." How dare his son not be as successful as him.

"He really does know how to get to us, doesn't he?"

Kevin smiled. "We keep letting him."

"What does that say about us?"

"Insanity runs in the family?"

Maggie laughed. "Indeed it does."

Kevin's phone chirped. He pulled it out of his pocket and looked at the screen. Leti. "I need to take this."

"Who is it? Everyone you know is here." Maggie tilted her head to get a look at the screen. "What does Leti want? Put it on speaker."

"Hello." Kevin slid the phone to his ear. There was no way he was putting it on speaker. He didn't think she'd say anything that Maggie couldn't hear, but if Leti wanted her to hear it, she would've called Maggie.

"Kevin..." Leti's voice broke.

He wasn't sure, but he could almost hear a sniffle. Was she crying? "What's wrong?"

"I don't know what to do. They were in my parents' house."

"Who was in your parents' house?" He asked to make sure, but he had a feeling he knew exactly who had been there. And why.

"Some thugs."

"Are you okay?" He pulled his keys from his pocket and mouthed to Maggie, *I have to go.*

"Is she okay?" Maggie whispered.

"I'm okay," Lettie said, "but I could use your help."

Kevin nodded to his sister and walked out the front door. "I'm on my way. Are you home?"

"Yes."

"Are they gone? Did you lock the doors?"

"They're gone. The doors are locked." A dog whimpered in the background.

"Is Pork Chop okay?"

"They tied him down. He couldn't breathe." Leti hiccupped, and the distinct sound of a sniffle came across the line. "He's shaken up, but okay."

Pork Chop was making noise. He was alive, but that didn't mean they didn't hurt him. If anybody touched a hair on that dog's head, he'd lose it. She loved that dog.

"Where are you in the house?" Kevin slid into his truck and started it up, shoving the phone into the holder on the dashboard and hitting speaker. He threw it into drive and sped down the block like the back bumper was on fire and he needed to outrun it.

"I'm in my room." Her voice was muffled. "With the door locked."

"Stay there." He could only imagine how scared she was. If these guys got into the house and threatened the dog, she'd be terrified. Rightfully so. This wasn't a game. They needed to take security up to the next level.

But first he had to get to her. He had to see her and make sure she was all in one piece. He'd meant it that he'd lose it if anything happened to that dog, but lose it didn't even begin to cover what he'd do if anyone touched a hair on *her* head.

CHAPTER ELEVEN

KEVIN COULD PRACTICALLY TASTE his heartbeat. Salt and fear. She'd said the assailants left, but there was no telling if they'd stay away or if they were just hiding and waiting. He wouldn't feel better until she was as far away from the house as possible.

He hastily parallel-parked between a BMW and a delivery truck. It wasn't his best parking job, but he didn't care. He needed to get to her and get her out.

They hadn't really talked about it yet, but he wanted her to go away for just a bit. She needed to get some distance. The bastards knew where she lived.

In a perfect world, she'd let this whole investigation go. Knowing her, that wasn't going to happen, so staying under the radar was the next best thing. He tucked his phone between his shoulder and ear to free up his hands so he could unlock the glove box and get his gun from inside. A quick check to make sure it was loaded and he slid from the truck and ran across the street. All the lights were on at Leti's house—inside and outside.

"I'm here. I'm outside the house." Kevin had thought about hanging up on the way here and focusing on driving, but that wasn't going to happen. If he couldn't hear her voice, he'd just worry about what was happening at the house. It was easier to just keep her on the line. After all, it was hands-free. And she had asked him to stay on the phone with her. That was the clincher.

He took the stairs, two at a time, to the front door. Locked. Good. He was worried she might have been so freaked out that she'd forget to lock the door.

He knocked, gun up as he turned to stare over the front yard. A car drove down the street, parking at the end of the block. A woman walked a dog on the opposite side of the street. Nothing looked out of place. Nothing menacing.

Kevin jumped as barking came from behind the door. Pork Chop. The little guy was doing his job.

Metal tumbled on metal and the door flew open. Leti stood behind the door in a little black dress that should be illegal. She was all legs and arms and—heaven help him—cleavage.

Even though he wanted to stare and enjoy the sight of her in that dress, the red-rimmed eyes drew his attention. "Are you okay?" His eyes ate up every inch of her. He needed to make sure she was okay. Every inch. No blood. No injuries. His lungs felt like they had inflated for the first time since he'd picked up the phone twenty minutes ago.

Leti nodded as she picked Pork Chop off the floor. "I'm okay."

Kevin slid inside the house and rubber-necked around the open door. Still nothing. He shut the door with a click and slid the locks into place. He shoved his gun in his belt and reached for the dog with now-empty hands. "How is this little guy?"

"He seems fine." A tear peeked out the corner of her eye. "They choked him with his leash."

Kevin lifted the hair along the dog's neck, exposing the skin. There didn't appear to be any marks, but that didn't mean there wasn't any trauma. "Take him in the living room." He pulled out the gun. "I'm going to do a check of the house."

"Can we go with you?"

He wanted to say no. She would be safer here, but the look on her face said she didn't feel safer here. She'd feel safer with him. And didn't that make his heart warm a bit. Not that he wanted her to ever feel unsafe, but if she did, he wanted her to feel she could come to him.

"Let's go." He pulled her behind him and headed up the stairs.

"I didn't see anyone up here." Leti leaned into Kevin and whispered.

He turned to her and held his finger to his lips. They needed the element of surprise if anyone had stayed behind.

She nodded.

They walked up the remaining stairs and found the first door on the left. He opened the door and peered inside the darkened room. The only light came from the streetlamps outside the windows along the far wall. A king-size platform bed stood underneath the windows, bracketed by red-oak end tables. Each one held a large-format digital alarm clock and a phone charger.

"This is my parents' room," Leti whispered.

Kevin nodded and raised his finger to his lips. "Shh."

He stepped to a door at the other end of the room and slid inside. A bathroom with a walk-in closet. He ran his hand along the clothing, looking for hiding spots. He opened the shower. No one was hiding anywhere he could see.

Clear.

He walked out of the bedroom, followed by Leti, and opened the door across the hall. There were no streetlamps on this side of the house, so the room was darker. It was harder to see, but the room was smaller. The twin-size bed was so low to the ground, Pork Chop would have a problem sneaking underneath that thing.

There was no second door, and they'd chosen blinds instead of curtains on the windows. There was nowhere to hide in this room

"This is Mateo's room."

Kevin stopped mid walk.

Leti bumped into his arm. "What do you see?" She craned her neck around him.

"I don't see anything." Kevin held a finger to his mouth as he whispered. "You know this means quiet."

"I know." Leti pulled the dog closer.

"Do you know why we need to be quiet?"

"So the bad guys don't hear us."

He nodded. "So let's finish this in silence."

She slammed her lips shut and pulled a fake zipper across her mouth. She tossed the imaginary key and smiled. Although the smile looked rather sarcastic in nature.

They went through the rest of the upper floor and didn't find any bad guys. And surprisingly, Leti didn't offer any commentary. The key seemed to have worked.

Kevin walked back downstairs and checked the closet near the front door, Leti at his back. He then moved to the living room, which was open to the dining room. The kitchen. The guest bathroom. He turned to tell her it was safe to talk.

No Leti.

When had he lost her?

"Leti?" he whispered, but there was no response.

Shit.

A loud bang came from the kitchen.

He ran out of the bathroom, his gun held high. Leti's father stood near the counter, grocery bags in his hands. Leti was emptying bags that were already on the counter into the refrigerator. Pork Chop ran back and forth from Leti to her father.

Her father dropped the bags onto the counter with wide eyes. "What's going on?"

"Kevin!" Leti stepped between Kevin and her father. "This is my father."

"Of course. Mr. Ramirez." Kevin shoved the gun in

the back of his jeans and leaned in to shake the older man's hand.

"Kevin?" Leti's father shook his hand and looked at Leti. "Why is this boy waving a gun in my house?"

The fact that the man knew to look directly at his daughter while he asked the question meant he knew her all too well.

"I had a little problem at the office."

"What kind of problem?"

"I am so disappointed in these chiles." Mrs. Ramirez came in the back door carrying a handful of green jalapeños. "Marjorie's garden is thriving and mine is withering... oh, hi. Who are you?"

"Hi, Mrs. Ramirez. Um...I'm here with Leti." Kevin wasn't an um person. He didn't stumble over words, but here he was stumbling like a teen meeting his girlfriend's mom for the first time. Not that the comparison worked at all in this situation.

"Well I would hope you're here with Leti and you didn't come inside my home without an invite." She dropped the jalapeños in a bowl on the counter and started emptying a bag.

"This is Maggie's brother, Kevin," Leti said.

"Oh, how wonderful to meet you. Maggie is like a daughter to us." Her mother folded the empty bag. "Have you had dinner? Can I make you something to eat?"

"I ate at my dad's." Not really a lie. He'd had a few chips and he'd stolen a couple cookies while they were making dinner. So, he had eaten. Not that he wouldn't like something a little more, but he didn't want Leti's mom making him dinner this late at night.

His stomach rumbled.

She shooed away his words with her hands. "You need more food. Your father would never forgive me if I let you leave starving. I'll warm up some tamales."

"That would be wonderful, Mrs. Ramirez." His stomach groaned in agreement.

"Why don't you all go in the living room while I make some food." Mrs. Ramirez pulled things out of cabinets and put groceries away. "Fernando, I'm only making you two." She looked at Kevin. "He has to watch his cholesterol."

Kevin had no idea what to say to that, so he smiled and followed Leti and her dad into the living room. Once they were out of earshot of the kitchen, her father turned to them both. "Someone tell me what is going on here."

Leti's attention didn't move from the floor. She seemed hesitant to even begin this conversation.

Kevin figured he'd save her. "Well, sir..." he said, and was interrupted by Leti's, "So, I've been looking into Wacker Children's Association."

"Isn't that run by Stanley Welford?" Her father frowned.

"How do you know that?"

Her father smiled. "I'm a lawyer in Chicago. It's a small community."

"Really?" Leti's stare left the floor to aim at her father.

"No, I played squash a time or two with his partner,

Rick." Mr. Ramirez moved to the window at the front of the living room.

"Since when do you play squash?"

"I have a life outside of you children."

"I know that, Papá."

Kevin took a breath. "Sir, can you step away from the window?"

Her father frowned again. "Are you in danger?"

"I'm not sure." She looked at Kevin—to back up her "not sure" story or to just not contradict it, he had no idea. But he wasn't going to say anything. He'd follow her lead here. Her family. Her lead. Leti faced her father. "But we don't want anything to happen to you or Mamá."

"What would you like me to do, mija?"

"Elena has been asking you to come help with the kids. Why don't you and Mamá go spend a few weeks there."

"I have cases."

"You can prepare from there." Leti looked ready to beg. Her hands were folded and she was close to bending at the knee. "It's only an hour from the city."

"Time to eat." Mrs. Ramirez came into the living room and took a look around the room. "Why does everyone look so sad?"

Mr. Ramirez shook his head and smiled. "Not sad, mi amor. I was just thinking that maybe you were right. We should go visit Elena for a bit and help her out."

"Really?" Mrs. Ramirez looked as if she just found out Santa Claus was real and he was bringing her her own amusement park.

"Yes."

The woman squealed and jumped at her husband. "What made you change your mind?"

"I know how much we appreciated when your mamá came to help with Mateo."

"This is wonderful." She clapped her hands together. "We'll go next week."

"Well, no." He held his wife's hands together and smiled. "We'd need to leave tonight. I don't know how long I can work from her house, but this is the perfect starting point."

"Really? But my job?"

"I will take you to work this week, so you don't miss any time, and then you can schedule vacation for next week."

"That seems silly."

"Mi amor, it's what I'd like." Her father looked deep into her eyes. Whether she saw that there was more to the story or she just saw that this was what her husband wanted, Kevin wasn't sure. She smiled and nodded.

Mr. Ramirez kissed her forehead. "Go pack and I'll be up in a minute."

Leti's mother started up the stairs. "You kids eat those tamales. I don't want them to go to waste."

"Of course, Mamá," Leti said to her retreating back. The sound of a bedroom door closing upstairs was the only sound left in the house.

"Where are you going to stay?" Her father asked Leti.

"My place," Kevin said at the same time Leti answered, "I don't know..."

Mr. Ramirez looked between the two of them. It wasn't exactly a friendly look, but Kevin wasn't going to take it back. He would do anything to protect her.

"I'm going to stay at Maggie's place," Leti told him.

"Are you sure? There seems to be a lot of confusion as to where you'll be staying. No offense, you're a nice boy, but I don't like my daughter staying with someone she's not engaged to."

"That's so antiquated, Papá," Leti argued.

"Well, I am an antique." Her father didn't smile, didn't laugh at his own joke.

"I'm staying at Maggie's." Leti glared at Kevin.

"Good. That's settled. Now. Handle this, hija." Her father stared at Leti. The lawyer came through in his glare and his dominant stance. "I cannot keep her away forever. You have three weeks to fix this."

"And you." He turned to Kevin. "Keep my daughter safe. From a distance."

"Yes, sir." And he would. Keep her safe anyway. He wasn't sure about the distance thing. That might be asking a bit too much.

LETI WATCHED her papá walk up the stairs to start packing. She wanted him far away for what was about to occur. She appreciated everything Kevin had done. He'd come running. He'd checked the house. He'd made sure she was safe. Goodness, he'd even checked on Pork Chop.

So why did he have to mess it all up?

"Why did you tell my papá I was staying at your place?"

"I was just making an offer—and I am staying with Maggie." Kevin had the intelligence to look contrite as he answered. It didn't stop the fact that her papá now thought she was sharing a man's home. If her mamá had heard any of that conversation, she would have had a cardiac event.

"Well, next time you offer, make sure my father's not in the room."

"Noted." He smiled. Apparently the contrition part of the night was over.

She walked into the kitchen to grab her phone. At least she hoped it was there. Between everything going on, she wasn't really sure where she'd left it.

Thankfully it was sitting on the edge of the counter.

Can I stay at your place for a few days, she texted Maggie.

The response was almost instant. *Sure. Come grab the key*

Thanks

One decision down. "I'll make you a plate," she told Kevin, sliding four tamales onto a plate. "Do you want any salsa or crema?"

"I'm good." He grabbed a fork and sat at the table in the kitchen, unwrapping tamale number one. The smell of pork and spices filled the kitchen.

"I'm going to pack." Leti ran up the stairs, leaving Kevin with the heavenly smell. She walked past her parents' open doorway as they finished filling their own bags. She didn't have time to waste. She didn't want to hang out in the house any longer than she needed.

She stuffed a few bras, underwear, T-shirts, and pants into an overnight bag until the zipper would barely close. Pork Chop's favorite dog toy sat next to her bed. She needed to make sure her parents took that with them. She hoisted the bag over her shoulder before turning off the light and running down the stairs.

She dropped her bag behind the couch. She wasn't sure if her mamá knew she wasn't going to be staying here, and she didn't want to announce it.

Leti headed into the kitchen and pulled a paper bag from a lower cabinet, opened it, and tossed Pork Chop's toy inside. She added a box of dog treats and a small bag of his kibble. She then selected an unopened bottle of Pork Chop's seizure medication and added that, too. That would be more than enough to last for the trip, and her parents wouldn't need to worry about running out.

"What are you doing?" Mrs. Ramirez came up behind her carrying a small suitcase.

"I'm packing what you'll need for Pork Chop." Leti tossed the box in a bag.

"We're not taking the dog. I'll have the children to look after." Her mamá dropped her small suitcase at the door. "You can watch him here."

Her mamá pulled a towel from the roll. She ran it

under the water and began wiping down the counter. She moved the plate of food. "There are still seven tamales left. Want another one, Kevin?"

"No thank you, Mrs. Ramirez." Kevin was working on that fourth tamale.

"Can I make you something else?"

Kevin stretched and rubbed his stomach. "No thank you."

"I have to stop at the drug store this weekend to get more baby aspirin." Papá set down a couple of large suitcases.

"Maybe we should wait and leave in the morning?"

Leti could feel her heartbeat speed through her veins. They couldn't stay here. Not another night. Before she could say anything, her papá wrapped an arm around his wife. "Mi amor, Elena has been begging for us to come help so things can get back to normal, right?"

"Well, yes." Her mamá might have been exaggerating. From what Elena had told Leti, she wouldn't mind help, but getting back to work wasn't on the top of her list.

"Then let's go. I need to get out of the city." He ran a finger down his wife's face. "Today was a rough day and I could use some time with my grandchildren."

"I heard Sofia lost her first tooth." Leti tried not to be jealous. But it was hard. Elena was the pinnacle of success in her parents' eyes. A CPA with a gorgeous doctor husband, Elena popped out kids like a Pez dispenser. They'd just welcomed their third into the world three months ago. Mamá lived with them for the first month, but came back when Juan's mother came to take care of the kids. Juan's mother left a month ago, and Elena'd been on her own since. It would seem like the perfect time for Elena to have some private-family time. But in Leti's mamá's world, that meant the perfect time for her to go back. "Diego is walking. Don't you want to see him roam around the living room in real life?" And Leti was pushing that agenda.

"Of course. We'll go tonight." Leti's mamá cleaned up the counter.

"No, Mamá, I'll finish cleaning. You go."

"Are you sure?" Her mother looked around the kitchen. "Don't forget to eat the food in the fridge. Maybe you can invite Giovanni over and make him dinner."

Not going to happen. Not that she'd tell her mother that. Giovanni left her with crazy people. He literally ran.

"I'll eat all the food." Leti took the towel from her mamá's hand. "You crazy kids hit the road before it's too late."

"Okay, mija." Her father kissed her forehead and whispered, "Call me when you get to Maggie's."

"I will," she promised as she watched them leave. She hoped she wouldn't break that promise.

CHAPTER TWELVE

KEVIN WAS STUFFED. He wanted to eat the rest of the tamales, but he was afraid he'd explode. It would be like the alien movie, but with masa and pork.

Leti stood over the counter, bagging up the tamales. "For the road."

He might not be eating those tonight, but he was seeing more tamales in his future. That made him happier than he wanted to admit.

She grabbed a plastic bag from the bottom cabinet and started filling it with food from the refrigerator.

"I'm sure my sister has food," Kevin pointed out.

"I told my mamá I'd eat the food so it wouldn't spoil. I just need to grab my toothpaste and stuff, then we can go."

"Okay." He took the bag with Pork Chop's things and the other one with people food and set them by the back door. Pork Chop's bag tipped over, and Kevin picked up what looked like a bottle of medication. "What's this for?"

"That's Pork Chop's medication."

"Medication?" Did dogs have medication?

"Yeah, for epilepsy. He has seizures." Leti gestured for him to hand her the bottle. "I'm going to swap this for the open one. I don't need to take so much with us."

Kevin didn't want to think about what a dog seizure even looked like. He'd had a friend in the military who'd had seizures and that was scary enough. Kevin wasn't a doctor for a reason.

He finished cleaning the counter and then washed his plate and fork. They didn't need that sitting around the house while the family was away.

"I think I have everything." Leti came back with another bag and a dog carrier, and dropped those next to the others. "You don't have to clean up. I'll do it later."

"I figured I'd take care of it. We don't know when we'll be back."

"It shouldn't take that long, right?" She looked so hopeful. He hated to burst her bubble.

"Are you going to keep following up on the children's home?"

"Well, yes."

"Then I don't know how long it's going to take." It could take days or weeks to get the information they needed. Heck, it could be longer.

"You know you can leave if you want."

"I know." He picked up Pork Chop. "But we're in this together. Right?"

The smile that spread across her face lit the whole

room, her brown eyes glossy as she stared into his. "Yes. You and me."

Those words hit him straight in the chest. If he wasn't holding the dog, he'd wrap his arms around her and never let go. But since they had to get the heck out of Dodge, the dog was probably exactly where he needed to be.

"We should go." She held out her arms. "I'll put Pork Chop in the carrier while you check all the doors."

"Got it." He handed her the dog and headed for the living room. Checked the windows and doors. He was going to make sure Leti didn't come back to this house until it was safe, but considering she had a stubborn streak, there was no guarantee.

Which meant he needed to make sure it was on lockdown before they went anywhere.

AN HOUR LATER, after a detour to Chase's to pick up house keys and a garage fob from Maggie, Leti drove toward Maggie's house, with Kevin on her heels. Pork Chop was sound asleep in his carrier, which was belted in the passenger seat. Since Leti had let Maggie stay at her house a few months ago when Maggie was hiding from a local gang, she'd said Leti could stay in the house as long as she needed. No matter how much Leti argued that she couldn't take her house, Maggie wouldn't budge. Apparently she didn't think staying at Chase's for the foreseeable future was a hardship.

Leti had seen him without a shirt. Not that she had

her sights on her best friend's man, but she could see how looking at that all day and night wasn't exactly torture.

As they pulled down Maggie's block, her hands-free rang with an incoming call. Kevin.

"Hey," Leti said. "We're almost there."

"Yeah. Can you wait outside while I go check the house?"

"What if they're waiting outside?" She didn't think anyone knew about Maggie or would be waiting at her house, but after the night she'd had, she didn't want to sit outside and wait to find out. "Maybe I should go inside with you."

"Are you afraid to wait outside?" There might have been laughter in his voice.

She might have imagined that, though. "No, I'm just thinking the bad guys wouldn't go inside Maggie's house. They'd stake it out if they really wanted to find me. So why sit outside like a duck and wait for them to kill me."

"They're not going to kill you."

"Then what is all this for?" If they weren't any danger, she could go home and hide under her bed, where she felt safe.

"Well, I'm not going to let them kill you." He sighed.

"Then I should go with you."

"Okay." He either agreed or was tired of fighting with her. She'd take it either way. "I'm going to park out front. If you want to park in the garage, I'll meet you back there."

She watched him parallel park in front of Maggie's house, waiting for him to scoot in between a Turano Bread van and a minivan. Her stomach growled just thinking about the warm bread in that truck earlier that day. If she thought it still had some, she'd consider a little B&E.

But that wasn't really her specialty. And she was being escorted by a cop in training. She'd have to call her parents to bail her out of jail. That would be a fun conversation.

"Why did you get arrested?"

"I tried to steal bread from a truck outside Maggie's house."

"They didn't sell bread anywhere near Maggie's house?"

"Well, yeah. I would have had to leave her house, and it was just parked outside and did I mention free bread?"

"It's not free if you steal it."

"Well, Dad, actually..."

That would devolve quickly, leading to Leti spending a few nights in the slammer. She had no desire to visit the good folks at Cook County Jail.

Leti tapped the horn before she entered the alley. She drove down the narrow, pebble-covered path, garages and fences lining both sides. If she hadn't been to Maggie's house a million times and spent one too many nights drinking her weight in Margaritas on the back porch, she might not know which garage was Maggie's. But since she had, and ultimately released those same margaritas from her stomach in a spectacle worthy of the Exorcist in this very alley, she knew exactly when to click the remote so the garage door would open at the right time. She knew how to angle the car into the garage. She even knew how many steps it took to get from the alley to the porch.

Don't ask. Another night of poor choices, but that time, bourbon. Apparently hard alcohol and her didn't get along.

This was why she didn't drink anything outside of wine these days. At least wine didn't wreak havoc on her stomach.

She pulled her car into the garage and hit the button on the remote. The door closed, leaving her in the brightly lit garage. Alone. She sat and waited. No Kevin. She turned off the car to avoid asphyxiation.

She stared at the side door, but it didn't open. She shouldn't've closed the main garage door. Now she had no way to escape if a bad guy came in. Another minute, and the garage light shut off, cloaking the room in darkness.

Crackers.

She really, really should have left that door open. Shadows shifted and bent through the small windows along the top of the garage door. Either a car was coming down the alley, or the ghosts were getting antsy.

Her head fell back as her eyes closed. She made the sign of the cross over her chest. She didn't mess with ghosts even if she was just thinking about them in her head.

The garage seemed to be losing air at an exponential rate. It was like the top of Mount Everest without the beautiful view. Her heart galloped, and she fumbled for the remote. She needed an escape route. She needed air. She was opening the door.

The side door opened, and a figure stood in the opening. Leti would like to think it was Kevin, but she couldn't actually be sure. Broad shoulders. Short hair. Gun. That was all she could make out. That could be anyone. Good guy. Bad guy.

Shitake. She was in so much trouble.

Light flooded the room as the figure hit the light switch. Kevin stood next to the car and opened the passenger door. "Are you ready to go inside?"

Air flooded her lungs. She was so beyond ready. No bad guy. Thank goodness. She nodded.

"I checked the perimeter of the house. There's no one there." Kevin didn't seem to notice she was mid meltdown. Pork Chop was still sound asleep and didn't seem to care that she was about to lose it. Slept through the whole thing.

Lucky. She wished she could have slept through the whole darn thing too.

"I'll grab Pork Chop. Come on, buddy." Kevin snagged the dog carrier and then tapped the passenger door shut with his hip. "I'll grab the rest of your stuff after I check the inside of the house."

Once he left, the lights were on but the shadows were still there. Leti got out and hurriedly hit the locks on the car, catching up with Kevin on the back porch of the tan brick ranch.

"I have the keys." She pulled Maggie's keys from her purse and put them in Kevin's awaiting hand. He fumbled them one-handed, and Leti took pity on him. "Do you want me to do that?"

He smiled as he slid the key in the lock. "I got it."

The door opened with a click. He walked inside and Leti followed. Small slats of light came in the back window from the neighbor's back porch lights. She went to flip the switch next to the door, and Kevin's hand covered her fingers. "No light," he whispered.

She nodded and watched as he looked under the kitchen table and opened the pantry door. No bad guys in there. There wasn't really any food, either. Not that she needed Maggie's food.

Kevin handed the carrier to Leti and whispered, "Can you hold him for a minute?"

She nodded, and followed as he walked down a small hall into Maggie's living room. A white couch glowed against the pale gray carpet in the light spilling into the room from a streetlamp. Big curved windows with gray curtains faced the front yard, flanked by bookcases filled with encyclopedias and other books, with two orange chairs angled in front of them. Pork Chop wiggled and she was so startled she dropped the carrier. "Shitake," she hissed.

Kevin swung to look at her.

"Sorry," she whispered.

"It's okay." He nodded toward the side hallway that led to the bedrooms.

She followed behind as he peered into the hall bathroom. Clear. They walked down the hall and into Maggie's bedroom. The room was quiet. Everything was quiet. No one was here. Not that she thought anyone would be here.

The curtains were drawn, leaving the room in darkness and making her eyes useless. Her ears were on high alert, though. But there was no sound. Kevin stood next to her as light suddenly streamed from something in his hand.

Leti screamed.

The phone vibrated and hummed. But that wasn't what made her jump behind Kevin and stare at the curtains in terror. A noise was coming from the window. A low screech, like the window was slowly being opened.

"Who are you?" Kevin held up his gun with one hand as he pushed Leti behind his back.

Leti's heart stuttered as Pork Chop ran into the bedroom, barking at the scraping sound. How did he get out of the carrier? Leti scooped him up and rubbed his head, his barks turning to growls as she held him to her chest.

Another scraping noise came from outside.

Kevin stepped toward the window and threw back the curtain. The window was closed. The darkness outside made it impossible to see anything. "I'm going out."

"But..."

"I'll be right back." Kevin ran a hand down Leti's cheek. "Watch over Pork Chop." He ran out the door as another scrape came from the window.

Oh goodness no. She turned on her heels and followed him. There was no way she was going to stand there and get killed. If her name was going to be plastered all over the news, she was going out a hero.

She ran through the living room and whipped out through the open front door. Kevin's phone lit up the side of the house. After closing the front door, Leti followed the light, coming up behind him. "Is something out here?"

He whipped around, aiming his gun at her. The light from his phone pierced her eyes. "Crap, Leti, I almost shot you."

"Thank you for not shooting me." Clutching Pork Chop in one arm, she lifted her free hand to block her eyes.

"Sorry." He angled the phone downward. "I don't see anything."

The front yard was empty. A tall apple tree stood in the center, but there wasn't any wind to swing the branches. Kevin ran his light over the ground and the tree. Nothing. "Whatever it is must be gone," he said.

Pork Chop growled.

A low hiss came from somewhere near the house. Kevin flipped his wrist up, aiming the light at Maggie's bedroom window.

A black ball of fur with white teeth lunged out from the sill, screaming as it flew at her like it was caught in the Matrix.

Pork Chop barked, frantic now. Leti fought to keep him from going after the flying attacker.

"Reowr!" The cat screeched as it landed on the ground, back arched and claws on display.

"Go away! Bad kitty." Leti pulled Pork Chop closer

as every muscle in his body fought to get to that cat. Every muscle in her body fought to keep him away. "I'm taking him inside." Leti ran across the yard and up the front stairs. Once inside, she slammed the door behind her and put Pork Chop down. The dog jumped at the front window, barking, trying to see outside. Thank goodness he wasn't tall enough to reach the window.

Adrenaline spiked in her veins. Her body felt heavy.

Her arms stung.

Her hands ached.

"Take it easy, little buddy." Kevin came in and locked the front door.

"Was there anything outside? Beside an angry cat?"

"No. The cat ran away. It doesn't look like there was anyone or anything else out there."

"Thank goodness." She sighed. She was so exhausted from the night's events. All she wanted to do was fall under the covers and pass out.

"Let's get you into some pajamas." Kevin must have read all of what she was thinking on her face. Hopefully that was a one-time deal. She didn't like to think if he could always read her mind. Embarrassing.

She nodded.

"Did you want me to stay tonight? Just in case you need anything or if there are any weird noises."

"Isn't this where you've been living?"

"It is. But I can stay with my dad while you're here if you need some space."

"I don't need space. Would you mind staying?" She

didn't cry. She was calling it a win, because she really wanted to cry. She hurt more than she wanted anyone to know.

"I don't mind at all. I wouldn't have offered if I did."

"Okay." She nodded. "Please stay."

"Do you need help getting ready for bed?"

She wanted to say yes, but she had a feeling being in the same house with him was going to be hard enough without him watching her get half naked. "I should be okay."

"Good." He nodded as he looked around the living room, for what she had no idea.

"Thank you." She smiled. At least she tried. "For everything tonight."

"You're welcome." He grinned, but his smile was about as genuine as hers. "Try to get some sleep. If you need anything, wake me up. I don't care how late it is. I'll be in the room next to yours."

She nodded and headed to Maggie's bedroom. Having him so close should make her feel better, but somehow she had a feeling it would make it impossible for her to sleep.

CHAPTER THIRTEEN

WHY WOULDN'T her eyes just close?

Leti slammed a pillow over her face. Surprisingly, suffocating herself with a pillow didn't help. Although, given the nature of suffocation, she felt she might be doing it wrong.

She tossed the fluffy white puff across the room. She'd tried counting sheep and meditating. Nothing got her to calm down enough to fall asleep. Maybe it was the excitement from the day, or the dog snoring at her feet. Or maybe it was knowing there was a very hot man in the next room.

Zzort-shu-bbrr.

Maybe it was both.

Leti reached down and rolled Pork Chop onto his side. Quiet.

See? This was what she needed. Kevin down the hall meant nothing. Now that Pork Chop was silent, she could finally get some sleep.

She eased her arms under head and nuzzled in. She

could do this. Sleeping was natural. She closed her eyes and let the silence seep into her bones, letting her body relax into the bed.

Zzort-shu-bbrr.

Her eyes flew open. She could not do this. It was time to give it up and maybe get some work done. A nice cup of tea sounded good about now.

Leti slowly slid out from under the sheets, trying not to move the dog. At least one of them should get some sleep. He shifted position and continued his tyranny of sound. He didn't seem to care that she was leaving.

She pulled her laptop from its bag and headed out the door, keeping it open just enough for Pork Chop to sneak out if he needed.

After making a steaming cup of tea that was too hot to drink, she turned on the light in the living room and set up her cup on the table next to a chair near the windows.

She booted up the laptop and leaned back against the seat as Google filled the screen. She searched for Wacker's Children's Association.

Multiple pages with address information, administrative information, and articles about Stanley Welford popped up. Each article praised his philanthropic heart. Thank goodness she hadn't eaten recently or it might have threatened to come back up.

As she scrolled, something popped up among the Welford drivel. An accident. A nurse died after claiming there was impropriety at one of the children's homes. The trial never happened because the only plaintiff, the nurse, wound up dead in a drive-by shooting. The article said it was meant for someone else, that the nurse was in the wrong place at the wrong time, but her mother claimed she was the target. No one would listen.

Leti would listen. In fact she needed to talk to the mother of the woman—sooner rather than later.

Her fingers flew over the keys as she looked up the name of the nurse. Pauline Lidell. Something shuffled and scuffed down the hall, probably Pork Chop. "Finally realized I was gone, huh? The snoring was getting to be a bit much."

"I don't think I was snoring, but if you could hear that through the walls, either the walls are super thin or you have super hearing."

Leti jumped. Last time she'd checked, Pork Chop jingled and barked, but he had yet to talk. Kevin stood in the doorway to the living room.

He looked good enough to mount—and stuff. Like taxidermy, nothing weird. She was so lucky it was an inside thought and not outside words. Kevin wore a pair of sweatpants that might have been a size too big, as they slanted sideways on his hips. His chest was bare. All the muscles he'd been working for the police exam were defined. He looked good. Not that she actually noticed.

"Shouldn't you be sleeping?" Kevin asked.

"Pork Chop was snoring."

"Do you want me to give him a tongue lashing?" He smiled as he said the words, or maybe he smiled because Leti was sure her face was now at def-con red.

It wasn't her fault he said tongue lashing and all she could think about was what he could do with his tongue. She might volunteer as tribute to get that lashing.

Her face pulsed in embarrassment. Good news was, it probably couldn't get any redder. She just had to stop thinking about his tongue and lashing and his chest. She should focus on her sleeping dog. He was safe. "I don't think Pork Chop would listen if you yelled. He's sound asleep."

"Lucky dog." He hiked up his sweatpants and sat on the couch across the room.

"Yeah." Leti closed the browser on her laptop. Not like she was going to get anything done with Kevin in front of her looking like that.

"So, I thought you had a date tonight. Why were you home alone?" Kevin leaned back, trying to give an air of nonchalance. But the way he stared at her said he was very interested in the answer.

And Leti hated to give it. Not because she thought he'd care, but because it was embarrassing. And the last time she'd been on a date, she'd been embarrassed and who had been front and center but Kevin. It was like he had a gift of being at the right place at the wrong time.

"I went out tonight with Giovanni. Dinner. Darts. We went back to the house for a drink" —he didn't need to know her plans for after the drink— "we walked inside, and those men were there."

"So Giovanni left after the guys threatened you?"

"Not really after." This sounded so bad.

Kevin sat forward, his elbows on his knees. "What?"

"He ran out of the living room while the men were in the house."

"He saw the men and just ran?" Kevin growled.

"Did you just growl?"

"No." He coughed and covered his mouth with a fist. "Maybe. He didn't protect you?"

"Not really." She felt her nose crinkle as she remembered the shove. She'd been terrified. There was a man with a knife. In her house. And Giovanni just disappeared. "The men threatened him, and he said he didn't know me and then he pushed me toward the one with the knife and ran out the door."

The vein in Kevin's neck pulsed. "He what?" The growl was back.

This time Leti didn't think she should joke about it.

"I hope you're not planning on seeing him again."

"I think we're done." Which had been a bit disappointing. Not that she thought they'd be walking down the aisle anytime soon, but it was hard to find a good man.

"Although..." She probably shouldn't let the next words out of her mouth, but she couldn't seem to stop them. "Not everyone knows what to do when being held at knifepoint. He probably didn't know what to do."

"You can't honestly be making excuses for him. Yeah, most people wouldn't know what to do, but most people wouldn't run out the door in a swirl of dust."

"You might not because you've been trained."

"Yeah, but that doesn't mean I don't get scared. And I sure as hell wouldn't run out on someone who... someone who needed my help. You don't do that."

"Maybe he didn't think I needed help."

"Or maybe he didn't care."

"But you would care?" She would like to think he'd care about her. She'd like to think he'd jump in front of a moving car for her... Oh wait, he had.

He sat back and seemed to think about it for a minute. "I think anyone in the same situation would do the minimum to help out a fellow human."

Not exactly a declaration of love. Leti sighed. "So you would do that for anyone, given the situation."

"Yeah. I can guarantee I wouldn't push someone toward the knife and run the other way." Well to be fair that was a pretty low bar.

Kevin's smile was crooked. "Maybe your mother has another man she can set you up with. One who doesn't offer you up as a human sacrifice."

"I hope not." Leti flopped back in the chair. "I don't know why she seems to attract such deadbeat men. Some of them look so normal on the outside, but then they speak or act and the weirdness ensues."

"Makes for good stories."

"I don't want stories."

"What do you want?"

"What everyone wants." At least she thought it was what everyone wanted. "Love. Romance. Someone who wants to be with me. Someone who will protect me. Someone who will talk to me and laugh with me." Part of her hoped he'd jump up and say he'd do all that or something.

But he didn't say a word. He just nodded his head. "I'm sure you'll find someone like that someday."

"I'm sure." All the hope escaped from her chest, leaving a big, giant gaping hole of hurt. She knew she was being irrational, but she'd had a long day. A yawn stretched her jaw as disappointment welled in her eyes. She refused to let him see it, though. He didn't deserve to see her tears.

"You seem tired."

She wasn't sure she wanted to sleep. She took her closed laptop and her mug and stood up. "I should get to bed."

"Are you okay?"

"I'm fine." The song of every woman that was not okay and not fine. But wasn't about to let the man who broke her heart see he could do just that so, so easily. Another yawn threatened. "Good night."

"Good night."

She walked to Maggie's bedroom and shut the door. Pork Chop lifted his head and stretched. He came to the edge of the bed and started kissing her fingers and rubbing his head against her hip. At least he still loved her.

Not that she thought Kevin loved her, but she thought she meant something to him. Given that he said she might find someone someday and didn't jump up and offer himself—well, that told her all she needed to know.

He wasn't her someone. Not today. Not someday.

And all the doggie kisses in the world weren't going to ease that gaping hole in her chest. She kneeled down and Pork Chop nuzzled her chin. Although it didn't hurt to try.

HE WAS A TOOL. There was no other explanation. Kevin had Leti sitting right here in front of him saying she wanted someone to talk to her. Check. She wanted someone to laugh with her. Check. She wanted someone to protect her. Check. Check.

And all he had to do was say that someone was him. And he hadn't. He'd wanted to. He'd wanted to tell her to stop dating these losers her mom kept finding and be with him. But all he'd heard was his father's voice telling him not to be careless with his career, telling him he wasn't smart enough to focus on a relationship and the job.

This was his last chance. He was aging out. Shit. If he was smart, he'd just take his dad's help and be done with it. So what if the old man held it over his head for the rest of his life. It's not like his dad was going to live forever. He was getting old.

Thinking about disappointing the one parent he had left, and losing him, too, was not helping. It didn't wipe away the hurt he'd seen in Leti's eyes. It didn't make him want her any less.

He closed his eyes and leaned back on the couch. He was an idiot.

He opened his eyes and looked at the encyclopedias lining a bookshelf. Before he could stop himself, he stood up and grabbed the volume labeled "I". It wasn't very thick. He was pretty sure idiot was in there somewhere and he was pretty sure his picture was going to be next to the word.

Id

Idiom

Surprisingly, idiot wasn't there. Neither was his picture. They must not have gotten the memo. To be fair, the encyclopedias were old. Maybe he hadn't reached documented "uh-duh" levels back when they were published.

Although his dad had been telling him he was stupid since he was a lot younger than that. Their older brother Kyle had gotten a computer for his high school graduation. Maggie got these encyclopedias and a laptop for hers. They were "for college" his father had said. Kevin apparently didn't need those things. His dad had gotten him a cell phone, "to keep in touch."

Kevin closed the book and put it back. What the heck was his problem? He'd always been the underachiever. Why was it bothering him now? He should get to bed and just let it go. Staying in his sister's house wasn't helping. He needed to get out of here as soon as he possibly could.

Claws scratched against Maggie's bedroom door. There was no way Leti was sleeping through all that noise. But maybe he could help her out, take Pork Chop for a walk. He knocked, and the door swung open. Pork Chop came running out.

"I thought you were sleeping?" He couldn't help but notice the open laptop and the papers all over the bed in the middle of the night.

"I was trying to?"

"With the computer on?"

She sighed. "Can I help you?"

"I heard Pork Chop and thought I'd take him for a walk."

"Yeah." Her lips turned up into a pathetic attempt at a smile. "Sure."

"Are you mad?" Dumb question. Of course she was mad. He wasn't sure if he knew why, but he was pretty sure it was his fault.

"Nope, just tired."

"Tired." He didn't believe that for a second.

"Yes." She threw up her hands when he shook his head. "What do you want me to say?" she snapped.

"The truth. What's really wrong?"

"What could possibly be wrong." She laced each word with a heavy dose of sarcasm. "I thought there was something between us, but obviously I was wrong. You would have saved anyone the way you saved me. You just did what anyone would have done."

"That's not how I meant it." Although he had.

"Are you sure, Kevin? I'm sure I'll find someone just like the man I'm looking for, someday. Right?"

Yeah. He'd said all that. Just like that. "You're right."

"What?"

"You're right."

"Great." She reached over and got the dog leash off the dresser across from the bed. Held it out.

"You're still mad." He should get a prize for saying dumb things tonight.

Leti's eyes narrowed. "I appreciate the fact that I'm right, but that doesn't make me feel any less stupid for thinking we had something."

"But we did have something." The color drained from Leti's face, and he wished he could take those words back. He was blowing it. "We have something. Present tense. We do." He ran a hand down the tension building in his neck.

"What about the busty blond?"

He shrugged. "I cancelled our date, but to be fair you were just out with another man."

"Because you were out with half the female population of Chicago."

"Is that jealousy I hear?" He smiled, but she just glared back. "I'm sorry. I just didn't think you liked me."

"I invited you to stay. I called you."

"You had no one else to call." He wasn't sure he believed that, but said it anyway.

"I could've called anyone. I chose you."

"And I chose to stay." Warmth spread through his body. She didn't hate him.

"Then what was all that talk about me finding someone someday?"

"Fear?" He hated to admit it, but there was no other reason for what he said. Well, stupidity was also in the running.

"I've had enough of men running in fear to last a lifetime, thank you." Before he could say anything, she scrambled off the bed, shoved the leash at him and slammed the door the second he took the leash.

"Wait." Kevin stood on the other side of the door. Alone. Well, not alone. Pork Chop stared up at him with big expectant eyes. Not so much him as the leash dangling from Kevin's fingertips.

He couldn't disappoint that face. He clipped on the leash and walked through the house and out the back door, making sure to close it behind him.

I've had enough of men running in fear to last a lifetime...

Was she kidding?

She had a lot of nerve comparing Kevin to that tool, Giovechio—or whatever the hell his name was. That guy ran away while Leti was in danger. Kevin didn't want to talk about his feelings. That was not the same thing.

Kevin crossed the back deck and went down the stairs to the yard. Pork Chop ran to the end of the leash and lifted his leg in the grass. He scratched furiously with his back legs after he finished his business, tufts of grass flying in the air, and bounced back up the stairs with Kevin right behind him.

Before Kevin could open the door, a sound came from his right. He reached for the gun he usually carried at his back, but he'd left it inside. An oversight he would not be making again. He opened the door, slipped Pork Chop inside, and locked the door. He snuck down the stairs and around the corner. The gangway stood empty. Nothing there. The neighbor's house was quiet. Overall, the night was still. He checked the other side of the house and walked along the front yard. Nothing.

He made his way to the back door. If he saw someone with a gun or a knife, he'd do what he needed to do, but what if he had never been in that situation before in his life? As he looked around and saw darkness and the unknown, he almost understood being afraid.

That made things a little different.

Because things with Leti were different. He'd never felt what he felt with her with any other woman. And it scared him. He could admit it. But unlike Giovania, Kevin wasn't a coward. He wasn't going to run.

He unlocked the door, thankful that he had the key in his pocket or he'd be outside banging on the door. Heaven knew if Leti would even let him in at this point. Once inside, he locked it up behind him. Pork Chop ran in circles, the leash sliding on the floor behind him.

"Come here, buddy." Kevin kneeled on the floor. "Let me get that off of you."

Pork Chop ran to him, his tail wagging. Kevin unclipped the leash and rubbed under his chin. "I need you to back me up, buddy. Give Leti and me a minute to talk."

The little dog didn't seem to understand the words. He just kept waving his tail back and forth. Kevin stood up and got Pork Chop's toy from the bag on the counter before going to the living room. The dog wagged harder and ran after him.

Kevin took a blanket from the recliner, spinning it into a round bed on the couch. "Up." He motioned to the makeshift bed.

Pork Chop jumped up on the couch and laid down in the center of the blanket nest. Kevin put the stuffed toy next to him and patted his fluffy white head. "Be good."

Kevin approached Maggie's bedroom door and knocked. He checked his watch. He probably should have done that before knocking. Not that it mattered. It was late, but she'd been on her computer not fifteen minutes ago. She should still be up.

The door flew open and Leti immediately glanced down. "Where's my dog?"

"He's sleeping on the couch."

"Then why are you knocking?" Her tone said mad. Her body language said mad. Her eyes said he was lucky she didn't have a taser.

"I wanted to talk."

"Okay." Her arms crossed over her chest.

This was not going to be easy. "You were right, I was afraid."

"Was?" She looked ready to slam the door again. "You're not afraid anymore?"

"I'm terrified." He figured honesty was the best policy here. "You terrify me. I care about you. Which means I could get hurt by you."

"You don't think that scares me?" Her arms

uncrossed and she threw both hands up. "The differ-ence is, I'm willing to take the chance."

"So am I." He took a step closer and ran a finger along the side of her face. Her skin was so soft.

He leaned in and rested his lips on hers. Heaven.

Why had he waited so long to do this?

CHAPTER FOURTEEN

THE NEXT MORNING, Leti couldn't keep the smile from her face. Every time she thought about last night, her face probably lit up like a Christmas tree. Thank goodness everyone was busy, or she'd have a lot of explaining to do. Jessi was at her desk up front, Danni was upstairs computer-whispering, and Maggie and Kevin were staking out some cheating spouses.

Maybe getting to work would help, since she was at work and all. She dialed the number for the mother of the nurse who died at the children's home. The woman didn't answer. Of course.

"Hi, this is Leti Ramirez. I was hoping to talk to Cindy Lidell concerning Pauline Lidell. If you can call me back, I'd greatly appreciate it. Thank you."

"Who's Cindy?" Somehow, Maggie had managed to sneak in and sit down across from Leti while Leti was daydreaming or on the phone or turning bright red —or maybe all three.

"She's the mom of a nurse who was killed at the shelter on the South Side."

"Shit." Maggie leaned forward. "Someone died?"

"I don't think it's only one person."

"What are we going to do?" To Maggie's credit, she looked pretty upset.

"We?"

"Well you can't do this alone." Maggie rested her hand on Leti's. "We're in this together. So, what's the plan?"

"Actually, I need to find some information." Leti looked over the locations on the printout and found the one not on the website. "This location isn't on the website. I was thinking, if they were hiding something, this is the perfect spot."

Maggie pulled out her phone and tapped away. "Yikes. This is an old warehouse and it's not in a great part of town." She held up the phone screen. Leti got up and moved behind Maggie, looking over her shoulder.

The small screen showed a run-down warehouse with garbage scattered around the building. Painted gang signs covered the walls between the broken doors and cracked windows. A truck was parked at the loading dock, and two cars were out front right behind a for sale sign.

"Depending on when this was taken, this building could still be in use and maybe even for sale." Maggie moved the point of view of the image to the front of the building. "It looks abandoned, but there are cars and trucks outside. We could go there and poke around."

"Where are we poking around?" Kevin's voice came up behind Leti.

She jumped. Literally jumped. He was stealthy like his sister. It must be a family thing. They should come pre-installed with bells.

"There's a warehouse Leti wants to check out." Maggie moved the point of view to the back lot of the building.

Kevin scowled. "That doesn't look safe."

"It'll be okay." Maggie shook her head. "I'm going with her."

He'd tended to be overprotective before last night. Leti had a feeling that after last night, he was going to be worse than a dog watching a squirrel in a tree.

He shook his head. "I don't think it's a good idea."

Yep. He was going to be worse.

"Why?" Maggie's voice held all the indignation Leti felt to her core.

"Because there were men in her house who could have killed her last night. We shouldn't put her in harm's way by going to one of their buildings."

"It's not that bad." Leti couldn't even say that with conviction. It was dangerous, but that didn't stop her from needing to get to the bottom of this.

"It's way too dangerous for you two to go alone."

"Why is that? Why is it too dangerous?" Maggie jumped up from her chair. "Is it too dangerous if it's two men?"

"Yes?"

"So you and Chase couldn't go either?" Maggie's finger was jabbing at her brother's chest.

"Ouch." Kevin tried to move away from his sister's jabby finger. "Well, Chase is a cop."

"And I was a cop. A very good cop, by the way." Maggie pushed him further backwards with her finger.

Kevin lifted his hands to block her jabs, but given the ouches coming from his mouth and the winces flitting across his face, his hands weren't blocking nearly enough.

"We are very able women who can kick some serious ass. Do you have a problem with that?" She pulled her finger back. "Think about your answer very carefully."

"No?" His hands covered his chest.

"That didn't sound like you believed it." Maggie wiggled her finger and smiled.

Kevin twisted his shoulder toward her and snarled, "Would you grow up. I have no problem."

"Good answer. Was that so hard?" She punched him in the shoulder.

"I get it. You are two bad-ass women who can handle yourselves." He twisted further, lifted his hands and raised his knee. Smart move. "But I think Chase and I should go with."

"Really?"

"I think you can handle it fine, but it doesn't hurt to have backup. I'm sure Chase would agree. And if we were in the same situation, you would feel the same way."

"I hate when you make sense." Maggie sighed. "Probably because it happens so infrequently."

"Funny." He smiled and dropped his arms. Apparently he felt it was safe to stop protecting his body. He looked at Leti like she was the only person in the room. "But I know this is important to you."

"It is." If more people died and somebody covered it up, she had to do something. Especially since that same somebody was still taking care of children.

"How do we want to play this?" Maggie stared at Leti like she knew what the tarnation Maggie was talking about.

"Play what?"

"We can't just walk in the door. We need a gimmick. A play." Maggie clapped her hands like someone just gave her a birthday gift, not like they were trying to figure out how to get in a dangerous building with deadly people.

"This isn't a game, Maggie." Kevin sounded annoyed.

"It's not a game, but it's exciting to get back out in the field. And we'll be careful." Maggie smiled. "And you were right, having you and Chase backing us up will keep us from getting into a jam."

"Can you repeat that?"

"Repeat what?" Maggie looked at Leti, again. Leti knew the answer this time, but she had no desire to get in the middle of Maggie and her brother.

"You know what." Kevin playfully shoved at Maggie's shoulder. "Tell me I'm right."

"You're a child."

"I'm a child who's right."

Maggie rolled her eyes. "Jeez."

"One problem." Leti hated to bring it up since the two were getting along so well. "Chase is a good cop."

"I don't see that as a problem." Maggie smiled.

"Will he be willing to be backup for us to illegally enter a building? That feels like the opposite of a good cop."

"Well, it's basically an abandoned building," Maggie argued. "And he won't want me there alone. I'm sure he'll be okay as long as we don't ask him to go inside."

"How are you planning on getting inside?"

"So, I'm thinking we go in as a married couple looking for real estate for our clothing line. I started my organic streetwear brand a few years ago and then I met you, Lori. You brought a new style to the brand—an elegance that I fell in love with. At the same time, we fell in love and now we're looking to expand the company from our garage to a warehouse."

"That sounds... elaborate," Kevin said.

"You need a good backstory ready if you want make it believable."

Kevin looked from Leti to Maggie. "And you two are a couple?"

"Yes." Maggie wrapped her arm around Leti's shoulder. "Don't we make a good couple?"

Kevin paled. "I just have a problem imagining you two together."

"Why? I'm not that bad." Maggie pouted as she stared at her brother, and then looked back at Leti.

Leti saw when her best friend put one and one together—her brother's horror and Leti's panicked look. "Oh my goodness. You two are sleeping together!"

"Shhhhh." Leti put her hand over Maggie's mouth. The last thing Leti needed was Jessi and Danni giggling and gossiping about her love life.

Teeth chomped into her hand.

"Ouch!" Leti pulled her hand away, staring at the little teeth indentations. "You're a menace."

"Yeah, but I'm not bedding your brother." Maggie laughed.

Leti rubbed at her aching hand. "Yuck. Can we get back to the plan."

"The plan is all set, we'll go tonight." Maggie smiled. "We'll be business partners. You're the fashionista and I'm the business brains."

"Shouldn't I be the brains, since my specialty is literally numbers?"

"It's role play. Why would we want to act like every other day?" Maggie pouted. "Don't take my fun from me."

"I could go inside and you could be the backup," Kevin suggested, but stepped back when Maggie glared. "Or not."

"I've got to sit on a subject and grab some caffeine. But not in that order. I need that caffeine to stay awake. Virgil is not the life of the party." Maggie grabbed her purse. "But I'll call Chase and we'll meet at my house after I follow this client."

"Okay."

"Kevin, bring your gun."

"Of course."

"Leti, wear something trendy."

"I don't own anything trendy." Leti was more boardroom chic, not fashion-forward designer.

"You'll figure it out." Maggie laughed. "Maybe no one will be there."

"Then why the elaborate backstory?"

"What's the fun without the backstory?" Maggie said as she walked out the back door.

"Is this a good idea?" Leti thought it was until Maggie got involved. Now she wasn't sure.

"I would say no, but she's right. She's a damn good cop. And if she can talk Chase into being there if things go south, we should be in a good spot."

Leti wanted to share that optimism, but she was a pencil-pusher at best. An accountant. She worked numbers, not undercover. But she needed to figure it out because getting to the bottom of this case was important—she owed it to Erica and the kids. So she had five hours to become a fashionista.

LETI LOOKED RIDICULOUS. She was wearing a tight pair of blue leggings and a flowing color-block top that Maggie brought over. Leti was afraid to find out where the stuff came from, so she didn't ask. The over-sized neck opening drooped over one shoulder, revealing a bright red tank top. A red paisley scarf around her neck and a green headband completed the outfit. Apparently, she was a fashion guru.

She didn't look like a fashion anything. She looked like a rainbow threw up all over her, or she had trouble discerning matching colors. Either way, she didn't look like a designer.

"You look amazing. Stop messing with your dress." Maggie stood next to her checking her gun and stuffing it in the waist band of her jeans. Maggie got to wear jeans and a T-shirt. Apparently accountants didn't dress up at night. So why did designers?

"This isn't a dress." Leti pulled down on the hem of

the not-dress, but that made the shoulder dip deeper, almost showing one of the girls. "This is barely a shirt."

"Which is why you're wearing leggings. It's an ensemble."

It was something.

"Ladies. You should head in now." Chase walked over from checking out the building. A single light came from the main floor. "It looks like there's one guy in the main room."

"So no B and E." Maggie sounded disappointed.

"I'm a cop. So there will be no B and E. And no stealing. Get pictures and get out." Chase wrapped an arm around Maggie's waist.

"I got it." Maggie smiled as she looked up into his eyes. "We're going in to look at real estate. Nothing more."

"Just watch your back." He leaned his face toward hers.

"I will." Maggie whispered before he kissed her.

"Take care of her." Kevin said to Maggie before walking over to Leti. "And you, please be careful. If it gets hairy in there, just run. Come get us."

Leti nodded. She had no desire to be a hero here. She wanted to get in, look around, and get out. She didn't want any problems.

Kevin ran a finger along the side of her face. "I need you to come back to me." He kissed her lips and her bones melted. He was sweet and kind and everything about him made her blood boil.

"Let's go, girl. We got a building to fake-buy."

Maggie grabbed Leti's hand and they walked toward the crumbling building.

The flimsy handwritten for sale sign sat in one corner of the filthy lot. Tufts of grass poked out from the cracked asphalt. Garbage was everywhere. The building wasn't much better. Half the windows were covered with plywood or cardboard. Duct tape did not fix everything, as a bird's nest nestled in between the carboard and duct tape bandaging.

They entered through the front door. The warehouse was one large room with a handful of desks scattered throughout the space. The desks each had a computer and a printer, with paperwork strewn all over. Plastic containers were piled high on the bookshelves against the back wall.

A man sat behind one desk and, by the look of him, he was not happy to have visitors. He couldn't have been more than thirty, and skinny as a beanpole. But given the leather holster straps across his chest, he had more than enough power underneath the open Sox jacket.

Maggie waved at him. "Hi. We're meeting our real estate agent here."

"Why?" the man growled. His hand hovered near his chest.

"I'm Midge, and this is my partner Lori, we own M&L Clothing Line. We want to buy this building."

"It's not for sale."

"But there's a sign in the front." Maggie pointed in the general direction of the sign outside.

"That's an old sign for the building next door. I

don't think the owner is even in the country any longer."

"Oh. So this place isn't for sale?" Maggie pouted. "We could really use the space. We're working out of her garage. Our landlord is going to kick us out if we don't get all our stuff out of his way."

"Sounds like a problem."

"It is a problem. We really love our townhouse." Maggie walked toward one of the other desks. "I'm really disappointed. This is a great space, isn't it, Lori?"

"Beautiful." Leti tried to smile but she swore she saw something tiny move in the back corner of the space. "It's a shame it's not for sale." She couldn't even say that without gagging a bit in the back of her throat.

Maggie nodded. "I agree. Are you sure they aren't in the market to sell?"

"We ain't selling." The man stood up. "You need to leave."

"Okay. We had to try. Sorry to bother you." Maggie walked out the door and headed toward the car. Leti hot on her heels.

"Shit." Maggie caught up to her as Kevin and Chase ran up.

Kevin stopped in front of Leti. "Is everything okay?"

"No. So the real estate angle is out. The building is not for sale." Leti sighed. Those desks looked interesting. She wanted a few minutes with the paperwork on them. "What do we do now?"

"It looks like we need to shift to a little breaking and entering." Maggie waggled her eyebrows.

"Magpie...." Chase said her name as an exasperated sigh.

"I didn't say you had to break or enter."

"But I'm a cop and I have prior knowledge of a felony."

"Honey, we're not going to steal anything. We just need to find information." Maggie rested her hand on his arm. "They're killing people."

"We know this?" Chase turned to Leti.

"We know this." Leti was sure of it. "We need to find the proof."

Chase leaned his head back and sighed. "Okay. I can buy you five minutes."

"What?" Leti and Maggie both said the word at the same time.

Chase looked over at Kevin. "Take them to that door we found around back. Stay with them. I'll keep this guy busy up front here."

"Thank you." Maggie kissed Chase in a way that said she meant those words. Leti followed Kevin as he headed to the back door.

"We should wait for Maggie." Leti reached for Kevin's hand, and he nodded. "Are you okay?"

"Yeah." He shook his head. The words not matching the actions. "No, I'm not okay. I don't like you going right into their lair like this."

"We have to keep looking." Although, she'd really prefer to look when she was wearing real clothes with real pants. Or anything that covered most of her legs.

"I know, but aren't you afraid of what happens if they find you?"

"No. You and Chase are here." And she meant it. She knew they had her back.

Kevin nodded. "I will protect you, but I need you to be careful in there."

"I will."

"Okay, guys. We have five minutes." Maggie ran up to them, her hand resting on the gun at her hip, probably so it wouldn't fall out. "Where is the door?"

Kevin pointed to a back door that looked to be propped open a few inches.

"Did you find this open?" Maggie whispered.

"No." He didn't elaborate as the three of them approached the door.

Leti couldn't help but ask, "How did you get in the door?"

"I have some skills." Kevin smiled. "Let's go. We don't have a lot of time."

Maggie opened the door slowly and Leti walked in. Chase's voice came from the front of the room, but they were hidden behind a wall near the doorway. They stood behind the wall and waited.

"So is that your car?" Chase demanded.

"What's it to you?" armed beanpole guy snarled.

"It's parked illegally. I'm going to have it towed."

"What for?"

"Again. It's parked illegally," Chase said. "I'm going to go wait for the tow truck."

"Hey!" the guy yelled, and Leti could hear him scuff across the floor, like he was running. "Who cares if it's parked illegally? No one's around."

Leti dove for the first desk. "Okay, we only have a

few minutes." The computers were off. It would take too long to boot up, and if whoever was behind this had any brains, there'd be logins and passwords. If they'd brought Danni, she might've been able to make that happen, but honestly, she didn't need to be in the room to do her thing.

Danni always said that people were creatures of habit—check the desks and the computer for little notes with login and password information.

Leti picked up the keyboard, but there was nothing there. In fact, the paperwork on the desk looked like children's information. Names. Locations for placement. Circumstances that led them to the shelter. Nothing unusual.

"Find anything?" Maggie was lifting everything on a desk across the room.

Leti moved to another desk. "Not yet." The name on the desk said Pete. Her lips curved when she noticed Pete had a custom mouse pad with a vacation picture of a man and a woman on it. Leti flipped the pad over. Pete had all of his logins and passwords listed on the back of the pad. Leti took a picture with her phone. Danni would have a field day with this.

The desk was covered with folders and lists of kids' names. Not just names— social security numbers, dates of birth and death dates. Plastic boxes sat next to the desk, more folders inside. A number and letter was written in Sharpie on each box.

She picked a random page from the desk. More names. Taylor Walker. Pat Styczynski. Pat was a five-year-old boy who'd passed away in Minooka, Illinois in

1960. Taylor was born in Lisle, Illinois in 1958, and passed away in 1964.

Leti took a picture of their paperwork and checked the next page of the list.

Amanda Clark. According to the paperwork, she'd passed away in Chicago in 1953. But there was a line through the date and a check mark next to the name. Written next to her name was 54B.

Leti looked at the number and letter. It reminded her of the writing on the boxes. "Do you see a box 54B?" she whispered to Maggie.

Maggie poked at a stack of boxes on her side of the room and nodded. "Over here."

Leti hurried over and opened the box. It just didn't make sense. Amanda Clark passed away in 1953. So why would they still have her paperwork here? She sifted through the files until she found one for Amanda Clark. Amanda was currently placed at the shelter on the south side. Her adoption was pending. The Petersons of South Bend were going through the process of adopting her.

"What did you find?" Maggie stood over Leti.

"Amanda Clark died in Chicago in 1953, but she's currently pending adoption. Look at the social security number." Leti scrolled through the pictures she just took of the lists back at the desk. "The number on the file matches the number from the list back there."

Maggie shook her head. "How is that possible?"

"I don't know." Leti pointed to the desk. "Check this desk and see if you can find any lists with children's names and deaths—especially if it has their social security number. I think I might need to look into this when we get back to the office."

Maggie rifled through the paperwork on the nearest desk, pulling out her camera to take pictures of each page as she flipped them over one by one. "There are a lot of names here. But these kids died in Germany."

"Does it show their Social Insurance Number?"

"Yes." Maggie looked up from her photo shoot. "How do you know that?"

"We ran a background check on that German opera singer a few months back."

"That's right." Maggie took a picture of the page. "There are more names crossed out, but there are no box numbers or anything. This doesn't make any sense."

"We have to go." Kevin ran toward them just as the front door opened.

The guy screamed, "I'll call my boss, you jackass!"

Leti put the lid on the box and shoved it back where Maggie had found it. No time. They ran around behind the shelving and plastered themselves against the wall. Kevin stood by the back door. Out of sight. Ten feet between Leti and Maggie and the door, and they'd be completely out of sight as well.

"Cops ain't got nothing better to do than bust my balls." The guy slammed his fist into the desk at the front of the room.

Chase walked in.

"You gonna give me a ticket for jaywalking, too?" The guy dropped into the chair. "Maybe you wanna give me a ticket for disturbing the peace—even though there's no one here to disturb."

"Look." Chase shook his head. "I get it. The whole ticket thing is ridiculous. I cancelled the tow truck."

"Why?"

"You seem like a good guy." Chase pointed at something on the desk. "You're a Bears fan. Bears fans are all good in my book. See, I have this key chain."

The guy stared down at whatever was in Chase's hands.

Maggie dragged Leti across those ten feet to where Kevin now held the door open. He slowly shut it once they were outside.

They ran to their parked car and scrambled inside. Safe.

Kind of.

———

KEVIN SAT behind the wheel with the engine running. The women were in the car, which made him feel a heck of a lot better. He didn't like them inside that building. Even from across the warehouse, he could see the security guard's 9mm Luger in the chest holster and the .45 at his waist. That guy wasn't playing.

Chase opened the passenger door and slid inside. "Let's get out of here."

"Did you let him off the hook?" Kevin shifted into drive and pulled out of the parking lot.

"Yeah, I gave him a warning."

"Was he illegally parked?" Kevin wouldn't think Chase would lie about that.

"Technically, the red stripe along the front and sides of the building means there's no parking. It was legitimately illegal."

Kevin laughed. "So we parked illegally too."

"Technically, yes. I wasn't going to actually have the guy's car towed. That would be hypocritical." Chase turned to the women in the back seat. "Did you find anything?"

"We found a bunch of strange things," Maggie said.

"Names of kids that are dead," Leti added, "but they've been dead for years. Lists with names and social security numbers. But one of the apparently dead kids is in the process of being placed."

"How is that possible?" Chase asked.

"That is the question of the day." In the rearview mirror, white light streaked across Leti's face from the streetlamps.

"Maybe the kid has the same name," Chase pointed out.

"Makes sense, but the social security number matches," Leti told him.

"That's not right." Chase leaned his head back. The realization that they were into something way over their head must have hit him because he looked a little sick. Honesty, Kevin was already feeling it.

"Do you think they're making up children?" Maggie voice pinched with the concern they all seemed to be sharing. "What would that accomplish?"

"I'm not sure. Maybe they're charging the state

for additional kids." Leti's words tipped up at the end, like she didn't believe them. "But that wouldn't work. They wouldn't pass the state or federal audits with ghost children. They would need actual children to appear in front of the auditors."

"So are they kidnapping children?" Kevin didn't want to say the words. He didn't want to think that someone out there was taking children just to adopt them out. "What would that accomplish?"

"It would give them children in the system that they could charge for," Leti said.

"That sounds about right." Chase nodded. "It's always about money."

"I hate to interrupt, but where are we heading?" Kevin kept his speed under the limit. He didn't think they'd get caught after the warehouse, but he was not taking any chances. They took too many chances already tonight.

"Let's head back to the house," Leti said.

Maggie's voice raised an octave. "Look at this. It's almost like the information was copied from one kid to another."

The women kept up their conversation in the back seat. Chase turned around to look at Kevin. "So, I didn't get a chance to ask at dinner last night, how is the testing going?"

"It's slow."

"Have you passed everything?"

"Yeah, I have the medical this week, so we'll see how that goes."

"Eh, it's nothing." Chase shook his head. "How did the rest of the tests go?"

"I guess fine. They kept telling me I passed. They don't really tell you how well you do." Kevin wanted to know if he was doing well, but according to everyone he'd talked to it didn't matter how much higher you did over the passing score, just that you passed.

"All you need to do is pass. It's one or the other. So that's good."

That's what he'd heard, but it was good to get confirmation.

"Have you been working out for the power test?" Chase said.

"Yeah." It was the test he had been most nervous about. It was over, but he figured he should keep up the training for the police academy. "I did everything with time to spare."

"You got the mile and a half down?"

"Yeah, no problem. I can run that in just under fourteen, so I'm good."

"I can run it, but I don't think I could do it under fourteen. Once you stop training with the clock, you lose it." Chase shook his head. "I forget. How many minutes do you have to run it in?"

"Fourteen and a half." Kevin pulled down the alley to Maggie's house.

"You got that, then."

Kevin pulled the car into the garage. "We should check the house before you go in."

Maggie reached across from the back seat and punched his shoulder before pulling out her gun.

"Don't be an ass. Leti and I will check the house. You two check the yard."

"Fine." Kevin wasn't going to fight with her again. His sister was vicious.

Maggie crossed the yard and went up the steps to the porch, her gun drawn, with Leti trailing behind.

Kevin waited for them to walk into the house before headed toward the front of the house, choosing the narrower walkway along the right side. Lights came to life as he moved, revealing absolutely nothing.

"I don't like this." Chase walked up behind Kevin. "This whole thing is unsafe."

"Me either. These two have a gift for finding trouble."

"That they do, but it leads to getting bad guys off the street, so it's not all bad. Unless you're in love with the woman, then you're constantly worried about her." Chase looked over at Kevin. "So are you in love with the woman?"

Kevin didn't even know where to start with this, so he stuck with his usual answer. "No."

"No?"

Once they got to the corner of the house, Kevin checked down the block in front of the house to make sure no one was loitering around. "Why do you sound so surprised?"

There wasn't anyone out even walking a dog. He never realized how quiet the neighborhood truly was.

"Because I have eyes." Chase laughed. "Are you just living in denial, or have you just not figured it out yet?"

Kevin couldn't help the laugh that ripped from his chest. "Denial."

"Been there, brother. When your sister and I first started dating I was an idiot."

"When did you stop?" Kevin eased into the front yard.

"Being an idiot?"

Kevin nodded.

"I'll let you know when it happens."

"I'm sure Maggie will let me know way before you do."

"Yeah, she'd probably throw a party." Chase checked the cars lined up along the front curb. So did Kevin. Not one of them was occupied. "I think we can head inside," Chase said.

"Yeah." Kevin followed Chase around the other side of the house to the back yard.

Once they were inside, with the door locked behind them, laughter echoed down the hall and into the kitchen.

"We really suck at this," Leti said.

"I can't do it." That was Maggie, sounding frustrated.

"Click on there."

"It won't work."

"Where's Danni when we need her?" Leti said as Kevin and Chase got to the living room.

"It's a diagramming software. We don't need Danni, dammit." Maggie poked at the laptop and glared. She slapped at the keyboard and shoved the thing over to Leti before draping her arm over her eyes and leaning her head on the back of the couch.

Leto scowled at the laptop. "Apparently we do."

"What are you two trying to do?" Kevin asked.

"We're trying to diagram what we know so far in the case." Leti shut the laptop and jumped up from the couch. She opened a computer bag and sifted through the contents, coming out with a stack of purple Post-it notes and a pen.

"So, what do we know so far?" Leti asked.

"They have a secret warehouse not listed on their website," Kevin suggested. Leti wrote something on a Post-it and stuck the note to the edge of a shelf in the nearest bookcase.

"If you had Post-its, why were we messing with that stupid computer?" Maggie tilted her head to the side but didn't move otherwise.

"Because a secret warehouse with dead children's names and socials?" Leti pointed out.

Maggie hummed. "The question is, are they reusing those names and socials?"

"And if so, where are they getting the kids?" Leti made a face like she didn't even want to think about that scenario. That meant children were being abducted, and no one wanted that.

Kevin said what everyone was obviously thinking. "Do they even exist?"

"Yeah." Leti nodded. "If this is a scheme to defraud, who are they trying to defraud?"

This was leaving them with a lot of questions and not a lot of answers. It was a mess.

"Maybe the nurse knew something." Maggie shifted her arm to cover her eyes. "That's why she ended up dead, too."

Leti paced in front of the bookcase. "I need to talk to her mother, but she's not returning any of my calls."

"We could try the shelter where she worked," Maggie said slowly.

"How?" Leti paused her pacing.

Maggie jumped up and clapped. "Lori and Midge want to adopt."

Leti narrowed her eyes. "They do?"

"They really do." Maggie smiled.

Kevin hated being the voice of reason when it was obviously bursting his sister's bubble. "Why don't Leti and I go in to adopt, and you can be our lawyer? It will draw less attention and get all three of us inside. It will be harder to keep track of us that way. And then you can poke around while we talk adoption."

"Fine." Maggie crossed her arms. "Boys screw up all the fun."

"How am I screwing up anything?" Kevin would never understand how her mind worked.

"You're right. Leti can still be Lori and I'll be Midge. I'll be her business partner and a lawyer, but we've put everything on hold while you and your boyfriend Kastle, here, are trying to build a family."

"That's way too complicated." Not that Kevin wanted to actually adopt a child, but having Maggie tell everyone their business was not how he wanted to spend any morning.

And he did not look like a Kastle. Dumbest name ever.

"Shush." Maggie flailed her hands at him. "It's perfect. Let me see what I have for us to wear."

Maggie latched onto Leti's arm and dragged her down the hall into her bedroom, leaving Chase and Kevin sitting there.

"So, what was that?" Maggie had been acting weird lately, Kevin could admit that. But this was weird even by her newly weird standards. Kevin thought about asking her about it, but she was also so cranky he'd been avoiding the conversation.

"I think Maggie's missing undercover work." Chase shook his head as he rubbed the back of his neck. "I caught her wearing a wig at Starbucks a few weeks ago."

"A wig?"

"She said she was watching a mark, but then a woman walked out of the washroom and sat down with her. Maggie was having coffee with her. She was wearing the wig to hide her identity—like Superman and Clark Kent or something."

"Was the woman the client?"

"No, the client was the boyfriend. She was having coffee with the girlfriend."

"She had coffee with the target?" That was a conflict of interest. Wasn't it?

"She said she wore a disguise in case the woman had a video camera at the house. She didn't want the girlfriend recognizing her."

Kevin did not get this at all. "Wait a sec. Why was she going in the girlfriend's house?"

"She wanted to see if this other guy's clothes were there."

"How would she know who the clothes belonged to? It could've been the boyfriend's."

Chase snorted. "She said she'd know."

The logic just wasn't there. Kevin shook his head. "Yeah, she's missing undercover."

"I'm hoping this case will get it out of her system."

Kevin knew his sister and he doubted it. He just hoped that it wouldn't give Leti the bug, making her want to track down more and more dangerous cases.

"How do I look?" The smile that lit up Leti's face was electric, but it was the outfit that had Kevin swallowing his tongue.

She wore jeans that left little to the imagination, and a short sweater that rode dangerously high. If she had to raise her arms, she was going to give everyone a show. She pulled down a pair of sunglasses and hid those eyes. Striking a pose, she rested one index finger at her lips. "I'm Lori, and elegance is always in style, darling."

Maggie laughed. "That is amazing."

Kevin looked at Chase, who looked back, eyebrows raised, and shook his head the tiniest bit. Kevin got it. Leti was liking this way too much.

And there wasn't anything Kevin could do about it.

CHAPTER SIXTEEN

LETI SAT across the desk from the social worker named Felice. A sweet woman with brown skin, short black hair, and Birkenstocks. She pushed her glasses up the bridge of her nose as she read the paper in her hand. "Thank you for filling out the application in advance. You'd be surprised how many people show up with nothing and expect to adopt."

Leti figured having some of the paperwork done ahead of time would encourage the staff to let them poke around. It would prove their seriousness. So far, it seemed to be working.

"Your application is impressive." Felice adjusted her glasses and smiled. "It's lovely to see such a successful, devoted couple in here."

Kevin reached across the short expanse and grabbed Leti's hand. She tried not to glow like a giddy schoolgirl, but the way Felice's smile widened, Leti felt like she'd failed.

"It says here that you're an artist, and Kastle owns his own company."

Kevin nodded with a strained smile. Leti knew the feeling. She had no idea what an artist did. And she had a feeling he didn't know much more about company ownership. Hopefully, Felice wouldn't ask.

Leti knew she shouldn't have let Maggie fill out the application last night. But she'd been so tired and Kevin had looked at her with those eyes and Maggie had offered. She figured, what could it hurt?

Her head. That's what it hurt. Now she was an artist and Kevin was the owner of… something.

Maggie was supposed to just get them in the door, not make their fake lives so appealing the shelter staff would start seeing dollar signs. Leti was afraid the staff were going to start throwing kids at them. Literally.

Felice frowned. Leti didn't know whether to be happy or alarmed. "You've stated on the application that you want an infant. Are you sure you wouldn't be interested in an older child? Bringing an older child into your home can be so rewarding. There are so many deserving children ready and waiting for a nice home like yours."

The thought of taking home a child of any age made Leti break out in hives. She wanted kids eventually. Very much. She was just really nervous about being a mom. She scraped her nails along the skin on her arms, but it didn't seem to get to the itch. Maybe Maggie knew what she was doing, filling in the application for a baby.

"We really were hoping for a baby of our own.

Right, Kastle?" Leti looked at Kevin and smiled. All part of the ruse.

"Yeah, Lori, a baby of our own." He patted her hand.

Felice frowned as she wrote on the application. She pulled off her glasses and slid the paperwork into a file folder at the side of her desk. "It was wonderful meeting you both. I'll be in touch when we have a child available in your preferred age range." She stood. "I heard you might be interested in donating to our location. Magdelina can take a check."

"Is that it?" Leti's disappointment was real. She still had nothing. A commotion came from outside the door. Children ran and screamed down the hall.

"Isn't there something we can do?" Maggie stepped away from the wall. She'd been so quiet through this whole thing, Leti had almost forgot their fake lawyer was there.

"Unfortunately, there aren't any babies available," Felice said slowly. Apparently she thought they were upset because there wasn't a child to take home. Little did she know they just wanted a tour.

Maggie walked up to Felice and whispered, "Maybe my clients have been a bit hasty. Can they have a tour of the facility? It might encourage them to go a different way."

The phone on the desk rang. "Of course. Let me grab this and we'll go." Felice smiled as she grabbed the phone.

"You need to open up your horizons, Lori dear," Maggie whispered once Leti stood up and took a few steps away from the desk. "I can't exactly poke around with her sitting in the office."

"I'm trying, Madge, but I don't know the rules."

"You don't know my name, either. I'm Midge."

Leti wanted to roll her eyes, but Maggie was right. She'd forgotten her name. Luckily she hadn't forgotten it in front of anyone else.

Felice covered the mouthpiece of the phone and said to the three of them, "I'm so sorry." Once she removed her hand, she spoke into the receiver. "I'll be down there as soon as I can."

She hung up the phone. "I would love to give you a tour, but one of my kids is having trouble at school. I need to head down to the high school." She walked out into the hall, to the office next to hers. "Jordan, can you give Mr. and Mrs. Turney, and their attorney, Ms. Steele, a tour of the facility?"

"Sure," a man replied. "I just need to deal with a little family emergency and I'll be right with you."

"Of course," Felice said, and returned to her office. She smiled at Kevin, Maggie, and then Leti. "I'm leaving you in very capable hands." She got her purse and left her office. Leti followed her in time to hear her say, "Hey kids, shouldn't you get to school?" before the woman headed out the front door.

In the hallway, two boys with golden blond hair stood in front an office door, and the same voice from a moment ago said, "Ryan, go get the permission slips from the printer."

The one boy dropped his backpack on the floor and ran down the hall. He ran back a second later with two papers blowing in his hands as he flailed them back and forth.

Leti glanced in the office as the man behind the desk stood up. He was a tall man—at least six feet. His blond hair nearly covered gorgeous green eyes. He was very nice to look at, but when Leti very casually checked his finger, he was very much married. Not that she was looking or anything, but old habits die hard.

The man took the pages and signed. He gave each boy a paper. "Now don't lose these."

"We won't, Dad." The boys each opened their backpacks a smidge and stuffed the papers inside the large section of the bag without unzipping the zipper more than an inch.

"Get to school," the man said, as both boys gave him a kiss on the cheek.

The boys grinned as they slowly picked up their school bags and put them on their shoulders. They were cute and sweet. And it made Leti want to have some cute and sweet little ones of her own. Again, eventually.

"Be good today," the guy told them as they walked away.

"Yes, Dad!" It sounded so realistic, like they might actually be good, but then they giggled.

"You two will lose your phones this weekend."

"We'll be good." They both smiled and ran toward the front door.

"They're cute." Leti watched them leave, pushing each other as they ran.

"They have to be, so parents don't kill them." The

man laughed. "Sorry, I'm Jordan. I probably shouldn't joke like that until you get to know me."

"My mom used to say the same thing. 'God made children so cute so parents wouldn't kill them.' I get it." Kevin laughed, a hollow-sounding guffaw. Leti didn't hear him talk about his mom very often. It was nice.

"You must have been a handful." Jordan laughed. "No judgement, so was I."

"I was. Once, when I was eight, I did something stupid, and she called me a son of a bitch. I told her not to be so hard on herself. She shouldn't call herself a bitch."

"No, you didn't." Leti had never heard that story before, but it sounded like a young Kevin. Maggie always talked about what a troublemaker he had been.

"I did. I'm surprised I made it to nine."

A laugh bubbled up out of Leti's throat. "Me too. How did you get out of that?"

"I hung out at a buddy's for a few hours. When I came home my dad looked at me like I was dead-kid-walking. He didn't yell. It was the one time he didn't yell. He smirked at me and said, 'what you said earlier was clever. Don't ever do it again. Now go see your mom.' I was terrified."

"You should have been." Jordan shook his head.

"I ran up to her and started crying and apologized. She never yelled. She just hugged me."

"Did you ever talk to her like that again."

"No. She was amazing."

"I wish I had gotten a chance to meet her." Leti held his hand. The look in his eyes said he was about to lose it. He didn't talk about his mom a lot. And she could tell he truly loved her. This whole conversation was hard.

"Are you okay?" Leti rubbed along his wrist. Hopefully he knew she was there for him.

He didn't answer. Hopefully it was enough.

"We should start the tour." Kevin seemed to be ready to move on.

"We should." Leti agreed. There was so much to unpack in that one story, but right now they had a job to do.

KEVIN DIDN'T LIKE this at all. He didn't like talking about the past. He didn't like remembering. He had been such a little brat. And his mom had put up with it until she hadn't been there to put up with it anymore.

He missed her. It's not like he even remembered much. He was young when she'd died and every year after morphed her memory into faded shadows. But from what he remembered—the feelings, the love, the few moments—he'd been happy with her around. His father had been happy with her around. They hadn't been happy like that or even a family like that since she'd died.

Some parents just didn't know how to be a parent. That was his father. When he'd lost his wife, the only parent who knew how to take care of the children, he'd been lost. And Kevin and his siblings had suffered.

"Are you okay?" Leti leaned over and asked the

question. He didn't want to answer, because he had a feeling she wouldn't like it. He wasn't okay.

"We should start the tour." Kevin shoved all the memories and the loss down his throat with a gulp.

"We should." Leti squeezed his hand. He could get lost in that touch—just forget everything. Unfortunately, they didn't have time for that right now. Watching Jordan look around the room brought Kevin back to the present and kept him there. He wasn't complaining.

"Wasn't there a lawyer too?" Jordan asked. He must have noticed that Maggie had slipped away. Even Leti looked a bit confused.

Kevin let go of Leti's hand and rested his on Leti's back instead, hoping she'd understand to just go with it. "She had to take a call from her office. She said to go on without her."

"Then let's go." Jordan walked through the open area and down the hall past offices. Kevin and Leti followed.

"So, what do you do here?" Kevin asked as Jordan badged through a heavy door and opened it.

"I'm the Center Director." He motioned to the doorway. "This is the entrance to the shelter."

As they slipped through the door, Kevin saw Maggie disappear into Felice's office. If there was something to be found, she would find it. He just had to give her time.

Beyond the door was a large room with a couple of couches surrounding a wall-mounted big-screen television. A toybox sat in the far corner, with tables and a play kitchen nearby on the far wall. A staircase was on the right.

"This is the playroom," Jordan explained. "We have the tables for the older kids to do homework.

"Whose toys are these?" Leti looked concerned, probably because she worried the shelter would steal the kid's toys. Given what they were learning, that wasn't out of the realm of possibility.

"The toys down here belong to the shelter. Any toys that the child came in with or has received are kept in their bedroom." He pointed to two separate doors underneath the stairs. "There are the bathrooms." He then pointed to another door across from the stairs. "That's the medical office. But we're going to head upstairs to the bedrooms."

He led them up the flight of stairs. The first open door was a child's room. It looked normal, like any other girl's room Kevin had ever seen. Not that he'd seen a lot, but he lived with Maggie. She'd been a girl once. Well, she was a girl still, sort of. Now she was a woman.

Darn. Why was he getting all PC in his head right now?

The floor was covered in toys, and clothes were thrown everywhere but in the pink plastic hamper. Glittery paper crafts were on the desk, and a unicorn had vomited pillows in its likeness all over the bed.

"The room is nice," Leti said.

"This is Jenny's room. She's been with us for a while. But the good news is that she's been placed with a nice family in Oak Park. We're just waiting for the paperwork to go through." Jordan led them out of the room. "Are you looking to adopt an older child?"

"Actually"—Leti grabbed Kevin's hand— "we were hoping for an infant, but it looks like we'll have to wait awhile."

"Well, that's true, unless you decide on a private adoption."

"Private adoption?" Leti said the words like they might bite.

If Kevin didn't agree that there was no way they were ready to start a family, he might be offended. But as it stood, they were barely together. They needed more time before they introduced kids—*if* they introduced kids.

He was thinking about kids, and they hadn't even gotten to their first road trip. They might not travel well together, and how would they take the kids to Disney if they couldn't travel without fighting?

"I didn't realize the shelter handled private adoptions," Leti said slowly.

Jordan shook his head as he pulled a card from his pocket. "They don't. This is a lawyer who specializes in private adoptions. You would need to use this lawyer and not the one you brought today. They won't work with outside representation."

Leti took the card, and her eyes went wide before she schooled her expression. Her face paled, and Kevin looked over her shoulder at the card pinched tightly between her thumb and forefinger. Rick Cullen. Kevin didn't know that name at all, but Leti obviously did.

"So we just call this guy, and he can help us?"

Kevin didn't like this at all. Given Leti's reaction and Jordan's insistence they could only use his lawyer—something felt off. "Is this legal?"

Jordan's face went from neutral to anger and then to smarm in the blink of an eye. "It's about finding homes for unwanted children. We do everything by the book."

Kevin smiled. The man hadn't answered the question. Classic misdirect. Whatever book they were following, Kevin doubted it was the letter of the law. "Sounds good. I find it's always important to ask."

The relief that washed over Jordan's features just proved he had something to hide. "It's smart of you to check. We all just want to help the kids."

"Exactly."

Jordan tapped the card in Leti's hand. "Make sure you tell him Jordan Strong sent you. He'll take good care of you."

"Thank you." Leti somehow found her voice and the color returned to her cheeks. "You don't know how much this means to us. I was so disappointed when I talked to Felice. This gives me hope."

Screaming came from downstairs, and Jordan turned around. "Sorry, I need to get this." He ran down the stairs toward the noise, followed by Kevin and Leti.

"Christy, are you okay?" Jordan reached the source of the loud sobs first. "What happened to your hand?"

Downstairs stood a young girl, maybe eleven or twelve years old. She carried a pink backpack stained red from the blood on her hand. "I caught my hand on the bench at the bus stop."

"Didn't my boys offer to walk you back?" Jordan asked her.

"They did. I told them to go to school so they wouldn't get in trouble."

"I'm not a nurse, but I'll do my best. Come with me to the medical office." Jordan pointed at the heavy door they'd originally come through. "Can you both show yourselves out, or do you have more questions?"

"No more questions." Kevin was lying through his teeth. He had so many, but all of them needed to wait.

"We'll be in touch with the lawyer." Leti smiled as she backed up to the door. "Thank you so much."

Jordan escorted Christy through the door to the medical office. After he disappeared, Leti opened the door to the hallway and held it for Kevin. Down the hall they found Maggie leaning against the wall next to Felice's office.

"You ready?" she asked.

"Yes." Leti ran for the door like her butt was on fire.

Maggie looked at Leti, then back at Kevin, and raised both eyebrows. He didn't literally speak eyebrows, but it was easy to guess she wanted to know what was going on.

He shrugged and they both followed Leti out the door—hoping to get far enough away so that Leti could tell them what had her spooked.

CHAPTER SEVENTEEN

LETI HADN'T TALKED the entire car ride. Not that she'd really had a chance. Maggie was rambling from the backseat about how she almost got caught by the front desk administrator numerous times. "Magdelina did not want to leave me alone in the offices."

"Do you blame her? You were there to steal files." Kevin shook his head, like what he was saying was obvious.

It might have been obvious to most, but not to Maggie. "She didn't know that." Her nose scrunched as if believed she should have just been left alone in the building with no supervision and was about to stick her tongue out at her brother.

"Did you find anything?" Kevin asked—which was probably a good thing. Maggie looked like she wanted to go on another rambling binge.

Maggie tsked. "Not much. There's no record of an Amanda Clark ever being in the system. So I'm not sure how she fits into the picture."

"I might know." Leti took a deep breath. "We're looking in the wrong place."

"Where should we be looking?" Maggie leaned forward into the front seat.

Leti handed her the simple business card. No logo or firm name, just a single name and a phone number. "At the lawyers handling the private adoptions."

Maggie pointed toward the building they'd just left. "That's not private adoptions."

"I know," Leti said, "but the Center Director gave me this card and said he could help me with a private adoption."

"Rick Cullen. Isn't this the guy who works with Enzo?" Maggie shook her head. "He was smarmy. He actually told me his last name was Cullen, like the vampires in *Twilight*. He licked his lips and said he likes to suck things, too."

"Gross." Leti made a face.

"Yeah, that was the last time I let Enzo introduce me to his single friends."

"Are they friends?"

"I don't think they're friends, just coworkers. Maybe a friends-because-of-work kind of thing?"

"So we should tread lightly when talking to Enzo."

"Probably." Maggie handed back the card. "What does this all mean?"

"I think they're using the names for the private adoptions," Leti told her.

"If children are getting adopted with these fake names, then there have to be children, right?" Kevin said.

Leti closed her eyes. All the hope that the organization was creating fake children's profiles and bilking Medicaid or donors went out the window. Heck, they might still be doing that, but they were using real children. And real children meant real repercussions for families.

"Maybe the children were abducted," Leti offered, but something felt off about that scenario.

"Wouldn't we be able to trace that?" Maggie leaned back against the car seat. "Wouldn't they show up on milk cartons and post office walls? They couldn't stop the Amber Alerts telling everyone the children were kidnapped."

"True." Leti agreed, but something still felt wrong.

"Maybe it is still just fraud, without the traumatizing of children." Maggie didn't sound like she believed her own words.

"I hope so." Leti sighed. "I'm going to text Enzo and see if he'll meet us tomorrow morning. He might be able to help."

"That's a good idea. Just know, Rick knows me. So if he's part of this, I can't help except in the background." Maggie slumped, her body crumpling into a ball like being sidelined was physically hurting.

"That's okay, Jordan said that you can't be part of it anyway. We had to get rid of our lawyer."

"That's a huge red flag," Maggie said, throwing her hands up. "Since when can't you include your lawyer when adopting a child?"

"I asked if the whole thing was legal." Kevin's face

was awash with red and white from the streetlights. The blinker clicked a rhythm.

"And what was his answer?" Maggie leaned forward, disappointment seemingly forgotten.

"He never answered."

Maggie dropped back into the seat. "Shit."

"Yep."

"We need to find out exactly what Stanley Welford and the Wacker Children's Association are doing, and bring them both down." Leti's very bones were charged. She wanted to run and shout and tell everyone what they were doing. She wanted to act. She wanted them to pay.

"We don't know if it connects to Stanley Welford. It could be a coincidence." Kevin pulled down the alley to Busted.

"You believe that?" Leti wasn't sure why that line of thought annoyed her, but it was. Stanley Welford was a part of this. She didn't know how.

"No. I don't believe in coincidence."

Funny, neither did she. She just had to figure out how he fit into it all.

LATER THAT NIGHT, Kevin lay in bed trying to sleep. Leti had passed out the minute her head hit the pillow. She was beautiful. Her features relaxed. Angelic.

He loved looking at her.

He loved talking to her.

He was pretty sure he loved her, but he wasn't ready to admit that to anyone yet. Not even himself.

He'd been burned too many times. He'd lost every woman he'd ever loved, starting with his mom. His high school girlfriend left him after they'd gotten into a fender bender on the South Side. Apparently he couldn't keep her safe. He couldn't argue.

While in Afghanistan, he'd been engaged to Anna, and he hadn't been able to keep her safe either. She'd died on a mine while doing sweeps along the perimeter of a small town. That happened three years ago, and it still felt like yesterday.

Flipping to his back, he sighed. This wasn't working. Trips down memory lane didn't help a man fall asleep. It just led to indigestion.

Leti started but sank back into sleep. Thank goodness. No need for them both to count the shadows on the ceiling. There were twelve, in case anyone ever asked.

He slid out of bed, making sure not to jostle the mattress, before grabbing his cell phone from the nightstand and slipping it in his pajama pants pocket. Tiptoeing out of the room, he avoided stepping on the dog dancing at his feet.

Kevin waited for Pork Chop to exit the room before closing the door. Light from the windows washed the inside of the home in streaks, making it possible to see without turning on any additional lights. Not that he thought the lights would wake Leti, but he didn't want to take the chance.

Walking into the kitchen, he grabbed a bottle of water out of the fridge and made his way to the kitchen table. Pork Chop curled into a ball on the floor mat in front of the sink. The little guy was snoring within seconds.

Oh to be able to fall asleep on command like that.

But sleep was not his friend. It was hard to close your eyes when the dangers of the case were playing on repeat behind his eyes.

This whole case stunk. He wasn't sure what was going on at Wacker Children's Association, but he was sure it was shady as shit. He hoped Grayson found something, because he didn't like Leti getting any closer to this case than she already was. Kevin didn't feel he could protect her, and the closer they got to the truth without taking this dirtbag down, the more danger she was in.

He pulled out his cell phone and dialed Grayson. The man never slept either. There was something about knowing all the real dangers in the world that kept a man up at night.

"Hey, brother." The man was obviously wide awake. "What are you doing up this late?"

"Hey. Can't sleep."

"Woman got you up all night, huh?" Grayson laughed.

That was so true in many ways, but probably not in the perverted ways Grayson meant.

"You could say that. We're still looking into this case, and I was wondering if you found anything?"

"No small talk, then."

"Did you want to do small talk? Any new loves of your life?"

"Moving on." Grayson chuckled. He wasn't a love-them kind of guy. When Kevin had been heartbroken over Anna, Grayson had been trying to feed him a steady diet of random women. After a while Kevin gave in, but it didn't last long. Despite his reputation, it wasn't his style.

Grayson, on the other hand, was perfectly happy having the entirety of the female population rotate through his bedroom each night.

"It seems this Wacker Children's place has had some trouble over the years. Child abuse allegations. Medicaid fraud allegations. There aren't many agencies that have not been brought in to audit this place."

"Don't they get audited all the time?"

"Yeah, but not like this. About two years ago, the DEA was brought in to look at medication tampering." Two years. Around the time when Pauline Lidell was found murdered. A nurse could've noticed medical anomalies.

"Why would they tamper with kids' medication?" Did Kevin mention he did not like this case?

"They were over-reporting the need for Ritalin and pain meds."

"To what? Sell it?"

"The DEA closed the inquiry before anything was resolved."

"How was it closed?"

"I don't know, brother, but keep your head on a

swivel. Whoever got a federal agency to shut down an investigation has some pretty high reach."

Would Stanley Welford have that kind of pull? "What did you find out about Stanley Welford?"

"Not much. No military career. Went to college straight out of high school. Got his law degree. He's on the board at Wacker Children's Association, so there's your connection. But he's squeaky clean."

"So he wouldn't have the type of juice to shut down a government investigation."

"I mean, he runs in high-power circles. They all have ridiculous amounts of money. He's a big contributor to Mayer Ramirez's campaign. A Chicago mayor would have some clout."

If the mayor was involved, this was bigger than even he thought. He really hated this case.

"I'll keep looking, but be careful." Grayson made some noise on the other end.

Kevin heard a woman's voice. "Come back to bed. I'm horny."

Grayson whispered, "Go back to bed and I'll be there to take care of my girl."

"You didn't have to drop everything to talk." And Kevin meant it. He appreciated it, of course.

"I did." Grayson chuckled. "I'm too old to keep up with her."

"How old is she?"

"Twenty-two." He laughed. "I do not suggest getting into a relationship with someone who can run faster than you."

"Are you in a relationship?"

"Eh, she likes to think so. After what we've been through, there's no way I'm doing that again. You know how it is."

Kevin did. Unfortunately. He'd lost Anna back in the day. Grayson had lost his fiancé to a guy back home. After that, Grayson became a certified man-whore and tried to convert Kevin into his makeshift cult.

Kevin never really bought into it.

"At least you seem to be doing better. You found someone to keep your bed warm." Grayson was poking. Trying to get Kevin to admit to something—feelings or a relationship. Kevin wasn't biting.

"I'm just fine."

"You've gotten over the fear of losing them?" Grayson sighed. "I'm impressed. I can't seem to get over that particular hurdle."

"Yeah." Kevin wasn't quite there yet. Especially with people coming after Leti and the case not any closer to getting wrapped up.

"I don't think I can do it." Grayson sighed. "I can't go through all that again."

"Come to bed!" the woman's said in the background.

"Gotta go, brother." Grayson hung up before Kevin could say goodbye. Not that it mattered, they'd talk again soon. With their relationship it meant never having to say goodbye.

Kevin clicked end and headed for the back door. He stepped over Pork Chop and checked the locks. He'd checked them earlier, but it didn't hurt to double check.

Talking to Grayson was always good and bad. He loved talking to his friend, but darn it if he didn't see Kevin to the bone. Grayson knew Kevin better than he knew himself. It was annoying.

Kevin sat back at the table and thought about going to bed. With Leti. He didn't want to go back there. Grayson was right. Kevin wasn't ready to go through all that loss again. Although Grayson had been talking about himself. But that didn't change the fact that Kevin had no desire to feel all that pain again, either.

"Everything okay?" Leti stood in the kitchen doorway. She'd managed to wake up and come down the hall without Kevin hearing.

He was too distracted. Thinking about her was taking away brainpower he needed to stay ahead of the bad guys. "Yeah. I can't sleep."

"Me either." Leti shuffled into the kitchen and sat across the table from Kevin. "I hope I can get ahold of Cindy Lidell tomorrow. Pauline must have seen something with these kids, and I hope she told her mom."

"I spoke with an old Army buddy of mine, and there was an investigation by the DEA into Wacker Children's. It seems they were overprescribing Ritalin and pain meds. The complaint came around the time of the nurse's death."

"Maybe that's it then." Leti yawned.

"You should go to bed. This will all be here in the morning."

"Why don't you come with me?" She came up behind him and slid her hands down his chest. It felt so good and his body instantly reacted. It would be so easy to just give in and have one more night with her.

But that wasn't the right thing to do.

He removed her arms and stood up. "I need to do a few things before I sleep."

"I can help." She ran a hand down his abs.

Every nerve ending fired. Desire pooled in his gut. Her touch. Her mouth curved in a smile that said she wanted to do naughty things. And he'd partaken in a few of those naughty things already. He knew that they were good together.

But that didn't stop the fact that she was in danger and he was unlucky. And he couldn't lose her like he'd lost everyone else. His father never forgave him for his mother. His sister would never forgive him if something happened to Leti.

Thoughts of his father and sister cooled him down long enough to step out of her reach.

"No need." He moved around the kitchen table. Farther away from her roaming hands and warm body. He might not be able to say no another time. He'd pushed his luck the first two times.

Leti's eyebrow arched as she watched him cower like a coward. He never noticed how similar those two words were. Cower. Coward. But if the Cow fits...

"Why don't you wake me when you come to bed?" Leti knew. She knew he was a fraud. He was scared and weak. She was finally seeing him for what he was.

But he couldn't lie. "I think I might sleep on the couch tonight."

"Why?" Her arms crossed over her very perky

chest. If he was a stronger man, he'd be face-deep in that chest, not running. But he couldn't lose her.

"I want to make sure everything stays quiet. We're getting close, and the feds are involved. The stakes are higher." All very true.

Leti rubbed her hands along her arms. Rejection clouded her eyes. He was pretty sure he saw the moment her heart broke, and he'd been the one to do it.

He was an ass. Leti waved to Pork Chop. "Come on, honey."

The dog scampered after her, his collar jingling. It was such a happy sound, yet nothing about this night was happy. She shuffled back to the bedroom and looked back at him.

He nodded. There wasn't anything else to say.

She softly closed the door and was gone.

Kevin leaned against the wall of the kitchen and took in a cleansing breath. That was one of the hardest things he ever had to do. Now all he wanted to do was take a cold shower and try to get some sleep.

But given he didn't want to keep Leti awake, he didn't think the shower would happen. And given his body wanted her more than his next breath, he didn't think sleep was coming anytime in his future.

CHAPTER EIGHTEEN

THE NEXT MORNING, Kevin downed his second cup of coffee. He hadn't slept a wink last night. They'd gotten up early to talk to Enzo, and they were still waiting for him to appear.

He was late and Kevin didn't like late. Especially when it meant he had to sit around. He and Leti hadn't talked about last night, which meant it was a loaded cannon in the room. Any minute, the lit fuse would hit the gunpowder and an explosion would happen. It wouldn't be pretty.

Thankfully, Enzo walked in before Kevin had to think any more about his impending doom.

"This doesn't look good." Enzo took in the scene. Kevin had to agree. Leti, Maggie, Chase and Kevin were sitting in separate chairs, just waiting. Danni sat on the floor against the front of the couch. Not one of them were talking or joking around like they'd normally do. They had gone over what Grayson had said, but it didn't change anything. It just seemed to add an extra layer to an already messed-up situation.

"Have a seat." Leti motioned to the chair opposite her desk.

Enzo sat. "Did you find something out?"

"We went to the agency and filled out adoption paperwork to get inside. We thought maybe we could find more information about this list we'd found." Leti handed him a printed copy of the names with personal information.

Enzo nodded but didn't say anything.

"We didn't find anything," Leti continued, "but on our application we stated that we wanted to adopt a baby, not an older child. We were told there aren't babies in the system up for adoption as often, so we were advised to contact a private adoption lawyer." Leti handed him the card with just a name and phone number. "Do you know him?"

Enzo's face drained of color—which was impressive given his Italian heritage. He turned to Maggie, who nodded and said, "I'm sorry."

Enzo shook his head. "I can't believe Rick is in on this."

"Are you friends with him?" Leti didn't know if they were besties, but given Enzo's reaction there was some betrayal going on.

"We started at Welford, Simmons and Dunne at the same time. We interned together."

"Could this be a different Rick Cullen?"

"I don't know of another lawyer by that name." Enzo shook his head. "But anything is possible."

"We're supposed to call him and set up a meet to talk about adoption."

"Sounds like a good idea." Enzo scanned the paperwork in his hands. "So, these names... you think they're finding children and given them new identities."

Maggie nodded. "Yes, but we don't know where they get them. Maybe it's just unwanted children the parents are giving up for adoption." Maggie was grasping at straws, but they all were. The reality was just too awful to think about.

Enzo shook his head. "No. if they were legal adoptions, there'd be no need for cloak and dagger. They wouldn't have warned you to get rid of your personal lawyer. They'd have the law office on the card. The firm does handle legal adoptions."

This was not where any of them wanted this case to go. Abducted children sold on the black market. The kids might end up in good homes. Might. But these poor parents that lost their children? Heartbreaking.

Leti took a deep breath and waved a hand at Kevin. "There's more. Kevin found out that there was a DEA investigation a few years ago. They had evidence that the shelters were overprescribing drugs like Ritalin. But the case was closed down right away."

"That doesn't make sense." Enzo looked confused. Like they all were.

"They were probably selling them on the street, not giving them to kids. I don't know if that makes it any better," Chase said.

"Why take the risk, though? The foster care and adoption scheme has got to be worth more than small-time drug-dealing." Enzo shook his head again. There seemed to be a lot of that. Given the shit-show that was this case, Kevin wasn't surprised.

"Well, they didn't really have any risk, did they?" Leti said. "The drug case was closed right away. Someone must have paid to have it shut down."

"Or called in a favor," Kevin pointed out.

Maggie leaned forward. "That is one hell of a favor. They must have some powerful friends to shut down the Feds."

"Yeah." Kevin sighed. The idea that someone could shut down a federal investigation made him worried that they were in over their heads.

"Well," Enzo said, "we should probably see if this is the Rick I know or not. Are you two ready to call?"

Kevin stood up and walked over to Leti. He put his hand on her shoulder, and he wasn't sure if she jumped from his touch or just happened to be reaching for the phone at the same time. But given last night, he probably didn't want to know the answer.

LETI PACED as the ringtone sang from her cell phone speaker. Kevin sat across the desk staring at her. He seemed confused. He'd looked at her like he was somehow hurt when she'd pulled away. But what was she supposed to do?

He'd practically run away last night after she'd thrown herself at him. Hollyhocks, she was still embarrassed when she thought about the way she'd slid up and down his body like a horny teenager. And he had run like a scared virgin.

Since she had firsthand knowledge he wasn't a scared virgin, that meant he wasn't interested in her. When he'd realized he no longer was interested in her, she had no idea. But apparently he had changed his mind.

It wasn't the best thing she'd heard all day, but she wasn't going to beg him to want her. She respected him and herself way too much to play these games.

A man's voice came over the speaker. "Hello."

"Hi, is this Rick Cullen?" Leti asked.

"This is."

"My husband and I are looking to adopt a child."

"Okay, but why are you calling me?" He sounded so hostile.

Right—she'd forgot to follow instructions. "Jordan Strong gave us your number."

"Ah, okay. Have you filled out the adoption paperwork already?"

"I filled it out through the Wacker Children's Association. Is there additional paperwork?"

"No, I can get that from Jordan. I will need a copy of your and your spouse's driver's licenses and your social security numbers so we can do a background check. We'll also need to have you fingerprinted."

Maggie waved her hand to get Leti's attention. She mouthed, "Why the fingerprints?"

Leti picked up a notepad and wrote, *probably to check we're not felons?*

"Why do you need all that?" Kevin asked.

"We just want to make sure we're giving children to loving, deserving families."

"Makes sense." Leti didn't believe that part at all. But she wasn't going to let him know that.

"We'll have to set up an interview. I'll be in touch." And he was gone.

Leti clicked end and turned to her friends. "What do you all think?"

"That was Rick. I'd know his voice anywhere." Enzo sighed. "So it's not just my boss involved."

"No, this goes much deeper," Danni said, from down on the floor. Leti wasn't exactly sure when she'd gotten there. But if she said there was more, then there was more.

"What did you find?" Leti asked her.

"Wacker Children's is a subsidiary of Mercy LLC. It's owned by a shell company called S&W Corp. It was hard to get to it, but the shell company can be traced back to Stanley Welford."

"So we have him."

Danni shrugged. "We have to know what he's doing first, and we need to connect the private adoptions to the shell company."

"So we need more information." Disappointment crawled up Leti's neck. She just wanted this over. "And Danni, we need some driver's licenses and social security cards."

Danni smiled. "No problem."

"But the fingerprints are going to be an issue. We'll need to put that off for as long as possible."

LATER THAT NIGHT, Kevin drove around with no specific destination. Yeah. He was being a wimp. He'd had his medical evaluation late that afternoon. He should be happy. That was the final hurdle to get into the police department. Now it was the final waiting game.

He should go to Maggie's and wait, but instead he was avoiding it. Maggie was there with Leti. It's not like they needed him.

And he didn't need to think about how crappy he'd been to her. She didn't deserve it. But then she deserved better than him.

So there was that.

His phone buzzed. At a light, he reached for it. If he was smart he'd let it go. He didn't want to see how Leti was looking for him or how he was disappointing her.

He grabbed the thing and looked down. His father. Red light washed over the screen.

Compassion Society of Chicago is coming this weekend for a donation pick up. Come this week. Anything left will go.

Fire burned in Kevin's veins. His father would do anything to erase his mother. But this was ridiculous.

The light stuttered to green.

Kevin hit the gas and switched lanes. Thankfully, there wasn't anyone around to get in the way. He barreled down the block, toward his father's house.

TWENTY MINUTES LATER, Kevin walked in the front door of his dad's house and found his dad carrying boxes up from the basement.

"Dad?"

"Oh, hey Kevin." He slid the box on top of another in the corner of the living room. "You want to help carry boxes?"

"What happened to giving us time to go through everything?" Kevin tried to keep his cool. He tried, but his dad just asked him to help with this whole farce.

His father sighed. "Kevin, you've had years to deal with it. I asked you to pick out what you wanted. Your brother and sister did. Why can't you? How many times did I ask?"

"I don't know, Dad." Kevin wasn't sure which question he was answering, but the answer was the same for both. "I was in the military."

"You were, Kevin. Past tense. You're here now." His father took a towel from a pair of stacked side tables and wiped down his hands.

"Are you getting rid of Mom's tables?"

"I bought new furniture." His father twisted the towel in his hands. He had the audacity to look like he was nervous. That was the least he should be.

"So you're just getting rid of it all?"

His dad dropped the towel as a sigh whooshed past his lips. "I need to move on, son."

"So I get nothing."

"I told you to take what you wanted."

"I haven't been here that long. I haven't even had time to get my own place." Kevin's voice rose as the blood pressure pulsed in his ears.

"You've had time. You choose not to take care of it."

Kevin shook his head. It didn't matter what he said. His dad wouldn't care. "Whatever, Dad."

"Yeah, whatever. I get you don't want to take the time to do what needs to be done. That laziness has always been your downfall."

There it was. Kevin was inadequate. Kevin was lazy. It was like his father was a walking thesaurus of every bad adjective and they all applied to Kevin.

"You started moving her things to the basement before she was in the ground. You couldn't wait to get rid of her."

"Get the hell out of my house," his father roared.

"Gladly." Kevin would happily leave. The man who claimed to be his father was a complete asshole. Always had been. Given the trajectory of his life, he always would be. "If you don't watch it, you're going to die alone. Miserable and alone."

"Where did I go wrong with you? Maggie and Kyle were never like this."

"Yeah, yeah, they were perfect and I was a constant disappointment. You don't need to remind me."

"I didn't say that."

"You didn't have to. You found plenty of ways to show me how much I disappoint you every day of my life. I get it. I'm the reason Mom's dead. I shouldn't have left her alone that day. It's my fault, so I should be punished for it."

"That's not what I said..." His father actually stuttered. Apparently he didn't like to be slapped with the truth.

"What I don't get, is why didn't you just send me away? Why didn't you just have me live with someone else? Why keep torturing me?"

"I didn't..."

Kevin shook his head. He didn't want to hear it. Not anymore. He was done. "Do what you want with Mom's stuff. I don't care anymore."

Kevin walked out the door, and didn't give a shit if the door hit him on the way out. As long as he was gone.

He'd put up with his father for long enough. It was time to be done with him.

LETI HAD KIND OF HOPED that Kevin would be here, but he had his medical evaluation. So having Maggie as a babysitter was expected. What wasn't expected was having her still here at ten o'clock at night.

The two of them sat on opposite ends of the couch watching TV, slippered feet touching. The final scene of *Deadpool* finished as they both laughed. "You know you don't have to stay here," Leti told her. "You can go snuggle with Chase anytime."

"My brother would freak out."

"I think you're overestimating your brother's care for me." Leti knew he didn't care. Not the way she wanted.

"He cares about you."

"Not wanting someone to kill me isn't the same thing as caring for me."

"It's more than that." Maggie kept trying to paint her brother as a decent guy, but Leti wasn't so sure anymore. Maggie's phone chimed and she looked at the thing. Her brows drew together.

"Is everything okay?"

Maggie kept reading and nodded. "Yeah. I think so. Just my dad."

"Does he need you?"

"It feels like you're trying to get rid of me." Maggie laughed.

"No. It's not that. I just feel bad that you're stuck here like a prisoner."

"How is this prison? I got my girl, a glass of wine, and Ryan Reynolds on TV. I have everything I need."

"Please. You've been checking your phone all night."

"I haven't."

"It's okay. If I had a Chase waiting for me, I'd be checking my phone too."

"Kevin is waiting for you."

"He's not." The whole conversation was making Leti tired. She didn't want to talk about it anymore. She needed to talk about something else... anything else. "Tomorrow, we need to go to the house and pick up more of Pork Chop's meds. I should have just grabbed a full one, but I wasn't thinking."

"It's not safe. Can't we call the vet and get a refill?"

"That's the thing. I don't have any refills left, and there's no way they'll give me a new prescription so soon. It's a huge hassle."

"Okay. So what happens if he doesn't get his meds?"

"He'll start having seizures. He'll trip and lay around because he's just not feeling right. You can see it in his eyes."

"So, it's bad." Maggie curled her lip. "We're not letting the little guy suffer."

In appreciation, Pork Chop raised his head from his sleeping position on the floor. He stretched and repositioned himself before his eyes closed again.

"Yeah, it's not pleasant for him."

"Okay. We'll have to take care of him."

"Good." Leti stood up and smiled because she wanted Maggie to head there with her, but she'd go alone if she had to. "I should go to bed. Did you want to take your room?"

"No, I'm heading to Chase's. I'm sure Kevin will be

here any minute." Maggie had more faith in her brother than Leti.

"Goodnight." Leti reached the bedroom and heard the back door open. She left the door slightly ajar as she slid off her slippers.

Maggie's voice came from the living room. "Where the heck have you been?" She was obviously angry. There was an edge to her tone that Maggie didn't use often.

"I had the medical evaluation. You know, because I'm trying to become a cop." His tone wasn't much better.

"Why weren't you here earlier? Your doctor appointment was at five. It's after ten."

"I know how time works. I didn't know you were keeping tabs on me."

"I wasn't, you ass." Maggie's voice raised a few octaves. "Why did you stop at Dad's?"

"Don't get in the middle of this, Maggie."

"I'm trying not to. But what did you say to him? He was upset." Maggie was quiet for a minute. They both were. Then she continued. "What's wrong with you?"

"Yeah, it's all me." Kevin's voice lowered. "I'm the problem and everyone else is blameless."

"Kevin. You've been acting weird."

"I'm trying to help with the investigation while trying to get on the force. I'm stressed out, Maggie."

"Is that why you're treating Leti like crap?'

"I'm not treating her like anything."

Maggie sighed. "She was worried about you."

"She shouldn't be."

"Why?"

"Because she's not my mother."

"Given what I'm assuming you two have done together, I would sure hope she's not your mother." She sighed again. "You haven't been treating her right. You're hot one minute, cold the next."

"Did she tell you that?" Kevin's tone said he didn't like them talking about him. Not that it was any of his business what she did, but Leti felt better knowing she hadn't revealed any secrets.

"No. She didn't say anything. I have eyes. I mean, you seem to like her but then not. I don't want you hurting her. What is she to you?"

"She's nothing."

Leti's heart deflated. She actually felt the tear where the air slowly leaked from her chest, leaving a giant, gaping hole.

"You're an idiot." Maggie was close. Kevin was an idiot, but so was Leti. She fell for him.

Leti didn't want to hear another word. She was done. She closed the door and locked it before sliding into bed. The sooner this case was over, the better. Then Kevin would get his job at Chicago PD and she'd never have to see him again.

KEVIN WAS nervous and he had no idea why. They were standing in the living room of the obviously heartbroken Cindy Lidell, the woman whose daughter was killed during all this mess. At least they thought she was killed because of all this. They still hadn't found anything out.

Pictures were scattered on shelves that lined every wall. Pictures of Cindy with a younger woman, probably her daughter, both of them smiling and happy. Kevin walked along the shrine of photos, taking in all the smiles. Ceramic figurines wearing nurse scrubs lined the shelves between the frames. A plaque read *Nurses do it best.*

"Are you a nurse?" Kevin asked as Cindy walked up beside him. She looked very different from the photos, shadows rimming her eyes and blond hair graying at the temples.

"No, that was Pauline's love." She picked up a

framed photo of the younger woman, this time wearing scrubs. A giant smile on her face. Her hair was similar, the eye color was different. The smile was the same. "This is her."

He took the memory from her as tears pooled in her eyes. "It probably seems weird that I keep all of this," Cindy said.

"Not at all." Kevin nodded to a figurine of a nurse kneeling in front of a boy, his hand wrapped in a handkerchief with a splat of blood. "That's a Hummel, right?"

"It is." Cindy smiled, and it almost turned up to her eyes.

"My mom loved them. My dad still has them. When I want to feel closer to my mom, I visit the Hummels." He would go into the living room at his dad's house and look around. He could still feel her there. Of course, now his dad was trying to get rid of them.

"It does offer a bit of solace, doesn't it?" She smiled. The first real smile since he'd walked into the small apartment.

He'd been mad at his dad for boxing up those figurines, but this—this wasn't healthy, having so many memories clogging up the space. Everywhere she turned was another reminder of the daughter she'd lost. How could she breathe?

"It's nice to have someone understand. Most people just judge me. They think I should just move on and let her go." She ran a finger along a frame with her and her daughter—all smiles. "It's hard to move on when you lose your best friend, and no one will believe you."

"What don't they believe?" Leti walked over and rested a hand on the woman's shoulder. "Because we will believe you."

Cindy nodded and moved to the couch. "Did you want to sit?"

"Thank you." Leti sat next to the woman and Kevin stayed off to the side. There wasn't another chair in the room, and he didn't want to get in the way.

"I'm so sorry." Cindy must have noticed him standing, because she jumped up from the couch. "Let me get you a chair."

Kevin shook his head. "It's okay. I can stand."

"No. That's rude." The despair in her eyes said this bothered her and they wouldn't get any information if they didn't get past it.

Kevin followed as she went through a door to the kitchen. He might not need a chair, but he didn't want her carrying one if she wasn't going to listen to him. "I can move the chair to the living room, if you can hold the door." He waited till she moved away from the chair, then lifted it up." He followed her back into the living room. "Where should I put this?"

"Right here is fine." Cindy pointed to a space next to the couch and then she sat next to Leti. "I'm sorry. I haven't had anyone over since Pauline left. It just didn't feel right."

Kevin's heart broke watching this woman. She didn't match the person in the photos. The photos showed someone happy and vivacious. Who seemed to have fun and enjoy life. This woman was a shell.

Dammit.

His dad was right. Keeping his mother's stuff out and bathing in her memory wasn't healthy. Kevin needed to get past his past or he'd be alone with a room full of Hummels.

He looked over at Leti and couldn't help his mind wandering. He didn't want the Hummels. He wanted her. He didn't want to lose what they had. He wanted to build on it.

She glared at him before resting a hand on Cindy's.

He might have to do a bit of groveling before she'd be willing to build on anything with him. But he hoped he hadn't messed up too bad.

LETI WANTED to hug this woman, scream for her, cry—all at once. She was obviously hurting. And this interview was not going to make things any easier. She was reliving her daughter's loss over and over again already.

"Are you alright to talk about this today? We can come back." Leti hated saying the words. They didn't have time to come back. If there was any other way, Leti would take it. But as it stood, they needed her help.

"Oh no. I'm good. You're already here." Cindy attempted a smile.

Kevin gave Leti a look like they should move on, or maybe he was looking at her like she was a nuisance.

Maybe both. He didn't seem to be liking her these days. She had no idea what she did, but whatever they had it was over. And now she just wanted him gone. The glare she gave him should have told him as much as she rested a hand on Cindy's hand. "If it gets to be too much at any time, please tell me and we'll stop."

"Thank you." Cindy's lips curved up as the pain crinkled her eyes. "But I want to help. I need the people who hurt my daughter to be punished."

"That's why we're here." Leti patted the woman's hand and Cindy pulled away with a small smile. "Your daughter was a nurse at Wacker's Children's Association, correct?"

"Yes. She worked on the South Side." Cindy smiled. "She loved that job. Well, she loved working with the kids."

"That must have been so rewarding for her."

"It was. Those kids relied on her and she loved them. They were run through the system like cattle. It broke her heart."

"How did they treat them like cattle?"

"You know. They ignored them. Ignored the complaints. If the kids had trouble that required time or money, they'd push it off with red tape and policies till the child was adopted. And if they weren't adopted, they'd just pretend it didn't exist."

"Sounds frustrating." Leti could understand why Pauline had a broken heart. Watching kids as they were overlooked and ignored couldn't have been easy.

"It was. Pauline tried to talk to her supervisor, but they didn't care."

"Did she talk to Jordan Strong?"

"That's him." Cindy's face clouded and a scowl twisted her lips. "He's an evil man."

"What did he do?" Kevin said from his chair. A dark look settled on his face as he leaned forward, his elbows on his knees.

Cindy bit her lip as she worried her fingers in her lap.

Leti wasn't sure why the woman wasn't shouting from the mountaintops. She'd seemed so eager to talk given, what Leti had read. But this woman seemed scared.

"Are you worried they'll find out you talked to us? I swear we won't say anything."

"I'm not worried about me." Cindy smiled. "I don't have anything to live for. I'm worried about you. The last person who went after these people ended up dead. They're not good people."

"I understand. But we have good people on our side. Police and the law. We'll be careful." Kevin said it like an oath.

And Leti agreed. She had no desire to let these men get away with this any longer than they had.

"Okay." Cindy nodded but her fingers still slithered around themselves. "Pauline noticed that one of her kids, Derek, had been diagnosed with ADHD. He was having trouble in school, but Pauline was told that he didn't need medication and that the doctor had suggested therapy. She watched Derek get worse and worse and she couldn't figure out what was going wrong. Turned out, the doctor had prescribed medication. They changed the paperwork so they could give the medication to someone else."

"Why would they do that?" Leti didn't understand. Why let a child suffer without medication? It didn't make any sense.

"They were selling it out of the park down the block," Cindy said, her voice low.

"Selling it?" Kevin said, sounding as shocked as Leti felt. Just when she thought this couldn't get any worse, Wacker Children's seemed to get worse.

"Was she sure they were selling it? I mean... how did she know?" Leti didn't want to call her daughter a liar, but she also didn't want to believe this. She didn't know why selling drugs was so far out of left field given all the things the association seemed to be doing. But it added one more thing to an outrageous list of felonies.

Cindy shook her head. "Derek started acting out with his potential adoptive parents. Once, they had him for a weekend visit, and they brought him back to the shelter early because he kept running away. He kept following a local dog. The couple were rethinking adopting him. So Pauline called the doctor to see what could be done. She thought maybe he'd change his mind about prescribing medication."

"Did he change his mind?" Leti asked.

"He said they could up the dose if it wasn't working. Pauline admitted she was confused, since Derek wasn't on any medication. The doctor said that he'd prescribed medication, and then wanted to know why he wasn't on it."

"So what happened to it?"

"That's the question. Pauline looked at Derek's paperwork to make sure, and it stated no medication. So she thought she'd ask her boss, Jordan. She knew she could trust him. They'd dated for over a year."

"Dated? How long ago?" Kevin asked.

"A year ago."

"Doesn't he have two children?" Kevin asked the obvious question before Leti could. Last they'd seen, he had two children who looked to be around ten or so. Of course, he could've been divorced. But Leti would have sworn she saw a ring on his finger.

Cindy sighed. "It wasn't her best decision. He told her he was in the process of getting a divorce."

"Was he?"

"I don't know. All I know is that he and his wife are still married."

"What did Jordan say when she told him about the paperwork?"

"He said there must be a mix-up, and he'd get Derek the meds. Later that afternoon, he brought her a baggie with a few pills. She planned to give those to Derek, but he was scheduled to spend a week with his new family, so she got a scrip from the doctor for a week's worth of medication. When she went to fill it, the pharmacy refused. They said they'd already filled two prescriptions for Derek this month."

"Two?" Leti wasn't positive, but she was sure that was fishy. "Could they have accidentally used the medication for another child?"

"That's what she thought at first. So she went back to Jordan, and he freaked out. Told her not to go behind his back ever again. If she needed medication, she should have come to him. He told her she overstepped."

"But she's the nurse. Medication is her job," Kevin said.

"Exactly. It didn't add up. So one night she went through his desk and found baggies full of meds. Ritalin. Opioids. She also found a list of kid's names. Some she recognized. Some she'd never seen before. A few of the names were for kids that had been in the shelter a few years before but hadn't been in the shelter in a while. She watched him over the next few weeks. Every Thursday he would put some baggies into the bank deposit pouch and give it to a courier."

"Would a shelter have a bank deposit every week?" Leti asked, brain kicking into high gear. "It's not like they bring in money that often, do they?"

"Jordan was known for being very charismatic. He could get money from a turnip."

Leti was pretty sure the saying was blood from a turnip, but Cindy's way worked too.

Cindy continued. "It might have been cash deposits other times, but not the times Pauline saw. She followed the courier to the park, and he opened the bag, handed baggies to a couple teens and kept a few for himself."

"So what did she do after that?" Leti figured she'd have to ask Maggie to surveil the park.

"She couldn't go to Jordan. He was obviously part of it. She'd met one of the board members at a black and white dinner a few years ago. She thought she could trust him."

Leti's veins went ice cold as a chill ran through her body. She knew whose name was about to pop out of this woman's mouth. And it wasn't good.

"Stanley Welford said he'd look into it, and asked if Jordan knew she was looking into this. She explained how she'd approached him once already. Welford said he'd help. A week later, Jordan confronted her in the hall. Told her to back off. She told him she had proof and she'd gone to the board, and they would have his job. He called her a stupid whore. Two days later she was accidentally shot in a drive-by."

Leti knew this already, but hearing it from Cindy made her feel dizzy. "Accidentally?"

"They said the shots were meant for a gang member who was in the shelter to pick up his son. She was in the wrong place at the wrong time. Mr. Welford tried to help. He was so upset my daughter was hurt."

Tried to help. Yeah right. It took everything for Leti to keep her eyeroll to herself and not use her outside voice. No need to be rude to this grieving woman who didn't know who to trust. "Did she find anything else before the accident? Or is there anything else?"

"She didn't, but it was weird. They never found her cell phone. She always had that on her. As a nurse she was always on call, so she never went anywhere without it."

"They didn't find it at the crime scene?" Leti felt naked without her phone. She couldn't imagine leaving it behind.

"No."

"Could someone have stolen it?" Kevin asked.

Cindy cocked her head to the side. "Maybe, but they left her purse with her credit cards and her money. The only thing missing was her phone. Why would they do that?"

"Do you have any theories?" Leti definitely had a few, but she wanted to hear what Cindy thought before sharing with the class.

"She had pictures with Jordan on her phone. He was probably afraid I'd go to his wife."

Leti said, "You mentioned that Pauline had proof that she brought to Stanley Welford. Do you know what that proof was?"

"I'm not sure. I didn't think to ask, I was so worried about Jordan trying something on her."

Cindy seemed to have had a singular focus on Jordan during all this. Not that he wasn't an awful guy, apparently worse than even Leti thought, but he was just a cog in the wheel of ickiness.

"Could she have taken pictures?" Leti asked her. "Maybe gotten pictures of the baggies, or the teens?"

Cindy's eyes widened. "Oh goodness, that's why they took her phone."

"It could have been partly to do with Jordan, but maybe it was bigger than his affair."

"I suppose," Cindy said slowly, "but he was unhinged. Once the relationship was over, he was horrible to her. Stalking her. Trying to get her fired. Giving her dangerous assignments. I just figured he didn't want all the crazy texts and threats he'd sent out there."

Yeah, Jordan was a heck of a lot worse than Leti thought.

"So, do you think he did this and we can prove it?" The anticipation and hope on Cindy's face was enough for Leti to want to say yes. But this didn't tie him to the private adoptions or tell them how those adoptions were working. She needed that before they could go after him for any of it. It didn't help that Cindy's emotions were a ticking time bomb and everything would go to heck if she got involved.

Leti did her best to project calm, concerned, and capable. "I think we have a good start, but I need you to keep this between us. Don't tell anyone, not even your best friend. If he finds out what we know, my life will be in danger as well as countless children." Leti stood up, ignoring the wobble in her knees.

"Of course." Cindy followed Leti to the door.

"Thank you," Leti said.

"We'll make him pay." Kevin looked so earnest as he said it, Leti believed he meant every word. And honestly, she wanted to make this guy suffer too.

Cindy opened the door and turned to Leti. "Can you do me a favor?"

"Sure." Leti held her breath. She wasn't going to do anything illegal, and given the story, this woman might be desperate enough to ask.

"Can you tell me after it happens?" Cindy twisted her fingers together. "I just want to know that he's in jail."

"Absolutely." Leti leaned in and Cindy latched on for a hug. The woman was frail and her breathing was heavy. She was holding the weight of the world on her shoulders. And Leti wanted to help.

Leti drew back. "We'll make sure you have front row at the trial."

Cindy's smile lit up the dingy hallway.

Leti was so taking this creep down. For Cindy and Pauline. For all the kids like Erica. No matter what it cost.

LATER THAT AFTERNOON, Leti sat next to Kevin at Café Calao, facing Rick Cullen across a table. She didn't like this at all. She didn't like willingly hanging out with bad guys.

And Rick Cullen was bad.

Most likely part of a drug ring, and maybe a kidnapper, killer, and thief. Even if he wasn't any of those things, he was evil-adjacent.

Rick's impeccably tailored suit gave him an aura of legitimacy. This whole thing was anything but legitimate. "As we discussed over the phone, I'll need your driver's licenses and social security numbers to get started. We can do the fingerprints later."

"I still don't understand why you need that." Kevin was playing the part of bad cop.

Rick adjusted his collar. He didn't seem to like the bad-cop vibe. "I need to do a complete background check before I would be comfortable placing any child with you."

"That makes perfect sense." Leti wanted to glare at Kevin, give him some sort of sign to stop with the bad-cop game, but she also didn't want Rick to think anything was wrong. She handed him her very not-legitimate driver's license and slid over the equally fake social security cards. "I brought these in case you needed them."

"I don't need the actual cards." Rick opened the camera on his phone and took a picture

She smiled. "I wanted to make sure you had every-thing you need. We've been waiting so long." She didn't mention that Danni had gotten them the fake cards about twenty minutes ago and they hadn't had time to memorize the numbers. Not that she had any desire to memorize fake numbers.

Kevin pulled out his fake driver's license and gave it to Rick.

"This is perfect." Rick pushed the cards back across the table. He opened his briefcase and pulled out a folder. Slid it toward them. "This is Josefine. She's six months old."

Leti used her index finger to open the file. A dossier and pictures were scattered inside. She picked up the one on top. A little baby with pink chubby cheeks and a smattering of dark hair. "She's beautiful." Leti would bet her parents thought so too.

"She is beautiful," Kevin agreed. He reached for Leti, but she pulled back. It was instinct. She wasn't thinking. But in her world, Kevin was the bad guy who was trying to break her heart.

Rick stared at the interaction like a hawk watching

his prey. A weird look in his eyes. Stiff shoulders. He wasn't buying their relationship. He was getting suspicious.

Leti reached over and grabbed Kevin's hand. She smiled at him. Nothing to see here. Just a loving couple and he wasn't a jerk who just up and left her bed never to return. He wouldn't do all that and not explain what's going on. That would be a horrible thing to do, and he was a good guy who deserved to raise this child.

Hopefully all that was not written on her face.

She tried to distract both men with a baby picture. "Isn't she beautiful."

Unfortunately, that was less of a man-type distraction.

Rick's smile didn't look friendly. "Jordan mentioned what a loving couple you two were."

"That's sweet." She dragged Kevin's hand closer to her. She could pretend.

Given the way Rick was eye-humping them both like he could see inside their soul, he didn't like what he saw.

Kevin pulled his hand away and sighed. "Maybe because that morning I didn't forget to put the toilet seat down."

Leti's eyes grew wide. What was he doing? They didn't give children to couples that fought.

Rick laughed. "My wife is the same way."

Or maybe they did. Rick's demeanor changed. His posture loosened and his neck relaxed. He was no longer watching them like he wanted to eat their souls. Men were weird.

"You mean your wife is logical?" Leti could play along. "When a woman goes to sit without a seat, we literally fall in. It's like a bidet without the clean."

Rick roared. "Yep. We've had this same argument." He closed his briefcase and tapped the folder on the table. "If you have any questions, reach out. Costs and requirements are in the folder."

Leti pulled out a page with numbers.

Whoa. Adoption fee. Transportation fee. Total cost? Six figures.

That number was enough to stop her heart. Did normal people actually have the money to adopt this way? How? The people who came to him must be desperate. And he preyed on them.

"Problem?" Rick asked.

Kevin shook his head, smiling. "Nope."

"I'll be in touch." Rick stood up and Kevin followed. They shook hands.

Leti inched out of the booth and shook his hand as well.

"Thank you," Kevin said.

Rick smiled. "I'm just glad I can help a nice family like yourself." He nodded before heading toward the front of the café and out the door.

Leti grabbed the folder in one hand and Kevin's hand in the other. They both headed out of the café without saying a word. She didn't know if they were being watched. She didn't know anything at this point. All she did know was that she needed to get this information to Danni. Hopefully, Danni could use it to find out who this child really was and what exactly they were dealing with.

KEVIN DROVE to Busted in silence. Not that he was alone, but he might as well have been. He'd tried to start a conversation with Leti but she wanted none of it. He'd tried talking about the meeting, the weather, and even about the Cubs. What Chicagoan didn't want to talk about the Cubs? Whether you loved them or hated them, there was always something to say.

But nothing. She faced the window like all the secrets of the world were harbored in the landscape as they passed by.

He still had one ace up his sleeve. "How do you think Pork Chop is handling staying at Maggie's?"

"He's fine. He wasn't really eating the first day or so, but I think it was more about not being able to find his food bowl." She turned back to the scenery. They were passing rundown warehouses, so calling it scenery was generous.

"Now he's an old pro, then, huh?"

She grunted.

He was losing her. He needed a new topic. Before he could come up with something brilliant, because let's face it, brilliance wasn't his forte, Leti turned to him. "By the way, I need to go to my house tonight."

Of all the things he'd thought she'd want, going to her house wasn't one of them. "Why?"

"I need to get more of Pork Chop's medication."

"Can't we just get some from the pharmacy?"

"I don't have any refills left. It's too complicated, and he only has enough for tonight."

"We'll go tonight, then. I don't want the little guy to suffer." And he didn't. The way Leti smiled, he realized that was the right answer. Pork Chop meant a lot to her, and the little guy meant a lot to him too. He was good dog.

The ice in the stare out the window—her attention had returned there—had thawed a little bit.

His phone rang. The name on the screen said it was Maggie. He used the hands-free to answer the call. "You're on speaker."

"Hi to you, too."

"Hi." He thought she'd want to know she was on speaker, not be bogged down with pleasantries.

Leti laughed. "Hi, Maggie."

He couldn't win. He wanted to make her laugh like that. Yeah. He was jealous of his sister's ability to make her best friend laugh. Pathetic.

"How did it go?" Maggie asked.

"Weird." Leti wasn't kidding. It had been weird. At one point, he was sure that Rick could see through right through them. He thought playing up the fighting married couple was the best option to make sure they didn't appear suspicious. Of course, if Leti hadn't been avoiding his touch, they wouldn't have needed all the pretense. Of course, if he hadn't been acting like an ass, she wouldn't have been avoiding his touch.

"We have the file for a child we can adopt. We're bringing it to Danni now," Leti said.

"Great. Kevin, I need you to drop off Leti and the file and then head over to Dad's."

That wasn't going to happen. "I have work to do."

"You don't."

"I need to watch Leti. We're getting too close." He wasn't lying.

"I'll watch over Leti until you get back."

"I need to take Leti to get Pork Chop's meds."

"Stop making excuses," Maggie snapped. "I will watch Leti and take her to her parents' house. You go see Dad. He has some things of Mom's he wants to give you."

Kevin wanted to say no. He didn't want to deal with his dad on a good day. Today was not a good day. But he wanted something of his mom's to remember her by. His memory of her was fuzzy at best. Looking at her things gave him a glimpse into her. It made her feel close, if only for a moment. "Fine, I'll go to Dad's."

"Good. Leti, I'll see you when you get to Busted."

"Bye."

Maggie hung up the call and Kevin leaned his foot back from the accelerator. He was not in a hurry to get to his Dad's.

"It's good that you're going to see your dad," Leti said.

"I guess." He sighed. "I think you should wait for me to go get Pork Chop's medication."

"I guess." Leti went back to staring out the window. She looked about as thrilled as he felt.

LATER ON, Leti and Maggie sat in Maggie's living room, poring over the documentation. Leti had given copies to Danni and she was working her magic, but Leti kept hoping they would find something, the smoking gun to give to the authorities.

Leti was waiting for the call from Rick, but she wasn't sure when he'd get back in touch with them. Not that she had the money to adopt a child, but that was probably why the impending contact was weighing on her mind.

"Has he called?" Maggie meant Rick.

"Not yet. And I've tried the number on the card multiple times and no one answers."

"Maybe he gets tired of parents calling all day and night wanting to know the status."

"Probably." Leti could understand that. Parents able to spend this kind of money would be pretty desperate, and that desperation might lead to overzealous use of the telephone.

"I don't see anything we can use." Maggie tossed the papers into the folder and sighed.

"Hopefully Danni has better luck." It was more than just hope. Leti needed Danni to have better luck.

"I'm sure she'll find something." Maggie closed the folder. "She's a master at finding the obscure."

"Yeah, I'm glad she's on our side."

"Amen. The woman could be dangerous." Maggie laughed and leaned back on the couch. She watched Leti for a moment, then asked, "So, how are things going with Kevin?"

The one topic Leti didn't want to talk about. Nice job, Maggie. "You know better than I do." Way to deflect. Leti was proud of her answer. It was easier to deflect than talk badly about her best friend's brother.

Maggie flopped her head back. "He's going through something."

"Yeah, well so am I, but do you see me treating him like garbage?" Anger burned in Leti's veins. Going through things didn't give anyone the right to treat people like they were nothing.

"No."

"Exactly. You don't do that."

"I know." Maggie leaned forward and shook her head. "My brother can be a real pain, but he's a good guy. He just has some issues."

"I get it. But I don't deserve to be treated like a side-note in someone's life."

Maggie nodded. "You don't."

Leti looked at the time. "I need to feed Pork Chop and give him his medication. After that, why don't we head over to my house and pick up the rest of the meds."

"You're in pajamas," Maggie said.

Leti shrugged. These blue plaid cotton pajamas were her comfort clothes. "We're not going to see anyone. We'll run in and run out."

"We should wait for Kevin."

"Why? I'm nothing to him." Leti stood up and walked into the kitchen, Pork Chop hot on her trail.

Maggie groaned. "You heard that. That's why you're so pissed."

Leti filled Pork Chop's bowl and added his liquid medication on top before setting his bowl on the floor. Once he began eating the kibble, she went into Maggie's bedroom and put on her gym shoes.

"He didn't mean it. You know that right?" Maggie stood in the doorway.

"Does that matter?" Leti stared at the sweatshirt Kevin had left behind for a minute, then shrugged it on. She wanted to believe that he didn't mean it, but who cared. He'd said the words. If he meant it or if he didn't, it didn't matter. She deserved better.

"I really want to say it does, because he's better with you. But you don't deserve that." Maggie's head hung down. "No one does."

"Thank you." Leti sat on the edge of the bed. It meant a lot that Maggie believed Leti deserved more. Sometimes Leti didn't always believe that. It was nice to hear.

Maggie smiled. "I love you, honey. You deserve the world."

"I love you too." Leti stood up and hugged Maggie. She was a great friend. Leti pulled away and got her purse and car keys. She checked on Pork Chop, who was now stretched out in his bed, chewing on a toy. "Are you coming with or are you going to make me go alone?"

"I'm not letting you go alone." Maggie opened her arm wide and stood off to the side. "Lead the way."

Leti didn't want to admit it, but she was thankful she didn't have to do this alone. It might just be a quick trip to pick up some meds, but it was good to have her friend by her side.

KEVIN WALKED into his dad's house and tried not to yell. The lights were off, but he could tell that the boxes were gone. He must've donated them already.

Great.

"Dad." Kevin stepped into the kitchen and found his dad standing over the stove.

"I'm making chili." His dad wiped his hands on an apron that said *chasin' capsaicin* and took a pull from a beer on the counter. He leaned against the edge. "Can I get you something to drink?"

"I'll take a beer." Kevin had a feeling this conversation was going to take more than a beer to get through, but beggars couldn't be choosers. And maybe a beer would make whatever this was going to be bearable.

His dad handed a bottle to him and took off the apron before walking to the dining room. He sat at the table, twisting his own bottle in his hands. Kevin followed. He had a feeling that was what was expected. But he couldn't bring himself to sit down. He wanted the freedom to run if he needed to.

His father wiped his hands on his pants and slid a piece of paper across the table. It appeared to be blank until he turned it over. "I wanted to be the one to tell you. Congratulations, you passed the pre-employment hiring. Welcome to the Chicago Police Department."

"You couldn't just leave well enough alone, could you? I told you I didn't want your help." Kevin couldn't believe his dad pulled strings. He told him not to. He told him he wanted to do this alone. "Do you think I'm just inept, that I can't do anything on my own?"

"You were always so much like your mom." His father looked at him almost reverently. It was unnerving. "You have her eyes and her stubborn streak. She was always so independent."

Kevin had never heard him talk about his mother this way. Or talk about how Kevin was like his mother. "She was?"

"Yes." His father flattened the paper and slid it further toward Kevin. "I was always in awe of her. It's why I'm always in awe of you."

Kevin didn't say anything, but his disbelief was probably written on his face, because his dad laughed and continued. "I never had to worry about you. Do you remember Kyle growing up? I had to stay on top of him for everything. I had to make sure he did his homework and practice with him. I couldn't let my guard down at all with him or he'd just stop everything. With

Maggie, things were a little better. She's more like you and your mom, but she gets distracted easily. I had to watch her too.

"But you never needed me. Never. Do you know how hard it was to watch you thrive without me? To see your mother in you and not have her here. When you didn't want to go on in school, you joined the military. You built a career there. You didn't need me then. And not now. Not even to get you into the Chicago Police Department. I'm the Chief. I could've handed you anything you wanted and you wouldn't take it. Do you honestly think your brother would've turned down something that was handed to him?"

"No." It was true. Kyle wasn't a bad guy, but he wasn't as strong as Maggie and Kevin.

"I didn't pull any strings, son." He took a drink from the beer. "I let you succeed and fail on your own. And just like I thought you'd do, you succeeded. Without me. It's what you always do. I'm proud of you."

Kevin pulled out the chair across from his father and sat down, not sure how to feel. He'd passed. On his own. But all he could think about was what his dad said. "So you treated me like I was an inconvenience because I didn't worship at your feet?" His father was exhausting.

"That's not what I meant." His father ran a hand through his hair. "Hell, maybe it is. I was wrong. I know you deserve a lot more, but I'm sorry."

"Is this why you wanted me to come here today?" Kevin could admit he was a bit disappointed. And yes, pissed. He'd thought he'd get a piece of Mom to take home with him.

"That, and I put all your mom's things back." His father pointed toward the living room. It was true. All the Hummels were on the shelves. All the pictures. In his anger, Kevin hadn't noticed. To be fair, the lights were off.

Kevin walked into the room and turned on the lights. "Dad."

It was just as he remembered. Hummels covered all the surfaces with pictures thrown in. Déjà vu. He almost cried. It was just like Cindy's house, a shrine to someone gone. A large boulder keeping him from moving on. Keeping his father tethered to the past. "You didn't have to do this."

"I don't want you to forget your mom." His dad came up behind him. "She is not gone because of you. I never blamed you. You couldn't have known she would pass that day. None of us did. Every day, I blame myself for going into work. I could see she was struggling, but she told me she was fine." His father stopped. Cleared his throat. "I never should have asked you to watch her that morning. I never should have left. That was on me, not you. You were a kid."

Kevin's heart ached. All the words—the actions he'd prayed for over the years. He'd wanted his dad to accept him. He'd wanted his dad to tell him it wasn't his fault. Every word hit him square in the chest.

After a long moment, his dad continued. "I always saw her in you, and maybe that hurt a little too much, and I'm sorry, but that wasn't your fault either. I always loved you and knew you'd be alright. I know it doesn't make it right, but keeping her alive for you, that's my way of making it right. I hope you'll take that as my apology."

Kevin didn't know what to say or do. His voice hitched as he pushed the words out. "Dad, thank you. This means so much." He cleared his throat of the emotion lodged there. "But you need to let go, and so do I. We can't keep living in the past like this."

They both looked at the living room covered in in breakables. His father laughed. "I wish you would have told me before I unloaded all this stuff."

Kevin snorted. "How about I help wrap it all up and I'll pick a few favorites, so I can keep a piece of Mom with me."

"Deal. Not today, though." His father took another drink of beer. "Chili is ready. Have some dinner. We need to celebrate. My son is going to join the police force."

"Sounds good, Dad." If someone had asked him yesterday if he'd be happy to share a meal with his old man, Kevin never would have believed it. What a difference a day made.

CHAPTER TWENTY-THREE

LETI OPENED the back door of her parent's house as Maggie kept an eye on things. They'd scoped out the neighborhood. They hadn't noticed anyone watching the house. The ride had been quiet. Maggie had been on the phone talking to Chase. He'd been busy all night on a case and they hadn't had much of a chance to talk.

So Leti tried to give them some privacy by thinking. That wasn't always a good thing.

But this time, it might be okay. She wasn't going to give up. Well, she was done with men who didn't want her. She wasn't going to chase after Kevin. That was over. And she wasn't going to let her mom set her up with these rejects anymore.

She could do it on her own. She'd take control of her own love life. She just had to close out this case and then she could find someone who thought she meant the world. And on that note, she was taking control of everything. It was time for her to find her own place and admit she wasn't getting her CPA. She loved working with her friends. She loved what she did. It was time to embrace what she wanted.

Leti held the back door open so Maggie could go inside. "I'm going to check the house." Maggie drew her gun from her holster and walked through the kitchen toward the living room. "Be quick."

Leti went to the cabinet and pulled out a bottle of medication. A full one this time.

Having weird men in the house with knives made a girl do stupid things—or overlook stupid things, as it were.

While waiting for Maggie to come back into the kitchen, Leti slid the meds inside her purse. And waited.

Her cell phone rang. Danni. Leti took a deep breath. "Hi."

"So, I found Josefine," Danni said. "You might want to sit down."

Leti leaned against the counter and braced herself. "Okay."

"Josefine was reported kidnapped three months ago, by a woman in Chicago. She's a druggie who lives on the South Side."

Leti had a bad feeling about this. "Does she live by Sentry Park?"

"She does." Danni kept going. "And she went to rehab after the night her daughter disappeared. She's been trying to get the police to help her find Josefine. The police report says she nearly overdosed the night the baby disappeared. There was something in the drugs and she almost died."

"Like someone was trying to kill her." Acid sloshed in Leti's stomach.

"And take her baby," Danni agreed. "There's a pattern. So far, I've found six women in the city with the same story. Different parks. Different drugs. The cops wouldn't know where to look or even try to look."

"Because they're just drug addicts." Leti closed her eyes.

"Yeah. Josefine's real name is Genifer Cooper. And her mom has been looking everywhere for her."

"Is this enough? Can we stop them with this?"

"I think so," Danni said. "Get Maggie and come to the office. We need to talk. I think he's laundering the money from these private adoptions through Wacker Children's."

That explained the large sums of money. Between the drugs and the adoptions, he was making a killing. No pun intended. "We'll be there in a half hour." Leti hung up the phone. "Hey Maggie, are you ready?" she called into the air. For someone who wanted Leti to hurry, Maggie was sure taking her time. Although the house was pretty big.

Leti walked into the living room and stopped. Maggie was face down on the floor with a man standing over her. A gun was in his hand.

Something hard tapped at her temple. Round and cold. She was assuming a gun. She'd never had one this close before.

"Don't move."

Leti couldn't move. Heck, she couldn't breathe. She

wanted to lift her hands over her head like they did in the movies, but they were frozen in place.

They were in so much trouble.

KEVIN FELT PRETTY good as he unlocked the door to Maggie's house. Not that he liked to admit to his sister that she was right, but she had been. Tonight with his father had been long overdue.

He didn't realize what a weight his father's disapproval had been. How much it hurt to think his father blamed him, heck that he blamed himself. But it really wasn't his fault. He always knew that logically, but it was harder to believe deep down. He still wasn't sure he truly believed it yet. It would take time.

But he needed to work on it, because he wanted to work things out with Leti—if she'd have him. He'd messed up and pulled away. He'd been there physically but he'd ghosted emotionally. It had been easier than admitting he was scared.

He was still scared. He was also tired of letting fear overtake his life. He wasn't going to live his life surrounded by the breakables of the past anymore. They were going in a box, and he was going to build his life around the present and his future. He just hoped Leti wanted to be part of it.

He opened the back door. Silence.

Pork Chop's collar didn't even jingle. The dog sat at the back door. Waiting. He should be basking in the women's attention, or the very least laying at their feet. Why was he at the door?

He looked around the kitchen, but there was nothing. "Leti?" He checked Maggie's bedroom as he walked by, and the light was off. No one was inside.

Pork Chop's collar tinkled as he followed Kevin through the house. He practically ran into the living room, hoping they were just being extra quiet. He didn't know what he expected. Giggling. Talking. The television covered in some half-naked MCU character. Nothing. They weren't here.

"Where did they go?" he asked Pork Chop. Or no one in particular. But deep down he knew where they went. She'd gone to get the little dog's meds.

She'd sworn she wouldn't go. Or maybe she hadn't. Maybe he'd asked her and she'd made some noncommittal sound. Either way, his sister should have known better.

His sister was smart though. He couldn't convict without proof. He lifted his cell phone and dialed her number. Voicemail. He dialed Leti. Voicemail.

He dialed Chase in a Hail Mary. Maybe the women had decided to grab ice cream, and told Chase but forget to tell him. Leti was still pretty pissed at him, but Maggie wouldn't have gone without reaching out.

But then again, the other option was she went to Leti's house without reaching out. Either option sucked.

"Hey man, have you heard from Maggie?" Kevin asked when Chase answered his cell phone.

"About an hour ago. They were heading to Leti's to pick up meds for the dog."

"Son of a..."

"Why?"

"Nothing. I told them I wanted to be there when they went back to the house. They're not answering their phones." Kevin didn't like where this conversation was going.

"I'm all the way on the north side, but I'm heading that way now. It might take a few minutes. Do you have your gun on you?" And from the panic in Chase's voice, neither did he.

"Always."

"Be ready to use it."

"Ten-Four." Kevin hung up the call and locked the house before running to his car.

CHAPTER TWENTY-FOUR

LETI'S CHEEK THROBBED. She'd never been punched in the face before. She didn't like it. Her eye felt like it was going to pop out of its socket. Her jaw pulsed. She didn't know why they kept hitting her.

She just couldn't understand. These men seemed to match the ones that had broken in that first night, but this time they weren't wearing masks. That didn't bode well for her. When they wore masks, there was a chance they didn't want her to recognize them. Now they didn't care. Not good.

"Please stop." Leti sat in a chair, her hands tied behind her back. Her feet tied to the legs of the chair. She never thought she'd let someone tie her up like this willingly, but it was hard to say no with the barrel of a gun to your head.

Her head hung down. She was so tired. Leti wanted to just go to sleep, but she didn't think Maggie and she would live through this. And there was no way they'd live through it if she passed out.

Maggie had been knocked cold before Leti had gotten in the room. She was tied up on the floor. They obviously didn't want her. They wanted Leti. And Leti was paying the price for whatever they wanted.

"We'll stop when you tell us what we want to know, sugar." The fat guy with bushy eyebrows tilted her chin up with his fingers so she was looking into his eyes. "Who do you work for?"

"I don't know what you mean. I work for Busted Detective Agency." Leti didn't want to get Enzo involved. It was bad enough she and Maggie were involved.

"Who hired you?"

"I found this on my own."

Bushy Eyebrows closed his fist and reeled it back. His arm flew forward, hitting Leti in the jaw. The impact tipped Leti's chair, and her head jerked with the force of the blow. The chair fell forward with a thump and her head snapped.

Skinny guy with the pinhead said, "She's not talking."

"She'll talk." Bushy Eyebrows pointed at Maggie. "Pull her over here."

Skinny guy grabbed Maggie's leg and dragged her closer to Leti.

"If you don't talk, I'm going to kill her." Bushy Eyebrows pulled his gun from his waistband and pointed the barrel at Maggie's head.

Leti didn't know what to do. She couldn't give them Enzo's name. She couldn't give them another person to kill like they'd murdered Pauline.

Pauline. She'd been a part of all this. Maybe it could work. "Pauline Lidell hired me."

"What?"

"Pauline Lidell hired me a year or so ago to look into her boyfriend. She thought he was cheating." Not a stretch. Once a cheater always a cheater, as they say. "While I was looking into him I found some financial anomalies and I gave her the information. She looked into it some more, but I told I'd help if she ever needed anything."

"She's dead, honey."

"Which was why I started looking into it again." She wasn't sure if they were buying it, but she had to own it now. Even if it meant she got another black eye. Or worse.

Bushy Eyebrow slid his gun back into pants and lifted his hand. Leti braced for impact, but there wasn't anything she could do. She closed her eyes, turned her cheek and prayed as his cell phone rang.

"Yeah," Bushy huffed into the phone. The *Peanuts* teacher was on the other end of the line, or maybe the cell phone wasn't loud enough for her to hear clearly. "She's saying she talked to Pauline Lidell."

More *wah wah wah wah.*

"We went over that."

Leti wanted to tell Bushy Eyebrows to put it on speaker, but she had no desire to be hit again. She opened an eye and watched as he talked.

"I don't think that's a good idea."

The noise from the phone increased, but she still couldn't make out any words.

"Fine." He ended the call and threw the phone on the couch.

"What's going on?" Pinhead stood by Maggie's body. She was still not moving but she seemed to be breathing, her chest rising and falling.

"They're coming here."

"The bosses?"

"Yeah." Bushy Eyebrows sat on the couch and retrieved his phone. He leaned back and poked at the screen. The bosses seemed to have bought her a little time. She just had to figure out what to do before they got here.

TEN MINUTES LATER, Leti was pulling at the ropes on her wrist. Her arms were exhausted. The joints in her shoulders sore and aching. The skin on her wrists were scratched to the point of raw, and the rope was barely loosened.

The front door to her house opened and in walked Rick, followed by an older man in a button-down shirt and tie. Bushy Eyebrows jumped up from the couch and stood next to Pinhead.

Rick walked over to where Maggie still lay on the floor. He kicked at her leg. "Is she alive?"

"Yeah."

Rick leaned down into Leti's face. "This one appears to be alive. Leticia Ramirez."

He knew her real name.

"Nice try with all that fake ID crap, but did you

really think we wouldn't recognize you? When someone comes after my money, I remember them."

"I didn't." She'd never tried to take his money.

"Don't lie to me," Rick yelled and grabbed her face. His fingers pinched at her bruised cheeks. She tried to pull away but he squeezed harder. The bruises burned. "You were looking into my business. That's my money."

"Rick, stand down," the older man said. He was obviously in charge.

Rick snapped his hand away, wrenching Leti's neck.

The older man looked at Bushy Eyebrows. "What happened to her?"

"She wouldn't talk."

"Seems a little overboard." The old man picked up a chair from the dining room and carried it over to where Leti sat. He sat in front of her. "Take these ropes off of her."

"Sir, I don't think…"

"I don't pay you to think. She's been through enough." He looked at Leti. "Are you going to try anything?"

She shook her head. She wasn't stupid. If her hands and legs were free, she might have a chance of getting out of this alive.

"See. She's not going to try anything." He leaned back in the chair as Bushy Eyebrows cut the ropes.

"So, Ms. Ramirez. Any relation to Mayor Ramirez?"

"No." She really wished she was related to him at the moment.

"That's too bad," he said. "Do you know who I am?"

"No." And she didn't. She had an idea, but she wanted him to tell her. Or not. Maybe if she didn't know who he was, he'd let her live when this was all said and done.

"I'm Stanley Welford."

Well there went that idea.

"You can call me Stanley, Ms. Ramirez. Who paid you to look into my businesses?"

"I was hired by Pauline Lidell."

"She's dead."

"I know." Leti didn't think Stanley was going to be easy to convince, and the two morons hadn't really seemed like they'd believed her. "I was working with her before she died. I offered to help if she needed anything else and when she passed, I thought I'd help.

"It's been a long time for you to just now get involved."

"I've been busy with other cases. I felt bad not sticking to my word, and her boyfriend was still out there."

"Her boyfriend? Do you mean Jordan?"

"Yeah, I wanted to see if he'd been cheating while he was with her. I wasn't sure if his wife had ever found out, so I was going to let her know."

Stanley laughed, a deep belly laugh. "So, wait. You're telling me all this is because you were looking into Jordan's cheating."

"She died before she got a full answer. We found out he was still married, but there was a chance he was dating someone else. She wanted to know. She deserved to know."

"She wasn't ever going to know anything ever again. Do I need to explain how death works?"

"No, but I could make his life a living hell. Tell his wife or his girlfriends about each other."

"I like you." Stanley laughed again. Apparently crazy, revenge-focused women were his thing.

"Does that mean I get to live?" She was pretty sure she knew the answer, but she thought she'd ask.

"Probably not."

"Maggie knows nothing about this." Leti pointed at her best friend. If she was doomed, she could at least try to save her best friend. "I didn't want her to know what was going on because it's a little crazy."

"She's the chief of police's daughter. I have no intention of making the CPD my enemy. That's why she's taking a nap. She'll be fine."

Leti's lungs pushed out a gulp of air. At least Maggie would be okay. Kevin would be upset that Maggie's friend was gone, but he'd survive. His sister would be safe.

"Leave the one on the floor. She'll come to and we'll be long gone." Stanley stood up. "Wipe this place down, then take this one to the cemetery and make it quick."

"Ms. Ramirez, pleasure meeting you." Stanley snapped his fingers at Rick. "Let's get out of here. Before the other one wakes up."

Stanley turned before he got to the front door and pointed at Leti. "And make sure you destroy her phone. I don't want anything she found to come to light. It would be sad if your friends all had unforeseeable accidents."

"What about her computer? Should we take that too?" Bushy Eyebrow asked. He might be a moron but on this he was smart. All her work was on her work computer. The partners just had to look. And they would.

"I have that handled. The agency is going to get one nasty virus." Stanley smiled as he walked out the front door. He called into the house before he shut the door, "Don't forget to wipe down the knob on this side."

LETI DIDN'T KNOW how computer viruses worked, but that did not sound good. Danni was going to kill this guy—which was good. Leti could hope vengeance wouldn't happen in her name, but anything in the name of Danni's network was fine by her.

Bushy Eyebrow yelled at Pinhead, "Grab her and let's go. I have things to do."

So Leti's death was cramping his style. She'd feel bad, but—uh, no. She needed to get her head back in the game. She didn't have much time if she was going to try something. Anything. She had to figure out what to do or she was going to be escorted to a local cemetery.

And never come back.

Her hands were still free. She had that going in her favor.

Pinhead pulled her to her feet. This was her chance.

CHAPTER TWENTY-FIVE

PINHEAD PUSHED her through the kitchen toward the back door while Bushy Eyebrows started wiping things down. He was busy, but there was still a problem. They were both armed and she was not. She looked over at the knife block on the counter. Kevin said that the amount of force needed was equal to your adversary's actions and intentions.

These guys had guns, and they were going to use them. On her. It was time she took it from him.

Leti turned to Pinhead and grabbed his right hand, exactly the way Kevin had showed her. She twisted with everything in her body. His wrist crunched as he went to his knees, exactly the way Kevin told her would happen. Except his head smacked on the corner of the counter with a terrible thud. His body slid down, his eyes closed. His body leaning up against the cabinet.

Heart in her throat, Leti fumbled the gun from his waistband before he woke up and tried to use it on her.

She aimed the gun at him and waited.

No movement. Not one inch. She used her foot to tap at his shoulder, and his body slid further down to the floor.

Oh no. His chest wasn't moving. She leaned over and checked his pulse. Kevins words kept playing in head, or she said it out loud. *Use just enough force to extricate yourself from the situation. Make it out alive.*

Leti couldn't look at Pinhead any more. She didn't want to think about the man who once was alive and now wasn't. Thanks to her.

It didn't matter. She didn't have a choice, it was him or her. Kevin told her to make it out alive. She chose to live.

"Let's get out of here," Bushy Eyebrows said from the other room.

She held up the gun and pointed it at the door Bushy Eyebrows was about to walk through. She wasn't exactly sure how guns worked, but she had an idea.

The big man lumbered into the kitchen. "Ready?" He was rolling a towel into a ball before he tossed it into the sink. His face went from shock to smirk when he saw her holding the gun. "What are you doing, little girl?"

"Don't move."

His smirk deepened. "You don't want to make this more difficult than it needs to be, baby."

"I'm pretty sure I do." She smiled. "If I'm going to die either way, I might as well go down swinging." She probably shouldn't have said that. It might give him ideas about swinging himself, given his current predicament.

He moved his hand to his gun.

"Put your hands up." She straightened her arms and tipped the gun toward his head.

His hands flipped up, moving away from his belt. "Calm down, sugar. Ain't no need to get crazy."

"I'm not your sugar, honey or baby. And I'm not crazy."

"Really? That gun you're pointing at me says something different."

For real? "You were pointing a gun at me twenty minutes ago and you're going to kill me."

Bushy Eyebrows smiled. "It's nothing personal."

"Neither is this."

"You know this won't stop me." Bushy Eyebrows took one step closer to her.

"Stop."

"I can't. I have a job. So if you want to stop me, you'll have to shoot me." He took one more step closer.

"I killed your partner." Leti stepped back and jerked her head at Pinhead. "I'll kill you."

Bushy Eyebrows grinned. "I see that. But even if you do pull the trigger, you probably won't hit me. No offense."

She was totally taking offense. "You're a big target."

He laughed. "I am, but that just means there's a lot of useless fluff to protect the goods." He had somehow moved within a few feet of her. One more step and he could grab her or the gun.

"Make it out alive," she whispered.

"What?" he snarled.

"Nothing." She aimed the gun at his chest, closed her eyes, and squeezed the trigger.

A loud roar came from her hands as the barrel kicked up and she stumbled backwards. Her ears rang. Her head spun. Bushy Eyebrows was splayed on the floor in the doorway. He didn't appear to be moving.

But wasn't that how all horror movies ended?

***

KEVIN PULLED up to Leti's house right behind the flashing lights of Chase's car. His heart raced as he ran for the front door, gun already in his hand, Chase on his heels. A loud bang came from inside.

Shit.

"Did you hear that?" Chase had his phone to his ear as he called it into the precinct.

Kevin flattened himself against the outside wall, and quickly glanced through the front window. Shit. "Maggie's down. I don't see anyone in the living room." Kevin tried the door, hoping it wasn't locked. Open. He slowly opened the door, wanting the element of surprise.

Chase took the lead, checking the closet near the front door. Kevin went through the dining room, inching to the opening by the kitchen.

Leti stood in the kitchen holding a gun. One man was face up on the floor.

Kevin paused, his gun raised. "Leti."

She looked at him with tears in her eyes. Her right

eye was swollen. Her lip bloody. Her cheek was already starting to bruise.

"Are you okay?" Kevin asked.

She didn't say anything, just went back to staring at the man on the floor.

"Is there anyone else here?" Kevin took a step, and saw the second body. Shit.

Leti swallowed. Shook her head. "No. I don't think so."

Chase walked in from the living room, his gun high. "The house is clear. Maggie is alive." He leaned down and checked the pulse of the man in the doorway. He looked at Kevin and shook his head. Dead.

"There's another one in here," Kevin said.

Chase slid past Leti and checked the other man. Another shake of his head. "Anyone else with these two?"

"I don't think so." Leti looked haunted. It broke Kevin's heart. "Rick Cullen and Stanley Welford were here, but they just left."

"How did they figure out who we were?" Kevin asked.

"The pictures on our driver's license."

"Ah."

Chase holstered his gun. He walked over to Leti. Slowly. "Can I have that gun?"

She looked at the gun in her hand like it was a foreign object that she'd never seen before. She didn't seem to know she was still holding it. She handed it to Chase. "I'm sorry."

"Why?" Chase ejected the clip and dropped it on the counter.

She hiccupped. "I killed them." Her eyes filled with tears. "They were going to kill me. Kevin told me to use the amount of force needed to extricate myself from the situation based on the intent. They intended to shoot me. They threatened to shoot Maggie. So I twisted Pinhead's wrist, like you showed me, and shoved him. He hit the counter and went down. Then I took his gun."

"Pinhead?" Kevin puffed with pride that she used the move he taught her.

"They didn't introduce themselves before they started using my face for a punching bag. So, he's skinny with a pinhead and he's fat guy with bushy eyebrows."

"You took Pinhead's gun. Then what?" Chase was holding back a grin.

"Then Bushy Eyebrows came in. He wouldn't stop. I tried to get him to stop. I tried. So I closed my eyes and had to shoot."

Kevin stared at her. "Please tell me you didn't actually close your eyes."

"I aimed first." She actually sounded offended.

Kevin moved closer to her. He was inches away. The darkness on her cheek and in eyes was horrible. He wanted to take it all away, but that would only make it worse. "How long ago did they get here?" He stroked her face ever so gently. He didn't want to hurt her more.

"I don't know. Right when Maggie and I did, I

think. They wanted to know who opened the case on them."

"Did you tell them?"

"Not really. I didn't tell them anything at first, which is why this happened. But then they put a gun to Maggie's head, so I had to say something. I told them it was Pauline."

"Quick thinking." Chase was typing into his phone.

"Did you see Rick and Stanley leave?" She winced as she touched the bruise at her cheek.

"No, we must have just missed them." Chase nodded toward the living room. "Reinforcements are here."

A voice came from the living room. "Detective?"

"In here." Chase turned to Kevin. "I need to lock down the crime scene. Can you watch over Leti and your sister?"

"Sure." He took Leti's arm and led her to the living room. Leti knelt at Maggie's left side and Kevin to her right. "Maggie, we're getting help. Hang in there." Leti ran a hand down her hair, moving a strand behind her ear. She looked terrified, and all Kevin wanted to do was make her feel better. But he had no idea how.

"I get it if you don't want to be with me anymore, especially now." Leti was talking but Kevin had no idea what she was saying. Or why. "I'm a killer."

"You did what you needed to. You did what I told you to do and I'm so grateful. My sister is here because of you."

"They weren't going to kill your sister." Leti bundled Maggie's hair and moved it away from her face. "They didn't want to make an enemy of the Chicago Police Department because of your dad."

"That doesn't change anything. I want you to fight for your life. I want you to make sure if you're in a situation where it's them or you, it's always you." He reached for her hand and leaned down so she could look into his eyes. He wanted her to see him when he said this. "I'm so proud of you. If I had lost you, I don't know what I would have done."

"But all the things you said…"

"I'm so sorry for all of that. I was an ass. I've been so locked up in my head lately and I was afraid of losing you."

"So you pushed me away and treated me like I meant nothing." It sounded so bad when she said it.

"Counterintuitive, I know. But I realized I don't want to live without you. So you can feel however you need to feel about what happened here tonight. I'll be here to pick up the pieces or celebrate or whatever you need. Just know, I'm thankful you stopped them. I don't know how you did it alone. But I'm glad you did and I'm hoping you'll find it in your heart to forgive me and you won't have to do anything alone again."

Her eyes narrowed slightly. "And when did you make this realization?"

"It was a process." He laughed. "It started at Cindy Lidell's. I watched how she let the past dictate her present, her future. I saw how I was doing the same thing to my father. And I don't want that for me or you."

"You can't just shut me out whenever you get stuck in your head."

"I won't." He squeezed her hand, a vow to her and to himself. Shutting her out wasn't fair to her or to him.

"Okay."

"Okay, you'll give me another chance?"

Leti smiled at him and his heart practically leapt from his body. For the first time in days, it felt like he was able to breathe.

He leaned in and gently placed his lips on hers. Soft, warm kiss that he felt all the way to his toes. She was here, alive and still wanted him.

Leti winced. Shit.

"Sorry." He went to touch her face, but didn't know where to touch that wouldn't hurt. He wanted to kill the guys that did this to her, but Leti beat him to it. Instead he said, "I do have good news."

"I could use some of that right now."

"I went to see my father tonight. I have an official offer letter from the Chicago Police Department."

"Congratulations." Leti leaned forward and wrapped her arms around him.

"Get a room," a faint voice said from the floor. Maggie.

"Sorry," Kevin and Leti said at the same time. They both pulled back and looked at her. Maggie's eyes were open, but they looked a bit cloudy.

"The paramedics have been called," Kevin told her. "Chase is locking down the scene. Are you okay?"

"Who are you?" She looked at Leti, confused. An

act if Kevin ever saw one. His sister was an ass. It must be a family trait.

"I'm Leti. Don't you recognize me with all the bruising?"

Maggie's eyes popped open and she tried to sit up. "What bruising?"

"Lay down, drama queen." Kevin put a hand on her shoulder.

Maggie took a good look at Leti's face. "I'm going to kill those sons of bitches."

"I already did." Leti said it so quietly. He wanted to shout it from the mountaintop, but for her it was hard. The first time, and hopefully only time, was something you never forgot. Right now, he just wanted to try to get that haunted look from her eyes.

"You should apply for the Chicago Police Department, Leti. You could be their sharpshooter or their hand-to-hand combat instructor." Kevin reached for her hand and squeezed.

"No thank you." Leti shook her head. "I think I'll stick to numbers."

"Are you leaving Busted?" Kevin understood. This was stressful and scary and she probably needed something less dangerous.

"No, but I'm going to stick to the side of the desk that doesn't include guns. I like taking down the bad guys. I'll just do it from a distance from now on."

"Excuse me." A woman stood over them carrying a case. "I need to take a gun powder residue test. Who fired the gun?"

"That's me," Leti said.

"You fired a gun?" Maggie's eyes widened. Leti nodded as she moved to the couch across the room.

A paramedic came in a few minutes later. Maggie told Kevin to go away, he was sucking up all her oxygen, so he figured she would be fine. He left his sister's side and walked over to Leti.

"Do you want me to sit with you?"

"Please." Leti sat on the couch as the tech cleared off the coffee table and covered it with plastic. She pulled out the tools she needed.

They didn't have Welford or Cullen in custody yet. But they would. His sister was safe. Leti was back in his arms, and she had no desire to do this type of work. Given how easily today could have gone to shit, he was taking today as a win.

EPILOGUE

ENZO SAT in his office and watched Chicago PD carry out boxes and computers. He knew it was coming, but that didn't mean it didn't hurt. His boss and Rick were going down, but it also meant the practice was being investigated. They'd never survive this type of scrutiny.

Rick was standing in the center of the office with an officer—probably on the firm's payroll. Or he was just using his charisma to BS his way out of something. It's what made Rick a great lawyer. Terrible person.

Chase walked into Enzo's office and handed him a piece of paper. The warrant. "We need to search this office." Chase had the decency to look contrite as the said the words, but his tone didn't give it away. He couldn't appear to be playing favorites.

Enzo nodded as he stood. He'd known not to bring anything personal to the office for the last week. He knew the evidence all pointed to a child-kidnapping ring and drug-dealing empire, but he didn't know when

CPD would get all their ducks in a row and go in for the kill. It was just a matter of time.

Chase pointed at the computer and the file cabinets. "Bag and tag it all."

Officers came in behind him and started going through his desk. Enzo had left everything unlocked. Why make it harder on everyone.

Enzo approached his coworkers in the center of the main room.

"Do you know what this is about?" Rick asked Enzo. Rick was playing dumb. Or he was just dumb.

"No idea. You heard the same thing I did. Before he was led out in cuffs, Welford told us to cooperate because he had it all under control."

"Welford must have done some shady shit." Rick's foot tapped and his lip twitched. He kept his eye on Chase. He had to know that the cops were going to come after him next.

Chase was called into Rick's office, and now he was sifting through paperwork handed to him by another officer. Enzo knew Rick was there the night the order was given to kill Leti, but Rick hadn't given the order. CPD said they needed more if he was going to spend the maximum amount of time in jail.

Chase nodded and smiled as he looked over at Rick. "Mr. Cullen." Chase walked over. "I have a warrant for your arrest."

"Me?"

"Turn around." Chase held out his cuffs.

"Why are you wasting time with me? Do you think I'm running the operation? Welford isn't even the head of this thing. I can give names," Rick jabbered during his perp walk out the door. Chase didn't bother responding, just shook his head.

Enzo knew Rick was full of it, but on this he didn't think the man was lying. When Jessi and Enzo had first started looking into the anomalies, they'd noticed they went up to the mayor of Chicago. They might have found what they needed on Welford, but that didn't mean they were done. At least Enzo wasn't done. Not yet.

Jessi ran into the room, her face a mask of concern until she saw Enzo. She ran up to him and whispered. "Are you okay? Maggie told me what was going on."

Enzo led her to a conference room and closed the door. They didn't need anyone listening in on their conversation. "I figured they'd be here sometime this week. I was ready."

"They have everything they need to take down Welford, but not the mayor," Jessi said. It had been over a year since they'd been threatened by the mayor's goons. "How do we take him down?"

"We don't do anything. I've put you and your friends in enough danger."

"Maybe, but they solved it. And they're your friends, too. Do you think they'll let you go at this alone? Do you think I will?"

Enzo smiled. "Do you miss me? Is that why you want me to include your agency?" He was pushing her, but the red that clawed up her cheeks was worth it.

"I just know on your own you didn't get as far as you did with our help," Jessi snapped. "And children are getting kidnapped. We might have shut them down for a short while, but if we haven't chopped off the head. They'll reorganize and be at it again."

Enzo had his doubts. "Have we shut them down?"

"Detectives are raiding Wacker Children's Association now. With everything Danni found, they can get these children back to their parents. Josefine is already meeting with her mom. She's going to be okay." Jessi smiled. "Because of you."

"That was Leti, Maggie and Danni."

"No. You were smart enough to ask Leti for help. They did it because you got everyone involved."

She wasn't wrong. Not that he wanted to admit it right now. Right now he was trying to figure out how he was going to make a living and pay for his condo. He was about to tell her just that when Jessi's cell phone rang.

She glanced at the screen and her eyebrows pulled together. "Hello... Wait... What?"

Chase leaned into the conference room as her voice got louder and louder. "Is everything okay?" he asked.

Enzo shrugged and mouthed, *I don't know.*

Jessi shoved her phone in a pocket. "Matty was in an accident. I have to go."

"Is he okay?" Chase seemed to be following along with this conversation a heck of a lot better than Enzo. Who was Matty, and why did Jessi care?

"They think so, but they want me to take him to his doctor just to be safe."

"Do you have a car?" Chase asked Jessi. She hadn't had one when Enzo and Jessi had hung out almost two years ago. Hung out. He'd had the best month of his life making love and playing house with this woman and now it was downgraded to hanging out.

"No."

"Officer Smith can take you." Chase turned to one of the men standing nearby. "I think we've got the crime scene locked down. Can you take Ms. Xu to her son's daycare to pick him up?"

Son?

Jessi's eyes were lined with tears as she followed Officer Smith out the door. Enzo just watched. When he finally found his voice, he looked over at Chase. "Jessi has a son?"

"Matty. Yeah, cute little bugger."

"How old is he?"

"Just turned ten months. Hopefully he's okay." Chase shook his head and walked toward someone calling his name. They could have been doing karaoke for all he knew.

Enzo couldn't think. He couldn't breathe.

Because he could count.

And if that age was right, Matty might be his son.

EXTRAS

Thank you for supporting an independent author. It would be great if you could leave a review or a rating wherever you purchased this book, or on Goodreads.

Would you like to know when my next book is available? You can sign up for my new release email list at http://www.vanessamknight.com or like my Facebook page at http://facebook.com/vanessamknightauthor.

ABOUT THE AUTHOR

Vanessa M. Knight has always enjoyed writing, and once she found mystery and romance, she was addicted. She props her laptop in the suburbs of Chicago with her family and menagerie of four-pawed claw-babies (AKA cats and dogs.) That laptop has partnered-in-crime to write contemporary romances with a dash of humor and splash of snark.

When she has a few moments to spare, you can find her singing off-key (but she assures everyone it's still considered singing), reading, kickboxing, or killing a few brain cells as she stares at the many sitcoms and dramas available through the Internet and TV.

For more information on Vanessa, including her Internet haunts, contest updates, and details on her upcoming novels, please visit her website at www.-vanessamknight.com.

Contemporary New Adult

Ritter University Series

Major Renovations

What Happens in College...

Christmas Breakdown

Rushing In

Sophomore Slump

The Make-up Test

www.ingramcontent.com/pod-product-compliance
Lightning Source LLC
Chambersburg PA
CBHW070411310726
48977CB00003B/643